Sentinel Five

Sentinel Five

The Redaction Chronicles Book II

James Quinn

Also by James Quinn:

- A Game for Assassins
- The Christmas Assassin (Short Story)

This book is dedicated to the members and patrons of the Special Forces Club, London.
It is a thank you for all their support and encouragement over the years.

"Spirit of Resistance"

A man who desires revenge should first dig two graves

Anon

Contents

Book One: The Returned   **1**

Chapter One   2

Chapter Two   9

Chapter Three   15

Chapter Four   29

Chapter Five   32

Chapter Six   43

Chapter Seven   48

Chapter Eight   58

Chapter Nine   65

Chapter Ten   74

Chapter Eleven   81

Chapter Twelve   102

Chapter Thirteen   107

Chapter Fourteen 121

Book Two: Redaction **131**

Chapter One 132

Chapter Two 136

Chapter Three 139

Chapter Four 146

Chapter Five 157

Chapter Six 160

Chapter Seven 165

Chapter Eight 172

Chapter Nine 174

Chapter Ten 179

Chapter Eleven 182

Book Three: Ronin **193**

Chapter One 194

Chapter Two 197

Chapter Three 203

Chapter Four 212

Chapter Five   216

Chapter Six   220

Chapter Seven   225

Chapter Eight   231

Chapter Nine   237

Chapter Ten   243

Book Four: Retribution   **250**

Chapter One   251

Chapter Two   254

Chapter Three   260

Epilogue   263

Glossary   267

A message from James Quinn   269

Acknowledgements   271

About the Author   274

Book One: The Returned

Chapter One

The four ghosts stood, huddled in the darkness of the night, hidden behind the crates, boxes and containers that lined the dockside. Ghosts, while not an accurate description, fitted their profiles perfectly. They were men who knew how to conceal themselves in the night, they wore black Dockers coats and knitted caps, and for the past hour they had managed to successfully stay concealed from the regular workers who moved supplies and cargo onto the numerous container ships. All were armed with razor sharp commando knives and all were ready to use them to lethal effect in order to complete their mission. This job needed to be done quietly, if it was to be a successful extraction.

Their leader stood at the forefront, his team flanking him. Colonel Stephen Masterman, Head of the Redaction Unit for the British Secret Intelligence Service, lifted the binoculars to his eyes and peered at the container ship's landing ramp as he waited for his agent to appear. The man they were waiting for was a half Portuguese/half Chinese heroin pipeline smuggler by the name of Raymond Yu. Yu was a sub-lieutenant in the almost mythical *Karasu-Tengu* organisation and had been persuaded to sell out his employer for a one-time payment from the British. SIS wanted the 'Raven' – the man himself, the leader – Redacted. The Chief's orders were clear. "Make him talk, Stephen, use whatever damned method you wish, but get the location of the

Raven himself," the Chief had whispered at their final covert meeting in London.

Masterman had searched and gathered intelligence, and plotted and planned. But so far, his target had been elusive. Yu's leader had money, intelligence and resources and knew how to stay hidden while still being able to strike out at his enemies and kill them. So far, the Raven had assassinated four of Masterman's operatives from the Redaction unit.

First, Spence had been slaughtered in Istanbul, then Trench had disappeared off the face of the Earth in Macau, then Marlowe... then Burch. All had been aimed at penetrating and assassinating the head of the organisation, all had been killed. Now Redaction was severely depleted; the remaining two Redactors had been assigned to cover a mission in the Middle East and Masterman had been left with little option but to call in a 'favour' from his old wartime Special Forces Regiment. He wasn't expecting trouble with the extraction, but just as a precaution, he'd felt it was best to have a small number of good men backing him up. Not that they were the men he would have preferred to have by his side, but they were good, nonetheless. His ideal back-up man was no longer a player in the game. He'd removed himself from SIS several years before, when he'd retired himself from fighting the secret war. Masterman had learned the hard way with agents that things could go awry quickly, so he contented himself with the seconded soldiers from the military elite. They stood in silence for several moments more and then, in the distance, he became aware of something new happening – a car, its headlights dimmed, pulled up just short of the gangplank to the nearest container vessel. Three men got out of the maroon Ford Falcon. They were tough-looking Chinese, dressed in sombre black suits. The bodyguards.

Masterman waved an almost casual hand to his men and watched as they moved away, melting into the darkness. He imagined them creeping nearer, getting ready to launch from a concealed position to eliminate their 'dead-eye's', should Yu and his security team decide to cut up rough. Once the Special Forces team were in position, he turned his attention back to the car and saw the man he'd been waiting for exiting the vehicle. He was tall and well composed, and even in this half-light, Masterman could make out the man's half Asiatic features. Yu and his bodyguard team began to walk towards the agreed rendezvous point, just north of Pier 41. When they were twenty yards away, Masterman stepped out of the darkness and approached them.

"Sentinel?" asked Yu, sounding relieved.

Masterman nodded and held out a hand. "Please, this way, we have a vehicle waiting for you."

The truck would take them along the harbour to a fast boat and from there, to a safe house down the coast where Yu could be de-briefed about the Raven. After that, he would be returned to his 'normal' life without anyone the wiser. He would be back at his office first thing in the morning and one hundred thousand US Dollars richer, thanks to British intelligence.

Yu turned, said something to his security team and began to step towards his new protector when the blast of automatic gunfire took out the two bodyguards to Yu's right hand side. Bullets pounded into their heads and the two men collapsed like rag-dolls. What followed was a hiatus of terror and confusion. Masterman was aware of his Special Forces team emerging from the shadows at speed, rushing to quickly move him to safety and provide body cover. Two of them died on the spot, before they were able to reach him. The men on the dockside were running and jumping to find any kind of cover, until they were able to ascertain where the sniper was located.

Masterman crouched down behind a crate, but was clearly able to see the scene before him. He heard the chatter of gunfire again and the last of Yu's bodyguard was taken in the back, sending him sprawling, dead, onto the cobbles. Masterman, ever the soldier, looked up and was able to see the muzzle flash from the sniper's position. He could just about make out the dark figure perched on top of a block of containers, the M-16 Assault rifle in the killer's hands was even now searching around for more targets. Masterman had spent enough time under fire in his career to recognise the maelstrom of a massacre and whoever the hidden sniper was, he was good. So far, all his shots had hit their targets with no misses. His priority now was to get his agent, Yu, out of the killing zone and to safety. He caught the eye of the remaining Special Forces soldier who was concealed behind a barricade and gave the hand signal for him to get to Yu and evacuate him. The soldier nodded, took a breath and was up and running. Almost immediately, Masterman was also on his feet and moving. Two targets! No sniper, no matter how good, could take out two targets simultaneously.

Masterman ran, but before he'd taken ten paces he heard the next volley of shots as they whizzed past him and he saw the soldier go down with a shot to the head. Masterman changed direction, frantically seeking cover from the sniper and jumped the last few feet until he was safe behind an abandoned stack of pallets. He searched around for an escape route... nothing... and then he remembered the car that Yu and his bodyguards had arrived in. If he could get Yu to make the mad dash to reach him behind the pallets – a little over twelve feet – then there was a chance that they could make it to the car and escape.

Masterman held out a hand, beckoning towards the man he'd been sent here to extract. "Come on, move, damn it! It's your only hope!"

Yu looked at him with fear. The men who had initially come to save him were now almost all dead and he had been compromised, betrayed, somehow! Masterman was aware of the shots getting closer, the rounds ripping the wood away from the pallets and then deflecting into the granite of the quayside. Yu closed his eyes for a moment and then, as if he had made a monumental decision, lifted himself to his feet and stood straight up, his tall frame elongated and his hands up in the air in surrender. He turned in the direction of the hidden sniper and called out. "I did not speak, I told them nothing! I would never betray the *Karasu*, I would—"

There was a cacophony of automatic fire and he was flung back onto the floor, his chest and face a mass of explosions as bullets ripped him apart. With his agent dead and his team massacred, Masterman ran for the escape option of the car. He almost made it, and if he'd been ten years younger, he probably would have. He was almost within touching distance of the driver's side when he heard a CLANK as a small metal object landed underneath the car. *A grenade,* he thought. The sniper was trying to flush out his hidden targets with grenades and—

The explosion decimated the car, sending shards of metal and debris outwards and Masterman experienced intense pain as metal from the vehicle tore open his back, the fire from the explosion scorched his face and the force of the blast lifted him, throwing him into the dark, cold water. Suddenly, his world was filled with blood, fear and blackness. He kicked out, pushing himself upwards, taking in a huge lungful of air when he reached the surface. He kicked again and swam away from the dockside shootout, putting distance between himself and the quay. Over to his left, he heard another explosion in the water. It was another grenade, but so far away, it had no chance of hitting him. *The sniper must have lost his bearings, going for a lucky pot-shot rather than a targeted aim,* he thought. It was in the last moments before his consciousness began to slip away when Masterman saw a dead man, a ghost; a man he knew had been dead for the past six months. He knew the man was dead, because Masterman himself had sent him on the mission he'd never returned from. The dead man stood high on the containers which had provided his sniper position, his rifle hefted one-handed as he began his descent. He took one more look around the area of devastation, perhaps to convince himself that there were no more survivors, and only then carried on climbing down the ladder.

"Trench... Trench... Trench," Masterman mumbled, as if convincing himself he'd witnessed an illusion. But this was no illusion. A dead man had come back to life and almost killed him. Masterman stared in disbelief, even as the freezing cold water begin to move his injured body further away from the dockside, drifting out along the harbour wall. And then he thought on the situation no more, as darkness overtook him and he drifted further and further away.

* * *

ASHDOWN FOREST, ENGLAND – 19th JUNE 1966

The elderly spy was dragged through the woods by strong arms. His dressing gown had spilled open, and his bare feet were cut and blistered from having been pulled and pushed along the earthen floor, after his slippers were lost somewhere deep in the forest long ago.

He knew not what his captors looked like. They were hooded, resembling something from a nightmare, and only slits in the black balaclavas revealed their intense eyes. He knew they were strong, certainly; capable, definitely. They had, after all, killed his police bodyguards, who were a perpetual adornment at the front of his private residence in Royal Tunbridge Wells. Then they had killed his wife, as she lay beside him in bed. He'd watched as they covered her with a blanket and silently inserted a long slim blade through the woven material... once, twice... and then she'd stopped moving. He'd been beaten, manhandled down the stairs and out into the cold of the night. Then there had been the drive, pushed into the boot of an anonymous car and driven at speed to who-knew-where. Judging by his surroundings, and the distance they'd travelled in the vehicle, he guessed he was somewhere deep within the maze of Ashdown Forest. His old spy skills, at least, hadn't failed him completely.

He'd been lifted from the car like a sack of potatoes and pushed deep into the darkness of the night, hands manipulating him, pushing him closer to his fate. The woods grew steadily thicker, the night mists rising from the ground giving his surroundings an ethereal quality, until eventually, just as he thought he would pass out from fear and exhaustion, they'd entered a small clearing. The area was no more than eighteen feet wide, and lit by a small paraffin lamp. And there, waiting like a patient executioner, was the man who had ordered that the elderly spy be hauled from his bed in the dead of night and brought to this place of horror. He was slim, fit looking, and dressed in a dark suit. His short-cropped hair and hard scowl gave him the look of a man used to getting his own way. He was the *Karasu*.

"The Raven, I assume," said the old man, weakly. His guards pushed him to the ground, so he was kneeling directly in front of his captor.

The cold wet soil swiftly soaked through his thin pyjama trousers and he shivered.

When the Raven spoke, it was with a power and authority that belied his small frame. It was a voice which didn't shy away from issuing violent demands. "There has been much bloodshed in our underground war... but it is not unexpected. Our business takes a heavy toll in lives."

"I understand that when you set out for revenge, you should dig two graves. Isn't that the proverb?" murmured the old man. He grimaced as the words filtered past his split lips.

The Raven ignored him, instead reaching behind his back to the scabbard which rested there. In one smooth and silent motion, he withdrew a gleaming, single-edged *Ninjato* sword. He held it up to carefully examine the blade's profile and then, satisfied, he lowered it to his side. "I have dug many graves, for many people. You dared to challenge me, dared to challenge my organisation. It is inevitable that I would destroy anything that stood in my way. You must surely have known that," he said.

The old spy nodded, resigned to his inevitable fate. "It is my job, my responsibility, to stop mad men. You were just the latest in a long line."

The Raven nodded, accepting the old man's final words. "And yet the *Kyonshi* will rise and grow, despite your attempts to destroy them. It is of no importance now. You have failed and the time has come for you to reap what you have sown." In one superbly fluid motion, the Japanese man torqued his body around and let fly with the razor sharp assassins' sword. A trail of silver flashed against the blackness, a whistle of steel against air, and then the head of Sir Richard Crosby, the Chief of the Secret Intelligence Service for the past twenty years, flew into the night.

Chapter Two

The small fishing village of Arisaig was looking particularly beautiful that morning, as Jack Grant emerged from his front door and took in the scene before him. Lights danced in the tiny cottages which were nestled along the coastline, breaking up the still-lingering darkness. The last vestiges of summer clung to the village and at that time of the morning, fog was still rolling in onto the land from the sea, giving the scene an ethereal quality. To Jack Grant, it always appeared as if a painting had come to life. The rain and the wind swept through the leaves into the gutter outside the small house. He turned up the collar of his waxed outdoors jacket and tucked his head down, so that his bearded chin burrowed deep into the top of his old, roll-necked jumper.

For the past year Jack Grant, a one-time member of the Secret Intelligence Service, had been working as the right hand man on his brother-in-law's fishing boat. He had left his old life behind, changed his appearance as best he could and settled down to the mediocrity of mending nets, fixing motor engines and hauling fish to market. While he was in no way contented, he satisfied himself with the fact that he was where he should be, with what was left of his family around him. This morning was the same as any other morning. He was up by five-thirty am, having breakfast while the rest of the family either slumbered on, or began to stir ready for work and school. Today though, he was driving down to Fort William to pick up an engine part for Hughie, his brother-in-law. Actually, for Hughie's aging boat, *The Tempest.*

He climbed into the battered and mud-splattered Land Rover, rumbled the engine to life and headed out of Arisaig. The drive was slow and carefree, with Grant taking in the stunning vista of the mountains which sheltered the village from the harshest of Scottish elements in any season. He'd been driving for no more than ten minutes when he spotted the vehicle following his old Land Rover.

He'd sensed it, before he'd seen it. A prickling of his skin, his senses trembling, the hairs on his arms standing on end – all were alerting him to the fact that he was being watched, observed, assessed and evaluated by persons unknown. Whoever it was, he was useless at vehicle surveillance. Driving a bloody big show-off car like a Jag made him stick out like a sore thumb in the rural environment. The only people who had flashy cars around here were the 'bookies', and gangsters from Glasgow, and they didn't tend to be visiting small fishing villages at five in the morning in Jack's experience. "Okay, sunshine," he muttered to himself, his eyes never wavering from the rear-view mirror. "Let's see what your game is."

Grant had watched the Jag's headlights, throughout the hour's drive down to Fort William. It had turned out to be so easy. Drive into the centre of town, dump the Land Rover and go about his business. It had taken him less than ten minutes of dragging himself around the stores and streets, before he'd identified his 'watcher', and then another five before he'd procured the name from his mental list of faces. Jack Grant recognised the face; a senior officer in Berlin, from bloody years ago. An Intelligence Corps Captain, attached to agent running. Penn, that was it. Jordan Penn, Jordie for short. Nice bloke. What a shame. *Well Mr. Penn*, thought Grant, *nice bloke or not, I'm about to spoil your day.*

* * *

Jordie Penn, former Captain in the Intelligence Corps, and now private security consultant to the rich and famous of Mayfair, had already had a pig of a day. He'd been on the go since three am. Jack Grant, his target, was routinely up and out early and therefore, he'd needed to be up at least several hours earlier, lying up in a spot along the route. He'd sat freezing his backside off in the Jaguar, trying not to let the windows steam up. He couldn't put the heater on, because that would mean turning on the engine and possibly alerting someone, so he'd had to leave the driver's window open to stop the condensation… and it was arse-numbingly freezing. Bloody hell!

Penn had enjoyed the drive up and through the Scottish mountains the previous day. He had taken in the majestic views of the Glens and the hills and had gloried in their ruggedness. He'd witnessed the clouds merging into, and hanging low over, the mountain peaks like some kind of camouflage. They were, he was sure, one of God's finest achievements. But it was the rain and the cold that was crucifying his part in the surveillance.

He had seen Grant – God, he had resembled a dishevelled fisherman – climbing into the Land Rover and heading off along the main arterial route down through the mountains, past Ben Nevis, and into Fort William. It had been slow going for Penn in the Jaguar, trying to keep Grant's vehicle in sight, while remaining unseen. Once they hit Fort William, it had been easier. More people, even at this early hour of the morning, had helped him to blend into the surroundings. Not that Jordie Penn was any kind of expert at hostile surveillance, far from it. His forte had been running a pathetic bunch of displaced persons as agents in post-war Berlin. So shadowing a target, even on UK soil, was something way outside of his remit. But… since his recruitment to this new operation he'd been doing an awful lot of things outside of his usual job description. The order had been given from the 'boss', so he was determined to see it through. "Follow him Jordie, get him on his own, then make the approach… bring him back into the fold," had been his brief the previous evening.

So Penn stuck to Grant as best he could. Up and down the high street, watching where he went. It was on his second tour of the same street he'd been down less than five minutes ago, when Grant made a sudden lurch into an entryway between two shops. It was probably the access road for deliveries. Penn took his time and peered into the concrete walkway, before he cautiously followed his target. The laneway brought him out into a courtyard, full of small industrial units. Several workers glanced up and scowled at him, before carrying on with their work.

"Where the bloody hell did he go?" Penn muttered, as he started to walk back out into the street. He was halfway along the laneway when he saw the dishevelled fisherman he'd once known in Berlin and… he was coming straight at him at speed! He exhaled sharply with the impact and Grant's fist tightened at the Intelligence Corps regimental tie at his throat. Pushed backwards, his feet were kicked out from under him, and his back hit the hard ground with not inconsiderable force. Above him, the furious face of Jack Grant glared down, his fist drawn back and ready to pound his face into a bloody pulp.

Jack Grant snarled. "Well, Mr. Penn, you better tell me what you want bloody quick – or you'll be picking your teeth up with broken fingers!

* * *

Penn had been dragged to his feet and wisely, he talked… quickly. He obviously knew of Gorilla's reputation for violence and he was wise enough not to test it. "Someone wants you to attend a meeting. Now. Thirty minutes' drive from here. A private meeting."

"Who?" snarled Grant, dusting the dust from Penn's jacket.

"I can't say. But it's a meeting you'll want to attend. It's a 'friend'." His face had flushed under the sudden onslaught of violence from the smaller man, but he was slowly regaining his composure.

A 'friend' was an informal name for members of SIS. Grant was intrigued, but he was more than determined to play hard to get, at least until he had more solid information. "Piss off. You think I'm going to just walk into a trap? You've been at the whisky, sunshine."

"I was told to tell you it was relating to your old offices, back at Pimlico," said Penn reasonably.

"I've been out of that for a wee while now, I don't know anyone there anymore."

"Nevertheless, my employer has taken great steps to keep this meeting secret. He's respecting your privacy, and your family's security."

At the mention of his family Grant's demeanour grew even more aggressive and he glared at Penn, fury invading his face. "How long for?"

"A few hours, no more, then you can return to your village," said Penn.

Grant weighed up his options and then issued a warning. "Any funny business and I start breaking limbs. Yours will be the first, Penn. Just so that you know. For the record… you understand?"

They travelled back in convoy, Penn leading the way in the Jaguar and Grant following close behind in the mud splattered Land Rover. The route from Fort William took them northwards, almost back to where Grant had started from that very morning in his tiny fishing village. Penn suddenly turned sharply to the left a few miles before the village, negotiating the Jaguar down a private road that was little more than a track. Less than half a mile away, through the fog and the rain, Grant could make out a large mansion house in its own private grounds. It was isolated and protected by the mountains standing guard around it on the banks of the Loch. Grant knew what it was immediately. Inverailort House was something of a legend within the quiet communities and villages in the Lochailort area. During the war, it had been one of the first Special Training Centres for the sabotage service and any number of fledgling Special Forces groups. Its grounds and rooms had played host to all kinds of nefarious black arts; small arms training, silent killing, explosives and sabotage.

Now though, the building was vacant and obviously in need of some repair. Even though the post-war years hadn't been kind to it, the house still stood formidably against the fierce weather and the elements. They parked directly in front of the main doors and Penn led the way up the stairs to the main doors. He produced an iron key from his pocket, turned it in the lock, and pushed open the large wooden door. The main reception hall was bright and airy, but with the look of a place used infrequently. The main staircase divided the hall into two large corridors and Grant estimated the mansion must have anything between ten to fifteen large rooms at its disposal.

"We go this way," said Penn, ushering Grant down one of the grand corridors. The smell of mould and mildew filled Grant's nostrils. They carried on for a good twenty feet, past heavily-curtained windows, until they reached what had once been the main dining hall. It had definitely seen better days. The wood was warped and cracked, there was an overwhelming smell of dampness and moisture, and darkness permeated the room making it appear smaller than Grant suspected it actually was. The heavy curtains in this room had been drawn shut and the room was poorly lit by faded wall sconces. It reminded Grant of a dour church he'd been made to visit when he was a boy.

He heard Penn close the door behind them and he stepped further into the gloom. Grant took only a few faltering steps before he heard the sound of rubber tyres squeaking on the dusty wooden floor. He made out a wheelchair at the far end of the huge dining table, and watched as it slowly pivoted to reveal the silhouette of a man. The darkness disguised the features of the man's face, but Grant would have recognised the voice anywhere. In truth, he'd suspected who had summoned him, even before they left Fort William.

"You look like you haven't shaved for a month," said the voice. It was deep, basso, commanding and in control. It was the man he'd fought side by side with, and the man he'd killed for.

It was the Colonel. Masterman. It was Sentinel.

Chapter Three

It had been a little over two years since they'd last met, at the funeral for a former Redaction team member who had been killed during an operation in Rome. Masterman, once a large and powerful man, now resembled a broken scarecrow. His frame had lost all of its bulk and his body was contorted at unnatural angles, almost as if he was wracked with pain whenever he moved. His complexion was pale, and sickly. The Colonel looked like a man ten years older than his true age. Except for the voice and of course, those eyes, which still held the familiar bombastic fire.

Masterman, to his credit, took the shock and surprise on Grant's face well. "I had a run in with some flying lead and explosives. It ripped apart most of my back, damaged my spine and broke one of my legs. Not to mention what it did to my face." Masterman raised one hand up to the scar tissue running across his face.

Grant eased himself into a chair; he could feel his legs trembling with shock. "Jesus, Colonel, you should have let me know, I would have come—"

Masterman interrupted, clearly not interested in any pity or remorse for his plight. "Pah, you had enough to deal with. I understand that now – you'd been through a rough operation. It hit you harder than you liked to admit and the best thing for your sanity was to give yourself some air to breathe, away from the death and the killing. Not that we didn't miss you, Jack. Many a time we could have done with your pistol skills, to assist us in halting a bit of trouble."

"What happened? Was it a mission?"

Masterman nodded, wincing with the movement. "I was ambushed by a dead man, or at least, we all thought he was dead." Masterman paused and Grant suspected he was using the extended silence, to decide how much to tell him. Finally he said, "It was your old team mate, Trench. We had word that he'd been taken out during an operation several months before in Macau, and I had no reason to doubt the information. Until I see him sitting in a sniper's perch, shooting down my security team and killing my informant in Australia."

For a moment Grant couldn't take it all in. Trench gone rogue! What the hell had been happening in the year since he'd left the Service?

"I never trusted the bastard, but to his credit, he was a damned good Redactor. Trench is working for some very bad people, it seems, and they're the reason I need you back in the game and operational," Masterman added.

"What? Me! I'm out of it, Colonel," spluttered Grant.

"Our country is under attack," said Masterman. "And the average man and woman on the street haven't even got a clue about it... yet. Besides you're never completely out of it... not in our game."

Grant stared at Masterman, trying to assess if his old comrade was serious. Masterman, Grant knew, wasn't prone to bouts of melodrama. He saw the fear in the other man's eyes and spoke. "Alright. Tell me everything."

"It started with an investigation," Masterman began. "The Chief had personally involved himself in the smallest details of the case. He judged it to be of such significant threat to the nation, that he took charge of it himself. The details, even now, are still hazy and unclear. I received a package a week after C was killed, containing copies of the evidence he'd accumulated. Sir Richard was a careful man and it seems he feared he would be a target for assassination. He had evidently chosen me to pick up the mantel and carry on the fight... little did he know, I'd been taken out of the game as well."

Masterman glanced down at his damaged body, pausing for a moment of reflection before he carried on. "It seems the Chief had been approached directly, by a former agent from his old wartime network, someone who had been part of an operation during the war in Asia. You know how it is; sometimes old agents pop up and try to make themselves useful again. Most of the time they're just after cash, needing a hand-out and missing the workings of the intelligence game, but according to the information I inherited; this agent was unique. This man had become aware of an organisation, one that if not controlled properly, could have been a threat greater than anything we've faced so far."

"What kind of organisation? Terrorist?" asked Grant.

Masterman shook his head. "Not exactly. It borders on a private intelligence network, subsidised by the use of mercenaries for hire, private assassins and illegal arms deals in the region. All to the highest bidder, I might add. There were even rumours that they'd waged a war with several Yakuza clans in Japan, but the Yakuza fought back by forming an alliance. It was a close run thing though, and the gangsters were lucky to make it out alive."

"So what was the information about?"

"Just rumours at first, talk of extortion, terrorist actions, the usual rubbish that we get all the time. But this one was a bit different… there was talk of a weapon, that if unleashed could have been devastating," answered Masterman.

Grant cocked his head to one side. "A weapon. Explosives? Missiles?"

"No. A biological weapon, something we hadn't seen before and way beyond anything our experts have at the moment. Even now, the details on it are a tad vague. The Chief communicated secretly with his former agent and requested more details. What he discovered seemed to shock him into action. According to his private diary, he immediately ordered the agent to come into protective custody and make himself known to the SIS Head of Station in Hong Kong."

"And did he?"

"No. The agent never made it. He was found with his throat slit, the day before he was due to meet with the Head of Station. Someone had gotten to him first, before we could question him in more detail. In the months following this event, the Chief's patience appears to have grown short and he targeted SIS resources at finding out more about the people behind this organisation, and the possible whereabouts of the bio-weapon."

Grant frowned. Whatever this bio-weapon was, it had been enough to have the Chief of the Secret Intelligence Service frightened. The whole situation seemed rather seedy and totally un-British. Since when did the SIS back down against terrorists? Something didn't add up. "What about Redaction? Couldn't you have sent the boys after them?" he asked.

Masterman paused, slowly moving his wheelchair until it was directly facing Grant. He pulled out a commando dagger from a sheath on the wheelchair, and pointed it at Grant like a schoolmaster instructing a pupil who is being particularly dense. "Redaction is gone, Jack. We were decimated. All your old team mates were wiped out by agents from this organisation. Following C's assassination and my shooting in Australia, the powers-that-be decided we'd outlived our usefulness and we should be scattered to the winds."

Grant stared at his former leader in shock. Redaction – gone? The elite of SIS destroyed? These men had been the action arm of the British Secret Service! How could all of them have been... murdered? "What about the Service? What state is that in?"

"It's a cabal," growled Masterman. "The lunatics have taken over the asylum, the Service is being stripped to its core and the politicians are in charge and they're making a right balls-up of it. At this rate, the Russians won't have to penetrate SIS – they'll be able to read all our secrets in the newspaper."

"Who's in charge? Who is the new 'C'?" Grant asked. He was finding it hard to absorb all the radical changes which had apparently taken place in his old Service.

"Some career diplomat, a bit of a fop in my opinion. Sir John Hart."
Masterman shrugged, his expression softening slightly. "He's not a bad
man, comes from a good family by all accounts. But he's out of his
depth, and hasn't a clue how bone-to-bone intelligence operations really work. He's leaning a lot on Thorne's arm and in effect, he's taking
his orders from him."

Grant's brow furrowed. The name sounded familiar, but he couldn't
quite place it. Masterman helped him out. "Sir Marcus Thorne, former
member of the Service way back in the bad old days, now Deputy
Chairman of the Joint Intelligence Committee. He stepped in when
the crisis began, helped negotiate with these... these terrorists. His
advice has been invaluable. He's been put in charge of re-aligning the
old SIS departments, and bringing new people up, to take over from
the old guard."

A kingmaker, thought Grant. Someone able to wield enough power
to nudge the pieces on the chess board to wherever he wanted them.
The hierarchy of the intelligence world always threw up such men;
power hungry, ambitious, ruthless and willing to decimate a Secret
Service to achieve their aims.

"So what is all this then?" said Grant, waving a hand at their secret
meeting. "If Redaction is blown, what exactly is going on with all this?"

Masterman smiled, the scars on his face wrinkling maniacally like a
cruel pirate. "This is private enterprise, Jack old boy. This is deniable all
the way. SIS doesn't even know we exist. They think we're all retired,
disabled, injured or drunk. This is about a debt of honour. This is about
pure and bloody revenge."

* * *

"Be a good chap Jordie and put the movie on," said Masterman. Penn
flicked the switch on a hidden movie projector, bringing it to life. A
white light lit up the opposite wall and the inevitable number count-
down began. The film started. It was dark and grainy, but clear in its
detail. The footage had obviously been taken from behind a two-way

mirror. What it showed was a small cell, no bigger than a standard prison cell. Except this cell had a small aperture built into one wall, which allowed something the size of a small suitcase to be pushed through in one direction. In the other corner of the cell was a young boy, no more than ten or twelve years of age. He looked like an Asian street kid, who had been imprisoned for some petty crime. His clothes were tattered and hung off his thin frame. He was huddled on the floor, his knees drawn up to his chest.

Grant looked more closely at the footage and noticed that in the bottom corner of the room, there were ventilation grills. Some kind of smoke or mist was being filtered through them and into the cell. Not in great plumes, but enough to make the small space cloudy for a few moments at a time. The boy barely seemed to notice, his head was down as if he was trying to block out his fate. While Grant watched, he began to twitch, almost imperceptibly at first, a flinch of a shoulder, a snap of his head, the shudder of a foot then an arm.

Grant turned to Masterman, a look of confusion on his face. Masterman, as if he guessed what the other man was thinking, merely pointed a finger at the footage and said, "Keep watching."

Grant turned back to the film and saw that the boy was now bent forward on his hands and knees. His whole body was shaking and convulsing, and it seemed to be... *stretching*, almost as if his bone structure was extending swiftly, visibly increasing the young boy's size. Without warning, the boy launched himself head first at the two-way mirror, and a large crack appeared where his skull impacted on the safety glass. Blood poured down his face from a gash on his forehead, but still the boy drove himself forward, banging against the glass with his fists, knees and feet. The glass was actually vibrating, from the level of punishment it was taking. Still trying to process what he was seeing, Grant was stunned when the small door in the corner of the room was lifted and, rather bizarrely, a goat was pushed into the cell before the door quickly snapped shut behind it. The boy didn't seem to notice the animal at first; still too busy using the mirror as target practice. It was only when the terrified animal bleated that the crazed boy stopped and turned. In a sharp movement he twisted his body around, leaping across the cell and onto the animal.

God he was fast, thought Grant. *He'd spied the goat and moved across the room in a blur of movement.*

Grant forced himself to watch the events unfolding. It wasn't pleasant and it wasn't easy, but force himself he did. The boy ripped at the small goat with his bare hands, manipulating it and pulling it down onto the floor before he set his mouth against the animal's throat. The boy's teeth found their target and when he bit deeply into the goat's neck, the blood flew. What followed was a cacophony of flying fur, snapping bones and an explosion of blood as the animal was ripped to pieces within seconds. There was a short cut away and the next scene revealed a guard wearing a gas mask entering the cell. He strode up to the boy, who was still pummelling the remains of the goat with his bloodied hands, and quickly shot the boy in the head with a pistol.

The scene abruptly cut away and the cell was replaced by a darkened room, possibly an office. A figure sat in shadow behind a desk, only the merest glint of light revealing him in silhouette. A single, well-manicured hand could be seen, the fingers drumming calmly on the desk. The rest of the body remained completely still, and when the figure spoke, his voice was deep and chilling. "I am the Raven, the gatherer of death, the demon of nightmares. I am here and I am nowhere. I will strike at the hearts of your children and take great revelry in the slaughter of your warriors. My legacy will be your torment for generations to come and you will learn to kneel before me, or face the wrath of my *Kyonshi*! The *Karasu-Tengu* will have his feast." The screen went blank as the spool of film wound off and the room was once more shrouded in blackness, the silence thick when Jordie switched of the projector.

"What the hell was that? Is that the bio-weapon at work?" Grant asked, his face stamped with a mixture of anger and disgust.

"We call it Beserker," said Masterman. "That's the codename we've given it. They call it *Kyonshi*, which is Japanese for living dead. We believe it's some kind of next-generation drug. It's far beyond anything we currently have. C's notes suggest that the weapon's initial purpose may have been targeted towards revolutionary-coup operations in third world countries; Vietnam, Bolivia and Cuba to name but a few. The toxin would be released in a confined space – say an office, or a high street – where it would interact with the local populace. The infected would begin to physically attack and kill their fellow citizens. As you can imagine, based on what you've seen in the film, it would cause widespread chaos and anarchy. Effectively, the country's own population would be fighting against itself."

"That's insane! Innocent people would be slaughtered. Soldiers and secret police are one thing, but bio-weapons are indiscriminate about who they target," said Grant.

Masterman nodded. "What we do know, is that it's still far from perfected as a weapon. The initial dose only lasts for up to thirty minutes and while it turns the subject violent, it dissipates quickly, providing the coup-plotters with only a short opportunity to take over. The fact that the virus doesn't work properly means the man who currently has control of it has decided to alter what it is to be used for. Military coup operations are out, so it seems, and bio-terrorism is in."

"And the film? Where did that come from?" asked Grant.

"A package was hand delivered to our Embassy in Lisbon containing the film and a note with a demand for five million pounds sterling, paid into an account in Switzerland. We received it the day after we discovered that C had been murdered."

"And if the five million wasn't paid?"

Masterman held up his hands. "Then the implied threat was that this bio-toxin, or whatever it is, would be released into a civilian crowd in British-held territories. The powers-that-be thought about it for all of an hour before they decided to pay up, bloody quick-smart!"

"What! I thought we don't work with terrorists?" said Grant.

"Ah, well yes, under normal circumstances that would be the perceived wisdom. But these aren't normal circumstances; I don't think any government in the world has ever had to deal with a threat like this before. Imagine if that was released in Oxford Street in London, or Princes Street in Edinburgh, or any of a dozen other soft targets. It would be catastrophic. So an arrangement was made to pay through deniable channels, as it were. Some friends in the banking industry made the arrangements and we simply reimbursed them."

"So what changed? They've been paid; surely that's the end of it?"

Masterman shook his head. "It seems the only good blackmailer is a dead one. We've heard rumblings that they're coming back for a second bite of the cherry. From what I understand, another communiqué has been received by the Prime Minister's office with demands for more money. It has to stop... and soon. The money is a way of buying us time until we can find and kill this maniac and his mob. Unfortunately, SIS won't commit to fighting back and with Redaction gone, they're impotent to say the least. That's where we come in."

Masterman handed Grant a piece of paper, containing a drawing of an evil looking, heavily-plumed blackbird, cradling an Oriental sword. Its beak was open wide as if to devour and the sword was held high as if to threaten. *No, not a blackbird,* thought Grant. The *Karasu-Tengu*. The Raven. A mythical Japanese demon, part-goblin and part-raven, which was a master in the art of single combat whether unarmed or with a sword.

Masterman continued. "Our people put the word out everywhere for information. We listened, we eavesdropped, and we spied. We got bits back... not a lot, just enough to help us make a start. The *Karasu-Tengu* himself was a mere rumour, a spectacle of bluff and deception. He was never seen and only whispered about on the streets where murder and damnation were the currency of life. He was known to disappear and reappear at will – quite often on different continents at the same time. He was a ghost to keep the street criminals afraid and tempered. Cross the Raven, and you will lose your head. It was a macabre version of a tale of power, ruthlessness and cunning. But who was the man in shadows? Who had made him the leader of the group which had taken the art of murder and assassins for hire to the next level? The evidence, at least initially, had been fragmented and incomplete. Myth, rumour and disinformation had corrupted the true facts about the leader and his origins. Then as reputations grow, the facts had been superimposed upon both the man and his deeds. The Raven and his assassins had killed across continents and had spread their wings to other criminal and terrorist groups. They were facilitators, able to infiltrate themselves into any situation. They could go where others could not and they could do what others could not do."

"So who is he? This Raven?" asked Grant.

Masterman frowned at that, as if not having a straight answer to a question troubled him. "Details of his true identity are sketchy at the moment, although I have someone working on it as we speak. Hopefully, they'll be able to shed further light on this man's identity soon. All we do know is that the Allies were involved with him in some way operationally during his time in Asia in the 1930's, but seeing as SIS and the OSS were involved with lots of agents during that period, it's proving to be a bit of a needle in a haystack. We'll get there in the end."

"So how do you get to him?" asked Grant, his mind already slipping back into operational mode and trying to work out the next play in the game.

"We've identified a small window of opportunity," said Masterman.

Grant inclined his head. "How small?"

"It seems C had identified a contract killer who was rumoured to be on retainer to the Raven organisation, an Australian mercenary by the name of Reierson. It seems he's one of their top gunmen. We've finally managed to track him down – if someone were to remove him, permanently –there would be a vacant position in the Raven's hit-team. What's more, it would be a role for an expert gunman. It would be our way in."

Grant began to nod in understanding; he could see where the Colonel was going with this –Masterman was after an infiltration agent. It was a dangerous position to be in within any covert operation.

"You eliminate Reierson and then we orchestrate getting you close to Trench. He'll bring you into their fold, an old comrade and all that," purred Masterman. "I need a man on the inside, Jack – a good man, someone who doesn't mind getting his hands dirty and playing rough with the enemy, someone to get close to the hierarchy of this organisation and get them to lower their guard, even momentarily."

"And then what? How far in do you want me to go?"

"All the way. All the way until we have the Raven where we want him, discover what he plans to do next and then you and the team can rip his bloody head off, once and for all."

"Can I just ask you one small question, Colonel?" Grant's voice was deliberately low and calm when he made the request.

"Of course."

"What the bloody hell has any of this got to do with me!" Grant snapped, in his usual cold and cruel manner.

Jack's outburst gave Masterman pause and it took him a moment or two before he recovered. He fixed Grant with his hardest officer's glare and spoke calmly. "Because you're lost Jack… or at least, you believe yourself to be. What you really need is a chance, an opportunity to get back into this war. You've had your sabbatical over the past year, stuck out here in the wilderness. Now it's time for you to come back and repay a debt of honour. Plus, we'll pay you for your time of course, we're not asking you to risk your life for free, there's coin in it for you at the end of the contract. My backers are men of means, shall we say."

Masterman fixed Grant with a glare from his one good eye and jabbed the point of the commando dagger down into the wood of the table. He thought back to all those months ago, on the day when he had been released from hospital. He'd called a meeting to be held at a private room in White's Gentleman's Club. In attendance were various members of the banking profession, a former Prime Minister, several recently-retired Generals and a handful of business leaders. Seven of them in all, all loyal to the late 'C' and all of them no longer affiliated with the present government or the intelligence agencies. Masterman had turned up, half doped up on drugs just to keep the pain at bay, and set out his thesis and plan. It had taken him a good three hours to convince them of what was needed, but eventually he'd triumphed. It was the kind of speech he'd given in the past when he sent young soldiers out to die on the battlefield. By the end of the day, he had resources and funding in place to go ahead with his unofficial mission.

Grant shook his head. "They'll never buy it, I've been out of it too long; I'm washed up, part of the old generation. A younger crowd will have risen up the ranks. Killers these days are ten a penny."

"That's exactly why they'll 'buy it', said Masterman. "You were something of a legend within the intelligence networks. If we can convince them that you're just as bitter and twisted as they are, as Trench is with the Secret Service, then they'll snap you up just as soon as look at you. A gunman of your reputation and skill willing to work for the highest bidder, a mercenary with a grudge. Gravy for them."

Grant considered it, working out the possibilities and risks. There was a big reward at the end of it, but the chance of discovery, torture and death... well, that had always been there, in all the jobs he'd done. In the end it was Masterman who broke his chain of thought. "Be a good chap and push me outside, let's get a bit of fresh air. It's as stuffy as hell in here. Do you know, I think the rain has eased off slightly?"

* * *

The sniper was watching carefully, and she saw them clearly through the telescopic scope of the rifle. The Colonel in the wheelchair and the gunman who pushed him out of the main door of the mansion and onto the drive. She was located on the hillside which towered over the mansion, concealed in the moss and the purple-tinged heather of the mountains. Today was another practice day for her. Finding a hide, laying up, staying hidden, and taking a shot every now and then. Practice. The rain had started at dawn and now, three hours later, she was soaked. But she didn't move, hadn't moved for an hour or more, except to occasionally stretch her fingers, keeping the blood circulating despite the cold. She moved her right eye closer to the scope of the rifle and studied the small, bearded man with the dirty blonde hair in detail. So this was the legendary Redactor who was famed for his skill at close quarter shooting. She thought he looked more like a vagrant.

A killer, no. A manual labourer, certainly. The man was both ragged and dishevelled.

If the vagrant who had once been a legend had tried to harm the Colonel in any way, she would have taken him out. The shot from this distance would have been no problem. It was well within her range and skill level and the rifle she'd been training with was more than capable of doing the job. It was a British-made Parker Hale Model 82. The Colonel had told her it was currently being trialled by several specialist units in the British Army. She'd been exhilarated when he presented her with the case containing the rifle, scope and ammunition. She'd removed it carefully, with almost reverence. In her opinion, it was well balanced, easy to use and above all else, accurate. It was a prestigious weapon and she coveted it greatly.

The next day, after familiarising herself with the weapon in the great hall of the castle, she'd walked out into the wilderness carrying the rifle in its case and several large turnips she'd found in the pantry. She'd walked a mile away from the house before setting the large vegetables on a small hillock, then she had climbed to the top of the great mountain overlooking Inverailort and the Loch. She'd unpacked the weapon, wiped it down and carefully loaded the magazine with four of the standard 7.62mm rounds. Finally, she'd flicked open the two legs that rested either side of the rifle's frame and settled down onto the ground, prone, sheltering against the harsh wind and fog. She had rested for five minutes, calming herself, slowing her breathing. It was a skill she'd taught herself over many years. Then, when she was ready, she moved the bolt action handle smoothly backwards and then pushed it forward, chambering a bullet.

The effective range of the M82 was around the eight hundred feet mark. The sniper judged that her targets – the turnips – were easily inside that distance, probably no more than six hundred feet. For both the sniper and the rifle, this was child's play. Through the magnified scope she saw the targets disintegrate with each squeeze of the trigger, watching them explode. One minute they were there and the next, gone. It was like a magician's disappearing trick and she was happy.

She'd found her zero and she hoped that she'd be allowed to carry and use the M82 against the monsters she'd been recruited to hunt and kill. It was a good weapon. The following day, the Colonel arranged for her to spend the day with a deer stalker and professional hunter from one of the big estates further up the Scottish coastline, and she'd overheard what the hunter and marksman had to say about her when he reported to the Colonel regarding her efforts.

"Well, Colonel, that wee lassie can shoot as well as any man I've ever seen. She has both the eye for it and the patience to wait for her quarry to move into the kill zone. She took down one of our biggest stags, a bugger we've been keen to cull for months!"

It had been the endorsement the Colonel was apparently looking for because he'd named her the first member of the team he was forming. *In many ways,* thought the sniper, *the Colonel reminded her of her own father.*

She placed her eye back at the scope and stared down at the forecourt of the house. She saw the vagrant turn and stand in front of the Colonel's wheelchair. Saw them speak for a minute or two, and then saw the nods of understanding from both parties. The Colonel heaved his frame up from the wheelchair, until he towered over the smaller man. They shook hands, as if sealing a deal, and then the vagrant turned and trudged back through the muddy grass to the cars, where Penn was waiting.

She turned the scope of the rifle so she could follow the Land Rover along the private road and out of sight. She wondered if the man known as Gorilla would be back, if he'd decided to be a part of their mission, or if he was returning to his life of obscurity.

Chapter Four

Twelve hours later, Jack Grant sat on a cold and lonely train station waiting for the final train of the day. The train would take him from Edinburgh Waverly Station southwards ever nearer to the heart of the British capital, and from there to the private safe house Masterman had arranged for him in Wiltshire.

Following his reunion with Masterman, Grant had stepped back into the Land Rover and driven in a daze all the way back to Arisaig. The miles had passed in a blur, had gone too quickly, if he was honest. He'd experienced many doubts and indulged in multiple arguments with his own mind during that journey. Should he climb on board for what was probably the craziest of secret operations? After all, they had no official licence on this. A private enterprise for revenge? Crazy! He should just go back to his sister's house and forget all about his old life, it would be the easiest thing to do.

But there was something of the risk taker in Jack Grant, always had been. It was what made him such a good Redactor in his day; the ability to face down the usually overwhelming odds. Yes, he could go back and tend to the house, work a fishing boat, look after his kin, perhaps even find a woman and settle down to a habitable existence. But Grant knew it would be a lie. He wasn't that man. He knew that here in Scotland, locked away in self-imposed exile, he was merely treading water, waiting for the next opportunity to arrive. He also knew he was a selfish arsehole to leave his kin, just because he'd been flattered into it by an old soldier. He'd been protected by Sir Richard Crosby, and he knew that Masterman had fathered that protection. He'd known that even before he left the Service, a security blanket had been put in place to protect his family and it had continued, long after he'd resigned in a fit of pique. Masterman had bent every rule in the book and called in all kinds of obscure favours, in order to keep his best Redactor hidden away from enemies.

But it was more than just a level of debt that Grant wanted to repay. In truth, Jack wanted back into his old life; the comradeship of a team, the sensation of a cold, hard gun gripped in his hand, the thrill of hunting a man down, the release he'd experienced as the hunter closing in for the kill. Seeing as he was having a moment of clarity and self-awareness, he admitted to himself that he also wanted to see if the Gorilla was still alive and kicking, hidden away in a deep part of his psyche, waiting to be reborn. By the time he'd reached the last mile of his journey, Grant had made his decision. His mind was a whirlwind, working out the details of the operation, and how he would break the news to the family. Whether it was the right decision, only time would tell.

He'd arrived back just as darkness set in and he'd stood in the kitchen and told everyone, as they'd sat at the kitchen table, eating their evening meal. He'd blurted it out, with no finesse or tact. He was leaving, going away on a job, would be gone for a few months… the details he couldn't remember, it had just been words he'd spouted. Vague platitudes, something about an old debt… but he knew he'd been trying to justify his actions. He'd looked down at their faces to be greeted with scorn, fear and rage.

Hughie had glared at him, clenching and unclenching his fat fists. His sister had roared and cursed at him. But it had been the reaction from the girl which had hit him the hardest. She'd simply fled the kitchen and stomped up to her bedroom. He'd left her alone, taken the brunt of the abuse from his sister and Hughie for ten minutes, before calmly making his way up the twelve stairs to the girl's bedroom door. She'd locked it and he could hear her crying, softly. He had tried in his ham-fisted way to calm and reassure her. She'd ignored him and eventually, he'd admitted defeat.

Grant had quickly scribbled a letter and sealed it inside an envelope, before handing it to his sister. "Make sure she gets it; don't hide it, May. It's important," he'd said, his rucksack in his hand, standing on the front step to the house moments before the door slammed, leaving him standing there in the rain. He'd suffered the shame of his actions, turning his back on his kin at the drop of a hat and walking away, back into the maelstrom of his old life. And all because someone had pushed the right buttons and asked him; asked him to be of use again, asked him to use his old skills again, and he'd agreed so easily. He'd folded like a cheap suit. Masterman was that good as a recruiter – of course he was – and it was why the man had been so successful in their secret wars.

Jack had turned and walked away to the Land Rover, looking back once more at the top bedroom window. He saw the face of the girl with the black hair. He threw his rucksack in the back of the vehicle and when he turned around to wave to her for a final time... he paused. She'd gone. He climbed in, started the engine and for the first time in many a year Jack Grant headed south across the English border.

Chapter Five

Grant was picked up by Jordie Penn when he arrived at Euston Station. From there, he'd been driven from London to a temporary safe house located on the outskirts of leafy Wiltshire, a six-bedroom domicile on the edge of some parkland. It was anonymous and ordinary enough not to gain any attention.

"The others will be arriving tomorrow, probably around lunch time. The Colonel will want to talk to you before then, and bring you up to speed before the rest of the team land," Penn said as he lifted Grant's overnight bag from the boot of the Jaguar. Masterman had been waiting for them in the dining room, where tea and sandwiches were the order of the day. *It was obviously going to be a working meal,* thought Grant. The former Head of Redaction must have been having a good day health wise, because he was walking with the aid of a cane and the wheelchair had been relegated to the hallway. Grant recognised this as being the 'boss' in war mode.

"Jack! Come in, come in! How was the journey? Good to have you back here. Take a seat," said Masterman, stepping forward and shaking Grant's hand. "We've a lot of ground to cover over the next few days, but first of all, I just want to make sure you're still on board for this mission."

Grant nodded. "I'm still in. I'm here." That seemed to be commitment enough.

"I thought I'd bring you up to speed on your fellow team mates, give you a brief rundown of who they are and what they're about," said Masterman, passing over a number of bland, tan files containing biographies for the rest of the team. True to his word, Masterman was keeping this operation under the radar and unofficial. There were no operational cover names, no mission headings and nothing in the files to suggest it had been officially sanctioned. They were privateers, operating without a licence.

It was always like this before a job. Getting your head into the files, to get as much information as possible before you hit the street. Grant took the first folder and opened it. The face in the black and white photograph staring back at him looked as if it was fit for the hangman. It was aged, with deep lines around the eyes, and hair slicked back with Brylcreem. The man had a tough, hangdog expression on his face. *In fact,* Jack thought, *he looked like a burglar.* Grant skimmed through the details, curious to learn more.

William 'Bill' Hodges was nearly fifty-five years of age. The file stated that he'd been a British Army paratrooper, before being recruited into Force 136, the wartime sabotage service based in Burma in 1944. Hodges was something of an expert with demolitions, explosives and booby traps, and more than a few of the enemy had fallen to his improvised little 'toys'. After the war, he seemed to have a penchant for getting into trouble with the law and he'd served a prison sentence for breaking into numerous banks in order to get at the safety deposit boxes. SIS had used him on several burglary operations against Iron Curtain targets. Grant's initial reaction, thinking he looked like a burglar, hadn't been far off the mark. "He's a bit of a lad, isn't he," commented Grant, who'd known a few 'scallywags' in his youth.

Masterman nodded. "He was a bloody good soldier by all accounts, an expert saboteur who gave the Japs hell. But... well, sometimes men who leave the military can't always adapt to civilian life. Hodges was a nightmare for the police, but for our purposes, he'll be invaluable. A good dems man can breach doors, set off distraction devices and bring a building down to hide any evidence with his little 'whizz-bangs'. Grant moved the Hodges file aside and picked up the next folder which, rather curiously, had two files inside.

"Ahhh, the deadly duo," laughed Penn, who was standing guard by the door.

The file contained the details of two former soldiers – very recently *former*. Up until last month, they'd been members of the post-war British Special Forces Regiment. Then they'd seemingly experienced a change of heart and 'bought' their way out of the army. Now, to all intents and purposes, they were technically unemployed. "Crane and Lang," Grant read. Both men were in their late twenties and looked tough and fit. Not the types you would want to meet in a dark alley. From the photos provided, they appeared to have been taken from the same mould. *Not exactly twins*, thought Grant, *but of a similar hue.* They certainly had an impressive operational pedigree; they'd hunted terrorists in Malaya and Borneo and worked undercover in the back-streets of Aden. Grant noted that they had several mentions in dispatches between them and both had risen to the rank of senior NCO's within the Regiment. When Masterman dragged himself out of the docks in Australia the previous year, it had been Crane and Lang who had been waiting at the emergency rendezvous to whisk him away to an SIS safe house for medical treatment.

"They're tough lads, Jack, but they'll respect you. They're your dogs of war for this operation. Good in a killing zone. Use them well," said Masterman, the pride for the men of his old regiment obvious and as strong as ever.

Grant assumed that when the mission was complete, and if they survived, the two Special Forces soldiers would be 'allowed' to return to the Regiment, almost as if they'd just been away on a short holiday. Oh, they would probably have to go through selection again, but if the current commanding officer was worth his salt, he would snap up the two Special Forces soldiers as quickly as possible. He placed the 'deadly duo's' file to one side and picked up the last of the folders. He licked his thumb and turned the page, expecting to see another hard-bitten ex-military type staring back at him... instead, he was greeted with a colour photograph, one definitely not taken by an army photographer.

The face was that of a woman in her late twenties, perhaps early thirties. She was of Asian descent, but with the uniquely exquisite look which hinted at her part-European parentage. Her long, jet black hair was tied back, revealing a delicate oval face and to the casual observer she might have been any nationality; Chinese, Greek, even Italian. Her features played a game with those trying to decipher her. She was to Grant's eyes... beautiful. But it was the eyes... the eyes provided the biggest mystery to her background, they were dark, almost black. He read down the page which accompanied the photograph. Her name was Miko Arato and she'd been born in Tokyo in 1938. The only other piece of information was that she was an accomplished marksman with a rifle, and an expert sniper. Confused, Grant threw the report back onto the table. "Hardly worth using any ink for all the good that was. Is this some kind of bloody joke?" he demanded.

Penn stepped away from the doorway and picked up the discarded sheet, placing it carefully back into the folder. Masterman fixed Jack with a hard stare and he could feel the weight of the man's fury bearing down on him. "There a problem, Jack?"

"A woman sniper? Bit unusual isn't it?" said Grant.

Masterman barked out a laugh. "Not a bit unusual, Jack, it's very bloody unusual! It's unprecedented, in my experience. Oh, you hear about peasant women in Russia during the siege of Stalingrad, but never a civilian in peacetime as far as I'm aware. She's a unique young woman and we're lucky to have her."

Grant wasn't buying it. There had to be something more, something he wasn't being told. "Okay, so what's her story? The others I can understand, undercover operators and Special Forces – that's their thing, that's what they're trained for, but what does this Japanese woman have to do with—"

"She's C's daughter," Masterman interrupted. "As the file says, her name is Miko. Miko Arato. Sir Richard and her mother met when he was working undercover in Japan in the 1930's. He was posing as a journalist and she was an assistant at one of the local news agencies out there. To say she was one of his agents would be a little… crude. Theirs was a working relationship initially, they were colleagues, although knowing C, he no doubt always kept his ears open in case of receiving any useful information. Later their relationship grew personal and a child was born – Miko."

"How did you find out about her?" asked Grant.

"In the documents that C had secretly sent me, there were details containing her address and some instructions about what he wanted me to do, in the event of his death. She was his secret family, apparently he'd visited her several times over the years when she was a child– without Lady Crosby's knowledge – in Japan," Masterman explained.

"So that's how she's involved in this operation. She's taken C's murder personally," interjected Penn.

"Once I told her about the circumstances of C's death, she expressed her desire for revenge," Masterman admitted. "I initially thought I could use her as an intelligence asset on the ground in Asia. Miko works as a tour guide for Japanese tourists, so both her English and her knowledge of European cities is excellent. She had what we call 'natural cover' for travelling, recruiting and organising. Then she showed me what she could do with a rifle. That knowledge changed everything."

"And you didn't think twice about including her in this mission? No matter how good she might be with a weapon, she's still a novice." Grant couldn't help thinking about the last time Masterman had introduced a young, inexperienced woman into a Redaction operation. His heart sank at the memory of the debacle which happened in Rome several years earlier.

"For God's sake man, she was his daughter! She loved her father – worshipped him – and the thought of some assassin getting away with his murder is something she won't allow to happen. Miko will be our eyes and ears on the ground, and when we track this 'Raven' down she'll be in at the kill."

Grant nodded; it was apparent from Masterman's strong reaction that he wouldn't be moved on this point. "Okay, tell me about this 'sniper' and how she came to be so good with a rifle."

Masterman leaned back in his chair, drumming his fingers on the handle of his cane and set about searching his extensive memory for every detail. "When her mother died, she was raised by her uncle on his farm. Apparently, he'd been a sniper during his time fighting against the Americans in the Pacific. After the war, he taught the girl how to shoot. Rather unusual, granted, but teach her he did, informally of course. The girl seems to have a natural aptitude for it."

Grant weighed up the story in his mind and decided to let any further arguments slide. Masterman had already picked the team, and there was no use arguing against the Colonel. He always made the right decisions operationally and Jack had to respect him for that.

The rest of the team began to arrive from eleven o clock onwards the following morning. The two soldiers, Lang and Crane, were the first to arrive and they were introduced to Grant, with Penn playing the part of host and conducting the introductions. Both men shook hands with Grant and he could see how similar they actually were. They both had that tough and resourceful independence that was a trait of elite soldiers the world over. Grant thought they would have made a couple of good 'bouncers' in some of the rougher London clubs he knew. He guessed they knew their way around a knuckle-duster and a head-butt.

A few minutes later, a taxi pulled up in the drive to deposit Bill Hodges, looking less like a burglar and more like an aging bank manager in his de-mob suit. He had a stilted walk, as if nursing an old war wound, and the manners of a spiv. "Good day to you all," he chirped. Grant had a feeling he would like this man, respect him, certainly. He just wouldn't trust him alone with the family silver.

When the introductions were completed, Penn spoke. "I'd better put the kettle on then, get a brew going?"

But Masterman shook his head. "No we'll wait, if that's alright with you lads, wait until the sniper arrives. It would be un-gentlemanly to start without her."

Ten minutes later, there was the faint noise of a genteel knock on the door. Penn removed himself from the room and returned a moment later, popping his head around and saying, "It's the sniper, Colonel. She's here."

* * *

She entered the lounge, moving gracefully, like a dancer. There was an aura of calmness about the woman that the other members of the team instantly picked up on. They all hurriedly jumped to their feet and stood nervously, Crane and Lang shuffling their feet, while the others lined up as they were introduced one by one to Miko Arato.

Grant was the last in line to shake her hand, which gave him more time to study her petite frame and dark beauty. She was wearing a fashionable floral print dress and her height had been raised by a pair of heeled shoes. Her hair was down and ran silkily over her shoulders. But it was the eyes, the dark eyes, which accentuated her beauty, even from a distance. They shone like onyx glinting in the light. With the introductions complete, they settled themselves and while Penn prepared refreshments, Masterman handed out files containing the latest intelligence regarding their future mission. "Read it through once," he said. "It will save me repeating myself, and then we can start."

Once they'd completed the read through and placed the files on the coffee table, Masterman heaved himself to his feet with the aid of his cane and began. He looked each of them squarely in the eyes, conveying the seriousness of the situation.

"This mission is pure and simply a Redaction. Oh, I know the unit doesn't exist anymore, but it's the type of operation I would conduct in the old days. Official or not, it's a Redaction by any other name. We have an opportunity – a rare one – to get to the heart of this organisation and bring it down. You're the best people we have for this job; you are all committed and fully capable. We get an agent inside this Raven's organisation and bring it down from the inside. Once you leave this safe house, you'll be officially cast to the wind.

You'll go about your respective drab and mundane lives, not raising a whisper and not giving any clue that we're part of something greater. You will be drunks, criminals, mercenaries, layabouts, and feckless… and that's exactly what I want you to be. I want the powers-that-be to think you're washed up and yesterday's heroes… rundown and gone to seed. The next time you meet, when you'll get together again, will be in the killing zone. Where that is, I can't say… yet. You'll receive the contact, recognise the activation code word – SENTINEL – and then be given the details. I expect you to move fast, within hours, and be on the road to the location. Penn will set you up with your emergency travel papers and enough money to get you accommodated. Once you're on the ground, we'll arrange for your weapons, equipment and transportation. You'll meet with Grant and then you'll be covertly infiltrated into the target's location. I missed anything, Jordie?"

Penn shook his head and turned to the team. "You do the job, get out and then emergency evacuation protocols are implemented. We get you out, and no one is any the wiser as to what happened. Simple enough?"

"Easy," mumbled Crane.

"Piece of cake, old boy," laughed Hodges, sipping his tea.

"It's anything but," Masterman warned. "But it's the job we have and it's the job we're going to finish. Put it this way – if *we* don't, no one will. You're all deniable – you don't exist. That's our greatest strength. We are ghosts. So remember why we're here. We're here because the powers-that-be have washed their hands of the whole affair, hoping it will go away if they pay enough money. We're here to stop a maniac from causing the murder of possibly thousands of innocents. We're here because we all of us, owe a debt to the late Sir Richard Crosby."

The team talked freely for the next hour, discussing ideas, tactics, and solutions to various problems. It was an open forum, something Masterman encouraged; after all, it was their necks on the line. 'The man on the ground has ultimate control', was something he'd learned from his wartime service. When they'd solved everything they could for the moment and talked themselves out, Masterman turned to Grant and said, "Jack, be a good chap and help me up; I think we should take a stroll in the garden." Grant assisted his old commanding officer – a mere touch of the elbow, nothing more – and the pair left through the patio doors leading into the garden.

* * *

Crane stood up and watched as the odd pair began their stroll. "So that's the Gorilla, is it? He's a bit of a legend amongst our lads. Been down to the killing house a few times. Knows his stuff."

Miko came and stood beside Crane, barely coming up to his shoulder. "Why do they call him 'Gorilla'?" she asked. Her gaze focused sniper-like upon the two men walking in the garden.

"It's a nickname he picked up from the bad old days in Berlin, or so the Colonel informs me. Nobody really seems to know why he's known as Gorilla, well, except Masterman – and the Colonel isn't one for telling secrets," Penn said absentmindedly, as he collected together the discarded files.

"I understand he's an exceptionally good shot," Miko said.

"From what I know, he's one of the best Redactors the SIS ever had, good with a shooter at close quarters," said Lang. The men returned to the table, leaving the small Japanese woman alone, staring out into the garden. Now that she'd seen Gorilla Grant up close, she experienced a sense of excitement and exhilaration knowing that this man, this ape-like killer, would be the one man able to get her close to the murderer of her father.

* * *

It had always been their way, to walk and conduct business; the tall British officer and his smaller, stocky subordinate. Sometimes, it had been around the streets of Berlin or London – today it was a splendid, typically English garden. But walk they did, rain, shine or snow.

"They all have a stake in this. They've all lost someone close to them. Miko her father, Crane and Lang their mates from the Regiment, and Hodges needs a road back to keep him from prison. And you have the insurance of protecting your loved ones for the future," said Masterman, digging the tip of his walking stick into the manicured lawn.

"What about you, sir?" asked Grant.

Masterman shrugged. "I'll have the knowledge that I've finished off the threat to this country by those madmen, and taken the head of the little bastard that crippled me."

Grant accepted this and nodded. "So they're my team. The five of us, working for Sentinel on a private Redaction, ready to storm on in there and put a bullet between the eyes of this… Raven, whoever he is."

Masterman smiled at the gallows humour. "It's not perfect, not by a long shot, and it's not how we would have done it in Redaction all those years ago is it? But they're resourceful and motivated, and that counts for a lot in this game."

Grant knew this to be true and had been on Redactions which offered far less chance of success than this one. He had survived all of them… just.

"You have everything you need, everything is in place. Just get next to Trench and get under that bastard's skin. You're our Trojan horse. Show them what you can do, how valuable you can be to them, so that they'll want to wheel you out in front of the top man. Show off their pet Gorilla, eh! When that moment happens… we pounce! Just remember, Jack, your cover is your best weapon; you're a cut-throat mercenary, a borderline alcoholic and a whore-monger. Everything that appeals to their base instincts! Be a darkened version of yourself. They'll want you corrupt and dirty, a ruthless killer who cares for no one. Give them your version of Gorilla the mercenary."

"You mean just be myself, then?" said Grant, with a touch of humour.

Masterman laughed out loud, in spite of himself. "Ha! Yes, I suppose so. You alright with that?"

"I'll give it my best shot," Grant replied with a hint of sarcasm. The two men shook hands for what may well be the final time. Something they'd done many, many times before. So far that 'last' time hadn't happened yet. "Just keep feeding me information as you get it, anything which can get me inside their head. I don't care where you get it from, Colonel, just as long as it keeps me alive," said Grant. Then he turned and walked away, heading toward Penn who was waiting in the Jaguar, ready to whisk him off to a London hotel for the night. He would be on the first plane out to Amsterdam the following morning.

Masterman watched as his old comrade and friend stalked away, the swagger and rolling gait returning to him after years of being in operational retirement. He hoped the Gorilla was back, and he for one, would be glad if he was. No one could shoot or kill like the small, pugnacious Redactor. He would do everything he could to keep the intelligence flowing for him, of course he would. However, he didn't mention his most clandestine of secrets to his tame gunman.

The other member of the team, one who was known only to Penn and himself – his little dormouse, the outside member of the Sentinel Five team – who was Masterman's spy, hiding away and buried deep inside the Secret Intelligence Service.

Chapter Six

Gorilla Grant sat in an armchair, facing the dead body of Reierson and admiring his handy work. It had been a long night of waiting before he could finally get at his target. But get to him he had, and now the man was dead.

Reierson had lived in a top floor apartment on the Amstelstraat. From the information Masterman had passed to Gorilla, it seemed the Australian killer used the Amstel apartment as his resting-up base between contracts. It was the place where Reierson felt at ease, with its postcard-perfect view of the Blue Bridge below it. Not that Gorilla had seen the *Blauwbrug* lit up in its finery that evening, because he'd been standing, barely moving, hidden inside the built-in wall cupboard in Reierson's lounge for most of the night. The cupboard held the meter for the electricity supply and seemed to be an ad hoc junk space, complete with ironing board, old work boots and rusty tools. It was small and cramped, but adequate for concealing him right inside the target's living space. He'd been there, peering through the wooden slats which gave him a perfect view of the room's layout, for a little over three hours. He'd been hot and uncomfortable and eager to get on with the job. The .38 revolver had sat heavily in his gloved hand.

Gaining access to the apartment had been a simple exercise for someone of Gorilla's skills. He'd watched as Reierson left his apartment building just after seven. The man looked like a wrestler, big and powerful. His neck was as thick as a spark-plug and it was appeared to be bursting out from underneath the collar and tie he wore. Reierson was going out for the night and wherever he was going, it looked as if it was for pleasure and not business.

Reierson's front door was well-secured with an advanced modern lock, something Gorilla would never have been able to pick without spending a good twenty minutes 'attacking' it. It would take too long and leave him too exposed. But at the next apartment along, security was minimal and their door was fitted with a standard mortise. So after ringing the bell and confirming the residents were out, Gorilla set to work with his picks, gaining entry in seconds and he made his way to the apartment window, where he let himself out onto the balcony and hopped across the four-foot gap onto Reierson's balcony. In the dark, no one on the street noticed a figure jumping across and then springing the lock on the balcony French windows before climbing through. Gorilla had quickly reconnoitred the apartment, discovering it was expensively furnished and for a man of Reierson's lifestyle, tastefully decorated. Perhaps he'd hired an interior designer. Obviously being a contract man for the Raven clan paid well. Very well!

Gorilla had the gist of Reierson before he'd even opened the file Masterman had provided. The man was a street level thug who had made it lucky. Ex-Australian Army, he'd been booted out for being an arse. Some low level underworld work, kneecappings, punishment beatings and the odd debt collection caper. Then he'd finally got enough brain cells together to figure out that he could make more money by using a shooter and offing people on contract. To his credit, he seemed to have had some success, mainly easy targets and fellow criminals to be fair, but he'd evidently done enough right to get him recruited by the Raven and his people.

After searching the apartment, Gorilla had decided on the least terrible hiding spot; the wall cupboard. Not perfect, but better than standing behind the curtains with his feet sticking out like some kind of fool in a farce. He'd settled himself in, checked his angles to make sure he had a clear view of the room through the slats and then began the long, long wait for his target. Three hours in and he'd been about to abort the hit. Perhaps Reierson had shacked up at someone else's place for the night, or maybe he was drunk in a bar somewhere and wouldn't make it home. Bloody hell, he could have fallen into the canal and be dead on a slab. Hopefully... It would certainly save Gorilla a job.

Just as he was about to cancel the operation, he heard the distant sound of voices from outside, followed by the scraping of a key in the lock and the door being pushed open. The light from the hallway lit up the dark apartment and two figures entered, one tall, slim and brunette and the other big and heavyset, holding hands. The door was slammed shut and then darkness covered the room once more. What followed was the inevitable fumbling and physicality of lovers. Even in the darkness Gorilla was aware of the couple hastily removing each other's clothes, and the noises of kissing and raw sex grew louder. The man, Reierson, lifted the woman up into his arms and carried her to the lounge before gently placing her in the centre of a deep white rug in front of the fireplace. Reierson flicked a switch and the faux electric fire sprung to life, bathing the room in an erotic red glow. He lay down next to the brunette and began to kiss her body, working his hands roughly across her breasts and thighs. Moments later there was a moan of pleasure as the Australian entered the woman's body. She wrapped her legs around him and the couple began to writhe together in rhythm.

Gorilla stood in the darkness of the cupboard, half watching, half preparing himself to make a move should Reierson do... anything. But after five minutes of the Australian pumping away at the brunette, Gorilla was satisfied that his target's mind was elsewhere, buried between the woman's long legs at that particular moment in time. The couple's lovemaking grew more vigorous and the decibel level went up a notch; Reierson seemed to be about to reach his crescendo and the brunette was making all the right noises in all the right places to encourage her client. Then there was a final gasp from Reierson... and silence filled the apartment once more.

What followed were the rudimentary workings of the professional woman as she quickly gathered her clothes and dressed, ready to move on to her next client. Reierson lifted his naked bulk off the rug, walked to the bedroom and returned moments later wearing a hideous silk dressing gown of orange and black, and carrying a wad of cash wrapped in an elastic band. He peeled off several notes and held them out in his meaty fist. The woman quickly took them and stuffed them into her purse. She reached forward and offered him a chaste peck on the cheek; in return, in good Aussie style, he gave her a resounding smack on her backside as she tottered in her heels towards the exit. A slam of the door and she was gone. Now it was just the two men in the apartment. *The difference, sunshine, is that you don't know what's about to happen,* Gorilla thought.

Reierson smiled, the smile of a man who was satisfied with his life. He stretched, and Gorilla heard his back and knees click, before made his way to the drinks cabinet and poured himself a large Rémy Martin, no ice. He flicked on the record player, something rock and roll that Gorilla didn't recognize and turned the volume up. It was someone singing about being a wild thing. Reierson sat back in a high chair facing the fire and the rug he'd just made love on. His feet tapped along to the music as he sipped his drink. Gorilla was pleased. The man was relaxed, off guard, and the volume of the music would help to hide what was going to happen next. He did one final mental check: catch to the inside of the cupboard loose, gloves on, gun primed. Check. He gently pushed open the door, took three long steps forward to reach the chair, brought the gun up to the side of Reierson's head and pulled the trigger, just as the drum beat of the song intensified. The boom of the revolver was lost in the maelstrom of music. It had been that simple, that easy and that brutal – and no more than three seconds had elapsed since he'd left the confines of the wall cupboard. Taking a life sometimes took no time at all and Reierson hadn't even been aware of what happened. One moment here, the next gone. Permanently.

Gorilla sat in an adjacent armchair and waited. He waited for the banging on the door, the wail of police sirens, and the screams of panicked neighbours. When none of that eventuated he knew he was in the clear. He turned to take one last glance at the dead man. The Australian was slumped sideways in the armchair, his head tilted to the left. There was a gaping hole in his right temple, from which blood still slowly pumped. Gorilla would give it another few minutes, then he'd turn down the volume level on the record player and make his escape.

According to the latest intelligence from Masterman and Penn, their mutual enemy Trench had been spotted in the hot spots of Hong Kong recently, by a friendly source inside Hong Kong Police's Intelligence and Security section. He'd last been seen in the company of the now-deceased Reierson, a known mercenary who was rumoured to have taken part in several contract killings. That alone was enough to flag him to the authorities. It seemed that Masterman's unofficial intelligence network reached far and wide, and they now had a clue suggesting Trench had returned to his old stomping ground of Hong Kong. *Regardless*, thought Gorilla, *his work here in Amsterdam was done and the next day he would be in the clear and winging his way to Asia.*

He did one final check of the apartment, confirming for his own peace of mind that he hadn't left any clues or evidence behind. Then he placed the deniable pistol on the floor, underneath Reierson's hand. To the entire world, it would look as if the man had committed suicide and then dropped the pistol onto the floor as his life slipped away. Job done and case closed. Gorilla unlocked the front door and gave the dark shadowed body slumped in the chair a final look. It was the Gorilla's first kill in a long time and it had been oh-so-very simple.

I'm back, thought Gorilla. *I'm back with a vengeance.*

Chapter Seven

The Caucasian moved confidently through the sultry heat of the busy market place. It was one of the rougher parts of the city and at that time of night, manual workers, traders and street criminals of all persuasions were making their way home or on to their next illegal enterprise. None of them mattered to the Caucasian, he wasn't threatened by them, wasn't scared that he was the only western man in the warren-like maze of the street market. He had a look about him which said 'This is one fight you're going to lose, if you try to fuck with me.'

For the past year his name had been Janner. No first name given, just Janner. Occupation: war zone photojournalist. In truth, his name wasn't Janner and he had no experience in the world of photography or journalism, but it provided a plausible enough cover to allow him to get in and out of countries in the region so that he could indulge in his real occupation – contract murder.

His name had once been Frank Trench, but he was that man no more. He was dressed in the fashion of the day. A light coloured safari suit with bell-bottomed trousers and boots with Cuban heels. His hair had been grown long, past his collar and he now sported a drooping moustache and thick sideburns, as was the current style. Long gone were the Cavalry officers' neat haircut, regulation moustache and three piece suits from Saville Row that he'd worn when he was a member of the Redaction Unit for the British Secret Service in London. This man was rougher around the edges and had the look of some kind of playboy/adventurer, but one who would carry a concealed weapon on his body in case of trouble, which in fact he did; a push-dagger in a covert belt sheath. He continued at his strong pace, his boots clock-clocking on the wet streets, making his presence known amongst the street rats. He liked that, letting them know he was approaching. One of them attempted to talk to him – small and whip-like, a heroin addict probably - and Trench sent a warning glare the man's way. The man cowed and disappeared back into the shadows, scarpering like a cockroach.

If someone were to ask him if he missed the patriotism of working for the Secret Intelligence Service, Trench would have told them to fuck off and pistol-whipped them. Poor money, high risk, no gratitude and no chance of promotion. He thought it had been piss-poor and was nothing like working as a freelancer for his new employers… the complete polar opposite, in fact. Good money, expenses paid, travel to the glamour spots of Asia and as many hookers as he could bang, plus the killing – the killing made it all worthwhile… that and the fact that he was no longer under the thumb of that cripple, Masterman. Yeah, that had been a good day for Frank Trench, the day he'd blown good old Sentinel to kingdom come… the Raven had been especially pleased with him after that hit.

His recruitment into the Raven clan had been less than orthodox, however. It had begun with his final job for Redaction, a little over a year ago, although he didn't truly know it at the time. A trip to Hong Kong, said Masterman, sandbag a senior member of a new and up-coming mercenary organization operating in Asia. The job itself had been easy enough. Picking up the target – a man called Angel – an arms dealer who moved guns for the Japanese underworld and who was reputed to be a main supplier. The job had been simple and after that, it had been nothing Trench hadn't done before. Drug the man, take him to an abandoned location – in this case a warehouse by the docks – interrogate him and then eliminate him. Simple. But there had been something in the way the man had spoken to him. Begged – well, they all did that at this point in the game, when you had a knife at their throat – but it was more than that. It was as if he recognised a kindred spirit in the Redactor. The man had offered Trench a deal. Let him go, give him his freedom and he would reward Trench, and the Raven would reward Trench.

"Why should I?" laughed Trench, flicking his knife eagerly in his fingers.

Angel had smiled in return. "Because, the Raven can offer you far more than Masterman has ever done… Trench."

Hearing his own name thrown back at him so casually had shaken him to his core and hearing the name of the Head of the Redaction unit, doubly so. These people knew the internal workings of Redaction! How did they have access to that information?

And so Frank Trench had taken the biggest gamble of his life and trusted the man he'd been about to kill. In truth, he'd been waiting for an opportunity, a reason, to move on to a new life. England was dead to him, SIS had used him, and he wanted to be more than a poorly-paid government servant for the rest of his life. So he'd crossed the line and gone rogue, faked his death, taken up a new job, a new face and a new identity. He'd shed Trench and became Janner, hired killer. After that it had been an easy fall, and his knowledge of SIS operations had helped the Raven to dispose of any more Redaction agents sent against him. They had fallen one by one… Spence, Marlowe, Burch and then finally nailing Masterman in Australia… and they all had Frank Trench's mark on them.

His rise over the past year had been meteoric and now he was in charge of talent spotting and running all the European contract killers working for the Raven clan. It had been plain sailing and easy money until last week, when one of his top gunmen, an Australian mercenary by the name of Darren Reierson, had been found with his brains blown out in Holland. The police reports said it was suicide, judging by the forensics – a bullet to the head. Trench wasn't so sure, there was a lot that didn't add up with the picture the police had presented… but what he did know was that he was one 'contractor' down and he had an important hit contract to arrange for the Raven in the next few weeks. Bloody Reierson! Damn him, whether he had killed himself or someone had done it for him!

He moved out of the shadows of the street market and onto the main thoroughfare, heading towards his favourite club, The Pleasure Dome, a first floor dive of a place just off Nathan Road, which offered a good selection of beers and an even better selection of go-go girls. Trench had been in Hong Kong for a little over a week, laying low and enjoying some much deserved rest and recuperation before working out the details of his next contract for the Raven. But for now, he had the night to himself, the bar in his sights and the thought of having enough hard-earned cash in his pocket to pay for two, or maybe three, of his favourite comfort girls. It was going to be a fun night.

* * *

Gorilla spotted Trench when he first entered the nightclub, thanks to the full length mirrors running the length of the bar. In truth, Gorilla would have known it was Trench anywhere. He had the same arrogant swagger and pompous glare he'd always had. Trench's new persona did nothing to hide that. It was the same old game of a 'hard case' walking into a bar. Gorilla knew the rules; he'd used them himself in the past, many times. You slowly stop in the doorway and give a short, sharp glare to the toughest looking bunch in the room. It was a look that says, "I'm here now, this bar belongs to me and you lot are on probation." Trench had played this game for years and played it well.

The bar was only half full, the late night crowd hadn't yet finished eating before moving into the Pleasure Dome's realm of drinks and girls, and what customers there were had found their own little island pockets of solitude. Gorilla for his part, played his role to perfection. Sitting on one of the stools at the bar, he had the look of a slightly down-at-heel and down on his luck traveller to Hong Kong, complete with hair that needed a good trim, a thick beard and an old suit which was fraying at the cuffs and pockets. He hoped he looked like a gambler who had put everything on red, only to have it come out on black. He was nursing his second drink of the evening, a Navy rum, and he was determined to make it last as long as he could. He watched as Trench made his way to the rear of the club, to a small reserved table, waving to several people on his way. It was a good position Gorilla noted – near a backdoor exit and allowing him full view of the people in the club. Trench scanned the room once, twice and then settled back to sip at the drink a waiter had brought for him. *Obviously a regular, if the waiter knows his poison,* thought Gorilla.

Gorilla continued to sip at his drink while keeping Trench's reflection under surveillance from the corner of his eye. The club was starting to fill up now; at least twenty people had come in during the last few minutes, mainly businessmen looking for a good time with the girls, but there was also the odd European couple, canoodling in the corner and listening to the jazz band playing – playing what, Gorilla didn't know, it sounded bloody awful and not like the jazz he was used to in London. This sounded like someone was torturing a cat.

A few minutes later and nearly at the end of his rum, he felt a tap on his shoulder and was surprised to see Trench's tame waiter standing next to him. He had a stupid grin and a large drink of dubious concoction sitting on the tray in his hands. "The gentleman in the private booth wishes to buy you a drink, sir," said the waiter in a half Chinese/half cockney accent. His bow tie was crooked and he looked about twelve, Gorilla thought as he weighed up this intelligence. Gorilla shook his head. "Must have the wrong guy, mate, I don't know anyone here. Send it back."

The waiter shuffled nervously, but stayed static. "Please sir, the drink is an offering from a Mister Janner, a very important customer... please, see for yourself."

Gorilla turned slowly towards where the waiter was pointing. He knew what was coming next – the face off, his first foray into Trench's new world. They locked eyes, and Gorilla squinted as if he was trying to establish who the man was... then he let dawning realisation spread over his face in the form of a frown. Still the staring contest continued. He turned to the waiter. "Okay, leave the drink, and thank him for me." By the time he'd taken his first sip of the cocktail – something rum-based which was quite good – Trench was stood next to him, hanging on his shoulder like a vulture. "Hello, Frank. Thanks for the drink, cheers. How you keeping these days?" said Gorilla. He was being deliberately blasé, keeping it light and sipping at his drink.

Trench smiled as he sat on the next stool along and stared at the smaller, dishevelled man. "I'm doing fine, thanks Jack, keeping the wolf from the door."

"I can tell. I like your costume," said Gorilla, indicating Trench's ensemble. "What you trying to do, get down with the hippy kids and the youths?"

Trench ignored him; the only sign of his annoyance was a slight flaring of the nostrils.

"You still in?" tested Gorilla. "You on a job out here?"

Trench smiled, and it was a cold hearted, stone killer's smile. "What, you mean you don't know Jack? Is that why you're here? You come to take me back to Blighty in shackles?"

Gorilla deliberately masked his face in confusion, and for the first time that evening, regarded Trench in full. "Sorry Frank, I haven't a bloody clue what you're talking about. I got out a little after Marseilles, after that blow up in Rome. I only went back to quit. SIS did me no favours, I'm afraid."

"Ah... I heard they treated you badly after the girl got murdered," Trench said cruelly. He obviously knew it was one of Gorilla's few weak spots and was testing him for his reaction.

"They can go fuck themselves," said Gorilla bitterly, before downing the rest of his drink in one.

Trench mused upon this. "Really... really... so what you doing for sheckles these days? Whatever it is, it obviously isn't paying *that* well."

Gorilla glared at Trench and then quickly calmed himself. "I was working a bodyguard job in Europe, decent work and the money was alright for a while..."

"So what happened?" Trench asked, pushing to get to the juicy details.

Gorilla shrugged as if it was all a matter of ancient history. "Ahh well... The boss, the client, was a bit of a prick. He seemed to take it personal when his wife tried to hop into bed with me..."

Trench burst out laughing. "You always were the thinking woman's bit of rough, Jack. So that's why he fired you? Banging his old lady... a bit of a looker, was she?"

Gorilla shook his head. "No, he fired me for breaking his nose when he tried to talk down to me. As I say he was a bit of a prick."

Trench thought for a moment, seemed to accept Gorilla's explanation for what had happened. The 'Gorilla' always did have a rage inside him, and a penchant for violence. "So what brings you to Hong Kong, Jack?"

Gorilla smiled. "Bit of a holiday, see some of the old stomping grounds, see if there were any work opportunities; that sort of thing."

"What? Bodyguard work? Don't think that's the right career path for you, Jack, and I don't suppose old busted nose will be writing you any recommendations in the near future."

Gorilla, laughed at that, despite himself. "Ha, yeah, no chance. Not necessarily just bodyguard work, I'll consider anything at the moment... my cash is running out fast."

Trench lapsed into silence, and Gorilla hoped he was giving consideration to offering him a job. He knew Trench would need a replacement for Reierson, and he imagined he'd be under pressure to recruit someone soon. The only question was; would he trust Gorilla enough to consider him? Gorilla decided to play it cool and make it seem as if he didn't give a damn either way.

"Yeah, well, thanks for the drink Frank, much appreciated, but don't let me keep you from your night out," said Gorilla, hopping off the stool and standing as if he was ready to leave.

Trench stopped him with a gently restraining hand. "Hang on a minute, Jack old boy, don't get so antsy, I might just have heard of a whisper of work. It could be right up your street, if you're still up to it."

Gorilla cocked his head, intrigued. "Go on."

Trench smiled his crooked smile. "How's about we go over to my table, get a decent bloody drink, shampoo, fancy a bottle of Krug and have a very, very serious chat."

* * *

Thirty minutes and several glasses of champagne later and Trench was playing his old games. Plotting, planning, scheming, weighing up the risks and desperately trying to get inside Grant's head to discover his motives – if any. Trench moved forwards, backwards and laterally in his questioning of Grant's timeline over the past few months.

But Gorilla knew Trench's tactics and ways of old and circumvented them effortlessly. He'd been well briefed by Masterman and Penn on how to 'play it'. His case officers had done him proud. "Show him a bit of ankle, Jack," Masterman had said at one of their last briefings. "But don't lift up your skirt too easily. You have your back-story in place, we've seen to that. The bodyguard thing, bit of dodgy dealing here and there. Just enough to hold you in place and keep them interested."

Penn had agreed and interjected. "Act keen, but not too keen, for God's sake."

Gorilla brought his mind back to Trench. He'd had enough of skirting around the issues and of letting Trench have it all his own way; now he needed to stir the pot a bit. "So what happened to you, Frank? You get pushed, or did you jump out of the SIS ship?"

Trench cocked a concerned eye and played it coy. The lie when it came was practised. "Well, I got out not too long after you. I had a little fall from grace, something to do with my expenses sheet not adding up – I forget the details. Point is, I decided that I wanted to try a different career path and make a few quid into the bargain."

Gorilla frowned. He schooled his face to suggest he wasn't connecting the dots of what Trench was feeding him. "So what we talking here, Frank – drugs? Muscle work for the opium and heroin gangs? What?"

But Trench was in a buoyant mood and waved away such trivial concerns. "No, these people are in a class of their own. They pay well for short term contractors and seeing as I'm in charge of their recruitment and so forth, there's every chance that I can make it permanent for you. I'm sort of their resident head-hunter. I won't lie to you, Jack, it's dangerous, but nothing you haven't done before. Think of it as Redaction, without the posh schoolboys and bloody red tape getting in the way," said Trench smoothly.

Or without the morals and ethics, thought Gorilla.

"Where you staying while you're here?" asked Trench.

Gorilla gave him the name of a two star hotel down in the rough end of Kowloon Bay, not far from the harbour. It was a battle to figure out which would kill you first – the perpetual stench of fish, or the insects making their home in the mattresses. Trench wrinkled his nose in disgust. "Bloody hell, sounds a right shit-hole. Things must be bad if you're staying there. Look, leave it with me, let me talk to my people. I'll see if I can put a word in for you. No promises though. I'll leave a message for you at your hotel's reception desk if I've got something for you. Who knows, Jack, it might be like the old days again, me and you working in tandem."

Gorilla stood and shook Trench's hand. He for one didn't remember the old days with quite as much fondness as Trench seemed to.

* * *

Twenty minutes after Gorilla Grant had exited the Pleasure Dome, Trench made his way to the rear of the club to use the house telephone. He checked no one was within earshot and then rifled through his little black contact book. Satisfied, he dialled in the number of one of his Kowloon contacts by the name of Sammy Hong. Sammy ran a team of professional leg-breakers, small stuff really, a bit of enforcement and protection racket stuff. Nothing really in Trench's league, but they did a good job and were known to be reliable. The phone crackled into life and Trench heard a high pitched voice say, "Wei."

"Sammy, "drawled Trench. "It's Janner. How you doing, you old dog? Fantastic! Look here, got a bit of a job for a couple of your boys. I've got a *Gwai Lo* who needs a bit of a testing. Can your boys pay him a visit... What? No, not killing him, Sammy, just rough him up a bit, broken nose, couple of missing teeth, that sort of thing. Busted fingers are even better... I'll pay double if it's done in the next day or so. Got a pen? Here are the details, ready..."

Trench reeled off the address of Gorilla's hotel, what he looked like and how he wanted the beating to go down – a suspected robbery, or as near as they could get to it. The testing was in motion. Trench had learned a thing or two about testing new men for his employer. He knew how to push them, to see if they had the right stuff. Even Gorilla, who'd been an old comrade in another life, couldn't be given a free pass. In truth, Gorilla Grant had never been Trench's cup of tea. He was too confident, too close to that cripple Masterman back in the day, and if Frank Trench was being completely honest, Gorilla scared the hell out of him. Plus, Gorilla was one hell of a gunman, which had made him one of the best Redactors. The question was, did Grant still have it in him or had he gone soft since leaving SIS?

Trench wasn't sure, but he was the sure that the beating Gorilla would be receiving soon at the hands of the professional leg breakers would tell him, one way or the other.

Chapter Eight

Less than twenty-four hours later and Gorilla was ready to see if he'd been allowed, however temporarily, inside the enemy's camp. He'd been contacted by Trench earlier that day and told to meet him that night in the restaurant of his hotel, the swanky Mandarin Oriental on Connaught Road. Apparently Trench, or Janner, or whatever he was calling himself these days obviously trusted him enough to arrange a meeting at his base while he was in Hong Kong. Gorilla took that as a good sign.

The moment Gorilla stepped outside his squalid room on the fifth floor and into the equally dilapidated hotel corridor, he knew something wasn't quite right. The corridor, no bastion of well-lit walkways at the best of times, was in complete darkness. He toyed for a moment with going back inside, but he knew it wasn't a realistic option for him... he'd always been the kind who goes forward into the darkness, come hell or high water. He began to slowly walk towards the end of the long corridor. He had a choice: straight ahead to the lift, or turn to the right and the stairwell. In the darkness, neither were perfect options, but his survival instinct told him that being trapped in a lift would mean death, whereas the stairwell would at least give him room to escape or manoeuvre.

He'd almost made it to the lift and was about to reach for the door handle of the stairwell when a figure stepped casually out of a small alcove which held a long-dead potted plant. Gorilla could barely make out the man's features, except for the fact that he was Chinese, athletically built and dressed in a dark suit and shirt. At the same time, a similar figure emerged from the other side of the stairwell door and barked something at him in Chinese. Gorilla had no idea what the man said; in fact, he had no need to, because they were both speaking a language now that Gorilla was intimately familiar with – violence. The first Chinese leg breaker stepped forward and threw a powerful roundhouse kick straight into Gorilla's stomach, and from that moment on all the talking was done and combat had become the speech of the night.

Such was the force of the kick, Gorilla doubled over as it impacted on his torso and no sooner had he crouched down than the other Chinese leaned in and with a ferocious yell, hit him hard on the side of the face. Gorilla experienced a flash of pain and then warm blood flowed from a cut above his eyebrow. His head was whirling, down was up and vice versa, then he felt his body being thrusted upwards and propped against the wall. Then came multiple blows to his stomach; snapping, punishing punches – not in a flurry, but in a controlled manner. He was fighting for breath and thought he would pass out at any minute.

He turned his eye toward the Chinese man who'd kicked him initially and saw that he was slipping a heavy wooden knuckle duster onto his hand. Gorilla guessed that the two Chinese must belong to one of the many Gung-Fu street schools; they were certainly well trained and knew how to inflict pain professionally. What he knew for certain, was that if that knuckle-duster came into play and got to work on him, he would be pissing blood for months and might never walk again.

The heavyset Chinese moved forward, rubbing the knuckleduster menacingly with his off hand while his partner held Gorilla in place against the wall. Knuckles craned his head forward and began to yell directly into Gorilla's face, almost as if he was psyching himself up for what was inevitably, at least in his mind, the end of the performance. *Bad mistake sunshine,* thought Gorilla. He might not have been a trained martial artist, but Gorilla Grant had earned his spurs in many a good street fight. It might not look pretty, but bloody hell, was it effective. *Just a few more inches Knuckles,* he thought as he slowed his breathing for what was about to come. A few more inches and... BANG! Gorilla thrust his head forward with full power and smashed it directly into the nose of Knuckles, who proceeded to fly backwards into the darkened corridor, blood covering his face. Like all good street fighters who'd been brought up the hard way, Gorilla knew that as soon as you deal with idiot number one, you have to deal with idiot number two. He turned into the other man, ducking his body down and delivered a devastating uppercut into the man's balls, heard his cry of pain and then he grabbed his ears, wrenching his head downwards before he brought his knee up into the man's face. He watched as the guy crumpled onto the floor. Not stopping his momentum, Gorilla went to work on the pair with a good old-fashioned football party; kicks to the heads, thighs and hands. His shoes took the brunt of the blows well, they weren't designed for the type of punishment Gorilla was dishing out to Knuckles and his friend, but that didn't stop him from putting force behind the kicks.

The men were down, but not out. Gorilla turned and searched for an escape route; the street would be no good, there might be more waiting outside. So the best choice was up to the roof and then across the buildings until he could get to safety and gather his thoughts. He ran for the stairwell and pounded up the steps that would take him to the roof. Behind him, he could hear the pounding footsteps of the Chinese strong arms... and he knew there was only one more floor before he'd make it. He didn't look back, instead concentrating on powering his legs to take him forwards and upwards. He dismissed the sounds of running feet behind him, hoping that the access door at the top wasn't sealed, or he'd be at a dead-end.

He by-passed the fifth and final floor doorway and kept running; from the corner of his eye he could make out the dark suited figures of the two Chinese thugs on the level below him. A few more feet and he found himself on the top landing, a musty, dusty place filled with empty packing boxes. There it was, the door to the roof – wooden and cracked with peeling paint and a weak-looking handle. He took a step back, braced himself and kicked out at the lock, it wobbled but held. Another run and kick and… the door flew open, shattering the lock. His eyes, already accustomed to the darkness of the hallway were more than ready for the sultry night outside. He was just about to make his escape when the bodyweight of one of the Chinese hitters cannonballed into him, taking them both to the ground. Gorilla was fast getting back to his feet, but the Chinese was faster and launched a lightning-quick kick at Gorilla's head, which he absorbed at the last second by throwing up a guard and grabbing the man's striking leg simultaneously. Gorilla pulled the man towards him and shot out three jabs with his right hand in rapid succession, straight into his jaw. The Chinese was out cold, but Gorilla wasn't finished with him just yet.

Gorilla was small, but he was strong. He lifted the man onto his shoulder in a fireman's lift and ran towards the edge of the rooftop, fifteen feet away. Sweat and blood was running down his face, and for a brief second, he thought his legs might simply give way underneath him. He made it though and he didn't even stop, he simply lifted and threw the Chinese man over the side of the building and watched as his body fell sixty feet into the darkness of the alley below. He heard the sickly crunch when the body landed. *There was no need for a second look,* thought Gorilla, *the man was dead.*

It was the sound of feet from behind that alerted him. Gorilla turned, wiping the blood and sweat from his eyes. He saw Knuckles waiting by the roof access door, his fists up and ready in a fighting stance. *Obviously wanting to try and finish what he'd failed to start,* thought Gorilla. This time the Chinese leg breaker had two wooden knuckle dusters pushed onto his fists. They began to move counter-clockwise, circling each other, seeing who would make the first move, like boxers in a fighting ring. There was only one way to go and that was through the access door, anything else would be a sixty foot drop to the death. Gorilla's gaze fixated on the wooden knuckles. He knew he would last three seconds once they hit his face. If he'd been armed with a hand-gun, this would have been over a long time ago. But Masterman's rules had been strict – no firearms. When they want to let him in, they'd supply the shooters, he'd said.

Gorilla could see the man edging ever nearer, a step at a time, his fists up and ready in a Wing Chun fighting pose, and while Gorilla didn't have a gun to finish Knuckles off, he did have something which had been with him for a very long time and was, in some ways, more deadly than a firearm. In the final second before Knuckles decided he was ready to attack and launched himself at the unarmed Caucasian , Gorilla did something he was very practised at. He reached into his jacket pocket and in one fluid motion – a flick of the wrist and nothing more really – a shard of razor sharp steel opened up and slashed twice at the Chinese leg breaker, just as he came into range. First to the left and then a sudden back cut to the right. Gorilla heard his wail of pain, before blood and viscous fluid sprayed in an arc of crimson and yellow.

The Chinese staggered backwards, his fists clutching at his eyes, screaming in pain. Gorilla stepped back, the cut-throat razor held at the ready in case a follow up strike was needed. But there was no necessity. Gorilla had cut across the man's eyes, popping both of his eyeballs and rendering him blind. Fight over.

* * *

Gorilla took the man to the ground and placed his knee down hard onto the back of his neck. Knuckle's face was a mask of blood and it was being pushed hard into the gravel on the rooftop. "English – you speak English, sunshine," said Gorilla calmly. He was all business now. The man said something in Cantonese, something guttural. Gorilla guessed it wasn't complimentary. "Okay, here's what I'm going to do. In exactly one minute, I'm going to lean your arms against the lip of the roof and stomp down on your elbows, one at a time, and break them. It probably won't be a clean break, because I've never done anything like this before, but it will be a break. So on the off chance that you *do* understand me, you've got forty seconds left before I go to work on you."

Knuckles thrashed about blindly on the floor, but Gorilla simply increased the pressure of his knee against the back of the man's neck. "Of course, you'll already be out of action for good, what with me cutting out your eyes, so broken arms won't get you back into the job market anytime soon, will they? Hey, what did you get paid for this? Twenty dollars? Forty? Doesn't seem like very much for being blinded and disabled. Twenty seconds left..."

Knuckles was panicking now, but in among his shouts Gorilla was sure he heard the word "Okay!"

"You sure you don't speak English? Oh well, never mind. We're out of time anyway," Gorilla said as he dragged the Chinese man by his leg to the edge of the roof. "So, I'm going to brace your arm at an angle and then with just a little hop and CRACK! Hopefully, that will do it." Gorilla placed the man face down and wrenched his hand onto the lip of the roof, holding it in place with his meaty fist so that the back of the Chinese man's elbow was facing upwards. *It looked so vulnerable and brittle,* thought Gorilla. *It wouldn't take much...*

"No, no, *no!*"

Gorilla didn't move, continuing to hold the sacrificial arm in position. Just because Knuckles actually did understand English, it didn't mean he was going to start revealing his life secrets.

"I tell you! I tell you!" the man screamed, pleading with his tormentor.

"Who's your boss?"

"Arrgghh! We work for a guy, tough guy work. Collect protection money," Knuckles said desperately, blood mingling with sweat on his face.

"Well, I don't need protecting," said Gorilla. "Who paid for this to be done? Tell me and I won't break your elbows."

"A *Gwaih Lo*, someone who did business with our boss. British..."

"Did he have a name?"

"I don't know... maybe..." Knuckles said, stalling for time.

"We can start on the knees as well as the elbows," Gorilla warned. "I mean; it's not like you can run away. Bloody hell, you'd probably just fall straight off the roof in a blind panic." Gorilla chuckled at the prospect.

"Janner, I think that was the name, Janner. That's the name the boss said. But we don't hear no more please... please..."

Janner. That was the name Trench had been using in the nightclub. The little bastard. Question was, did Trench suspect him, had there been a leak, or was this a test? Was Trench just seeking confirmation that the Gorilla still had his old skills? Either way, Gorilla promised himself he would have a reckoning with Trench.

"And you promise, you won't break my arms? My work, I need them for that!"

"I promise." Gorilla did what needed to be done and left Knuckles where he'd found him, by the door of the stairwell to the roof. Someone would hear his cries soon enough, and come to his aid. True to his word, Gorilla didn't break the man's arms. Instead, he'd found a length of discarded lead pipe and smashed all of the fingers on both Knuckles hands to a bloody pulp.

Gorilla thought that was a poetic form of street justice.

Chapter Nine

Frank Trench lay back on the rumpled sheets of the king-sized bed in his tenth floor luxury suite at the Mandarin Oriental, and exhaled a sigh of pleasure and relaxation. The Mandarin was his favourite hotel whenever he stayed in Hong Kong, a luxury he could now afford.

The young Chinese whore he'd paid for earlier had only recently scampered from the room, off to another client, maybe... *or maybe,* Trench thought, *he'd worn her out for the night.* Trench rated himself an excellent lover; well, maybe not a lover, but he considered himself great at sex. He turned his head to the right and looked out at the sparkling lights illuminating a dark Kowloon Bay. He was amazed by its beauty, it was almost hypnotic and he could feel the last of the stress and tension of the last few days easing. Sleep would inevitably take a hold of him soon.

He'd checked with his people within the *Karasu-Tengu* clan about bringing Gorilla Grant on board. Had sold him up well; ex-intelligence officer, expert Redactor, noted gunman, left SIS under a cloud.

The word had come down from Hokku, the Raven's second in command, to keep Gorilla under surveillance while the 'source' checked out his recent activities. Trench knew better than to question Hokku any further. This was sacred ground, things Trench rarely got to hear about: the clan's source, a person who was somewhere high up in British Intelligence. It was the holiest of holies. Whoever the source was, he'd been instrumental in setting up Trench for recruitment and delivering the rest of the old Redaction mob to be brutally murdered. Trench had only heard his codename in passing and even then, only by accident. *Salamander:* a poisonous, hidden creature who skates along silently beneath the surface. Who the source might actually be, Trench had brooded about many a time, but he was no closer to discovering the man or woman's identity. Less than five hours later he'd received a call from Hokku, to say that Jack Grant had been given an initial 'clean bill of health' from Salamander and the Raven had given permission to go ahead and recruit Gorilla. But Salamander would keep checking... just in case.

Trench's mind turned to more recent events. It was a shame about Gorilla. When he hadn't made it to their rendezvous at the restaurant downstairs earlier, Trench had naturally assumed that the two leg breakers he'd sent had gotten a bit too 'handy' with their Gung-Fu, and paralysed Gorilla at the very least. Still, it was better that he found out now that Gorilla had lost his touch, rather than when he'd come under the clan's protection. It was fair enough to lose your touch, if you were a sportsman or an actor, but in their lethal profession, it was a death sentence. *Never mind,* Trench thought, *he would send some flowers to the hospital tomorrow...*

Trench didn't know how long he'd been asleep when it happened. He would guess no more than thirty minutes. But sleep has a strange way of disorientating the unwary and Trench couldn't be sure of anything. When it did happen, it happened not gradually, but with rapid fire intensity. He was vaguely aware of the darkness of the hotel room, and caught some kind of physical movement from the corner of one barely-opened eye... and then he felt the weight of a body on top of him, kneeling on his chest. A strong hand covered half his face and he was aware of the sharp tang of steel at his throat, a gentle but lethal pressure resting near his artery. He risked opening the one eye further and aided by the ambient light from the city, he looked up into the bearded and furious face of Gorilla Grant.

"We need to have a bit of a talk, Trench, and if I don't get the answers I want— Well, let's just say you'll be making a bit of a mess on this fancy bedcover," Gorilla growled, a hiss of menace under his breath.

Trench's heart pounded away double time as he snapped into full awareness. Christ, he could feel the pounding of his heart against Gorilla's knee and he panted, struggling to think straight through the panic which was swiftly overtaking his senses. "Jack, look... *arghhh!*"

Gorilla had drawn the cut-throat razor an inch, only an inch, along the skin at Trench's neck, not deeply, but it was enough to let the prone man know Gorilla meant business. "Shut the fuck up Trench. Speak when you're spoken to."

Trench nodded as best he could and made a determined effort to slow his breathing and calm himself. He'd badly underestimated the smaller man, something he was kicking himself over now. But he was canny enough to know that if he wanted to survive this encounter with the little assassin, he would have to play it completely straight from here on in. Gorilla had a way of sniffing out bullshit.

"One question. Why?" asked Gorilla.

"You daft or something, Jack? I had to know that you were on the level, not with SIS anymore," replied Trench, some semblance of control returning to his voice.

The anger in Gorilla's voice was evident. "I already told you that... they can go and fuck themselves after what happened in Rome! I don't work for those pricks. It's me, on my own."

"Plus..."

"Plus what?"

"Plus, I needed to see that you were still capable, that you hadn't lost either your nerve or your touch, for Christ's sake. My people take their killing very seriously and they don't like gunmen getting the jitters at the last minute when a trigger needs to be pulled," said Trench reasonably.

Gorilla leaned in towards Trench's ear. "And you thought by sending those two cretins after me, that was the best way to test me? For the record, Trench, one took a dive off the side of a tall building and is probably being eaten by some back alley rats as we speak, and the other has lost the sight in both eyes and won't be playing the piano anytime soon. The whole thing took about five minutes for me to sort out. So a test? No fucking way. It was an insult."

They seemed to have reached an impasse and Trench, knowing how to work a situation, decided to try his hand and go for broke. "So where do we go from here, Jack? As I see it, you can open up my veins and scoot back to your shitty little hotel and shitty little life scrabbling around looking for a job… or we can both sit down over a decent scotch and you can listen to my proposal."

"I don't feel much like drinking to be honest, Frank," Gorilla snarled. "So you better tell me fast what your proposal involves or—"

"A job!" barked Trench, fearful that Grant was about to rip the blade across his throat from ear-to-ear. "I bigged you up to the powers-that-be and they want you to come on board. There's a vacancy. Starting salary of five thousand dollars a month, plus a bonus for special jobs and all expenses paid. They want you – us – to attend a meeting in Vientiane in a day or two."

"To meet who?"

"Their number two guy, name of Hokku. He's a bit of a crusher, but he holds the purse strings."

"Who's number one? I don't want to be dealing with a second in command."

Trench shook his head. "Don't go there, Jack, it's a road you might not come back from… arghhh!" Gorilla had moved the razor closer to Trench's throat again and another spot of blood appeared. Trench spoke faster. "The top guy is known only as the *Karasu* – the Raven. I've only met him once, briefly, he wanted to give me a look over to see what he'd bought when he'd hired me. He likes to meet the new talent. He's a shadow, very rarely seen."

Gorilla moved the razor away from Trench's neck and sat up, pushing Trench's head back onto the bed. "So, Vientiane? Okay, sounds good. What happens next?"

Trench sat up and looked his new colleague up and down. "How's about we get you some bloody decent clothes, and spruce you up a bit. I'll book you a room here and we can at least try to drag you back into civilisation."

* * *

Jack Grant studied himself in the mirror. After a decent shower and with his face cleaned up after his recent fights, he looked more like his old self. Trench had been good to his word and arranged a room on one of the lower floors. Not quite as grand as Trench's suite, but anything was better than the fleapit he'd been forced to stay in as part of his cover story since landing in Hong Kong. That evening, there had been two visitors to his room. The first was an elderly Chinese man who came to measure him for a new suit. The man had expertly taken his measurements, stood back, inspected Grant's body shape and then left without saying a word. Grant had no doubt that within a matter of hours, there would be a new, made-to-measure suit being delivered to his hotel room.

The second visitor had arrived not long after the tailor departed and Jack had been on the verge of crawling into bed. In truth, he was exhausted after the previous day's events and all he wanted was to get some sleep. So when a light knock sounded on his hotel room door, Grant assumed it was his new suit being delivered. What he didn't expect was the woman who stood on the other side of the doorway when he flung the door open. She was tall for a Chinese woman, elegant certainly, and dressed in a coral, above the knee *Cheongsam*. Her hair had been professionally styled, twisted up off her neck, and her smile fluttered between coy and seductive. Grant recognized her by type, if not by reputation – high class hooker.

"Good evening. My name is Willow," she said. Her voice was soft, cultured and playful.

Grant thought the name suited her perfectly. She was both graceful and charming. He shook his head, knowing where the conversation would lead and not wanting to get there too easily. "Sorry, I think you have the wrong room, I—"

She ignored him, pushed open the door, took two genteel steps forward and then closed it behind her. "I am a friend of Mr. Janner. He said that I should make you comfortable this evening. Everything is taken care of."

Jack knew what Trench was up to: bringing his new employee into line, wooing him, showing him the good life, making him loyal with luxurious hotels, clothes and women. Trench was nothing, if not predictable. It had been a little over a year since Grant had been with a woman. A late night dance at the local church hall had turned into a one night stand with a young widow from one of the nearby villages. It had been a release and nothing more, and he'd never seen the woman again. A night with this girl would have the same level of meaning, sexual certainly; fun definitely, but with no more emotion than he would experience when he killed a man he'd never met before. If it meant he could get close to Trench's employers, however...

The girl took a step forward, so that they were touching, her lips gently brushing his. "I am at your disposal," she whispered softly.

Grant returned the kiss passionately, bringing her closer to him by wrapping his arms around her back. Her body stiffened momentarily, and then she relaxed in his arms as the kiss became mutual. In that moment Jack Grant wasn't sure who had sold themselves for a greater price – her for the money, or him for his soul.

* * *

Later that night, once the girl had left, Grant rose in the darkness and quickly dressed. For what he was about to do, he had to hope luck was on his side. The rules were that once he'd made contact and been taken under their wing, he was to report in quickly. To simply phone his contact from his own personal hotel telephone was too risky, just in case Trench was monitoring his calls. So Grant decided to do the next best thing and use the phone in another, empty, hotel room on the next floor down.

Finding the right room was the hardest thing, it was really down to pure blind luck that the first hotel room he investigated happened to be vacant. The door and the locks were laughable, he could have tripped them in his sleep and he was inside within seconds. The room had a similar layout to his own and he quickly made his way over to the bedside phone, picked up the handset and dialled '9' to get an outside line. He heard the click as the line was accepted and then calmly dialled the contact number which would connect him to his case officer, Jordie Penn. He listened intently into the earpiece, heard the electronic burr and was rewarded with a sleepy voice.

"Yes," said Penn.

Gorilla went through the procedures. "It's 2308. I've made contact. So far so good. I'm not inside yet, but I'm getting there. I'm staying at the Mandarin, courtesy of my new employers. I'm off to Vientiane tomorrow morning. I'll contact you as soon as I can. Stay by the phone." He put the receiver down carefully. The whole conversation had taken less than fifteen seconds. Contact with the team had been made.

* * *

The next morning, Jordie Penn was on the surveillance watch. Seated in the foyer of the Mandarin, reading that day's edition of The Times, he looked like a respectable businessman waiting to meet with an important client. His appearance had been altered by the addition of a glued on moustache and a pair of horn rimmed spectacles. Penn thought the disguise made him look like an older version of Clark Gable. Outwardly he was calm, relaxed and in control, but under the surface, his heart was racing like a train. Penn hated this part of any operation, that desolate feeling you have knowing your agent will be going out into the 'wilds', far beyond the reach of his case officer. Penn had been an agent-runner for most of his adult life, and still the feeling of dread didn't abate when your agent was off the leash and running free. It didn't matter if it was Berlin, shoving agents off to get them over the wall, or running sources inside terrorist cells as he'd done in Cyprus during the campaign there; for the agent runner, it was akin to a mother giving up one of her children. It was bloody hard. But it was why Masterman had specifically recruited him to this private operation; not only was Jordie Penn a decent case officer, he was also a loyal Englishman and decent human being.

He sat forward and picked up his tea cup, took a quick sip, made a brief scan of the foyer but there was nothing to be seen yet. In his time Penn had sat and waited at checkpoints, inside freezing cold vans in the dead of night, and in steamy cafes waiting for his agents to come back from a mission. They'd been terrified and desperate men, ready to sell out their country for either financial or ideological reasons... but they were still his agents and despite his manipulation of them, he cared for and fretted over them.

But Grant was a different kettle of fish. He was a tough man, capable and with hidden resources; a born operator. But then they all started off like that, until they found themselves deep inside the enemy's camp and the job started to get to them. It didn't take long for an undercover agent to lose his equilibrium and get confused about which way was up. Those who survived came back haunted, those who were consumed by the deception of the trade usually ended up taking their own lives or being caught, tortured and executed.

He checked his watch – 10.30am – and it was as he was considering ordering yet another bloody green tea, when he caught sight of a movement over to his right. The elevator doors opened and out bundled a busboy, carrying two small suitcases. The busboy was closely followed by the two men Penn had been waiting to see for the past hour. Trench led the way with Grant close on his heels. Both men were dressed in new suits, well-groomed and had the look of people who were about to meet someone higher up the food chain. They reached the main doors of the hotel and Trench peeled off a bank note and passed it to the grateful busboy. As if by magic, a hotel car pulled up and the busboy loaded in the suitcases. Trench turned and called to his partner. Grant took one final look around the foyer of the hotel, but his face didn't betray that he'd spotted the ever-resourceful Penn seated at one of the tables, reading his paper and drinking his tea.

Penn, to his credit, just carried on browsing through the latest international news from his paper. He paid no attention to the two Englishmen as they climbed into the car and drove off. But then, he really didn't have to. Penn was satisfied. His agent was in play.

Chapter Ten

Despite its hotchpotch mix of Corsican opium smugglers, professional gamblers, warlords, militia, arms dealers and CIA spooks, Vientiane had a much more relaxed atmosphere than Hong Kong, Gorilla mused to himself. It was a city where 'people watching' was the norm and an unwritten code of rules governed the many disparate personalities from spilling over into violence. It was a city where Asian good manners were played out in a colonial French setting, and it seemed to work perfectly.

Gorilla and Trench walked through the busy side streets on their way to the meeting. They'd stopped in for a quick beer at the bar of the Constellation Hotel an hour earlier, partly because they were early and partly to get the pulse of early evening Vientiane. The *patois* mix of Chinese, Laotian, French and English permeated the air babble-like. They'd been in Vientiane for less than five hours and would be leaving again later that night by plane, for who knew where. It was a whistle-stop visit, leaving the two Englishmen with only enough time for their private meeting with Taru Hokku, the underboss of the *Karasu-Tengu* organisation. The meeting took place at the Tan Dao Vien Restaurant, which was noted for its excellent Chinese menu and convivial atmosphere.

Hokku had the face of a salaryman or an accountant – bespectacled, sombre and preened – combined with the body of a heavyweight Sumo wrestler jammed into a business suit. Grant also suspected he'd caught a hint of a tattoo from beneath the man's shirt cuffs. It was some kind of ideograph, possibly denoting his underworld connections and affiliations, Yakuza or something similar. 'A crusher who holds the purse strings' Trench had said of him and Grant thought that description was perfect. Trench introduced Hokku to Grant, the large Japanese bowing from the waist in respect, and with the formalities out of the way, the three men sat down in a private booth at the back of the restaurant. Trench called the waiter over and ordered Russian vodka and a platter of Dim Sum for everyone. Grant turned his attention to a dark-suited man sitting nearby, nursing a glass of water. *Bodyguard,* he thought.

"Mr. Janner speaks very highly of you Mr. Grant – or would you prefer I call you Gorilla?" said Hokku, his voice surprisingly delicate for a man so immense.

"Only my close friends and enemies call me Gorilla," said Grant. "And as of this moment you're neither of those."

Hokku accepted Grant's answer in good grace and continued. "I understand that you both worked together for many years, for the British."

Grant nodded. "Indeed, Frank... er, Mr. Janner and I have covered each other's backs several times."

"And I understand that you left your previous work for the British government under somewhat of a cloud," said Hokku, not even sounding remotely apologetic for being so cutting with his guest. Business was business and an employee was an employee.

Grant frowned. "I was involved in an operation, an operation that went wrong. Someone I cared for was killed and the British wouldn't let me go after the person responsible."

"So what did you do?"

"I quit and then went after the man anyway."

"What happened to him? This man?"

"I hunted him down and killed him," said Grant simply.

"You are that good?" asked Hokku, seeming surprised by the candour of Grant's answer.

Grant nodded. "I'm the best. "

"The best with a pistol, at least, Mr. Hokku. Grant was something of a legend within the intelligence community, his reputation as a Redactor was second to none," Trench added.

"So if you're asking me If I have any loyalty to the bloody British government then the answer is no. Any loyalty I did have died with me one night in Rome when my partner was murdered. These days I'm an army of one," replied Grant sternly.

The answer seemed to satisfy Hokku and make his mind up for him. "You know our business Mr. Grant. Mr. Janner has educated you on our work?"

Before Grant had a chance to answer Trench interrupted. "I've made Jack aware that the work we carry out is for a long-standing and noble organisation, one that takes its business very seriously."

Hokku nodded, as if this was an acceptable way to begin negotiations. "My patron and I do indeed come from a long lineage stretching back generations. However, we recognise that our business, if it is to survive, must adapt and change in the modern world. Our traditions are still sacred to us, but over recent years we have decided to recruit some of the top people in the world to work with us. People like Mr. Janner here and hopefully, your good self."

Grant liked this man's self-control and manner, typical Japanese, but he was under no illusion that he was dealing with a hard core killer, despite his polite manner and respectable veneer.

"Our organisation deals with difficult problems every day. We work for only the most powerful and influential individuals. We solve problems, or on occasion, create problems for certain governments and corporations. But above all else, we have a reputation for being discreet," continued Hokku.

Grant could easily imagine the problems the Raven clan dealt with; a coup in a banana republic, stealing corporate secrets, terrorism and assassination. Grant knew the range of services the Raven could provide, but he decided to play it dumb, as if he didn't fully understand what was being offered to him. "Are we talking mercenaries? If so, that's not really my area of expertise. I was a soldier once, but mainly in the secret wars. Not front line infantry."

Trench smiled. "Not quite Jack. Think of it as a bit more wide-reaching and subtle than that. Similar to what we used to do in the old firm, except that we'll be operating for a private enterprise."

"Would you have a problem with that, Mr. Grant?" Hokku asked politely.

"At the rate of payment that Mr. Janner told me about? No, I don't have a problem with any of that. I faced far worse odds when I worked for SIS and the army. When do we start?" said Grant

Hokku smiled. "All in good time. We have many operations happening all over the world, our contractors are expected to be on stand-by for whenever a job that suits their particular skill set is arranged. I suggest that you and Janner return to Hong Kong. We will make interim arrangements for you."

* * *

Grant and Trench took their cue, stood and shook hands with the giant Japanese man and left. Hokku followed their progress with his eyes and when he was sure they'd cleared the restaurant, he motioned for his bodyguard to follow them. He wanted to be sure that this 'Gorilla' wasn't playing a very subtle game. Once he was certain of the bona fides of the man, he would brief his employer personally... but until that time, this tough-looking Englishman had a question mark hanging over his head

* * *

Later that day at Vientiane airport, the two former Redactors conversation turned to the minutiae of their trade, to bring Grant up to speed with how the contractors working for the Raven clan were expected to operate. They were sitting in the lounge, biding their time waiting for their delayed flight, so being men of experience they knew to keep the conversation quiet and to the point.

"Frank."

"Yes, Jack."

"What the fuck have you gotten me into? What are they – Yakuza?"

Trench laughed out loud at Grant's openness and honesty about his concerns. Then he set out to educate his latest recruit. "Not exactly. It's complicated. As I understand it, they're a clan which was once affiliated to the Japanese underworld, but that was many years ago. In recent years, they've transcended that and moved into operations in South America, Europe and parts of Africa. Their Japanese name is the *Karasu-Tengu* Clan, which is traditional and old school. *Karasu* means Raven, so we keep it simple and just call it the Raven organisation. Want to know how it works?"

Grant nodded, keen to let Trench settle in to his subject matter and perhaps let some useful snippet of information slip.

"So the big man accepts a job from a client – who knows who, maybe an industrialist, maybe a politician who wants to remove a rival, whatever – the *Karasu* hierarchy set the rules and the terms. With me so far?" asked Trench.

Gorilla shrugged, he knew how a contract was picked up and administered. He'd been around this business long enough, but he thought it best to stay silent and have Trench give it to him verbatim.

"The next stage is, they pick the right contractor for the job, or to be more accurate, for their European contractors I pick the right man for the job, "continued Trench. "You're on retainer to us and when I call, you better be by the bloody phone. So the job comes in and your bloody ticket comes up, we give you as much information as you need to get the job done; target bio, surveillance photos, and itinerary. We usually supply the contractor with whatever he needs for the job – travel papers, weapons, expenses, forged documents – you know the drill. If he needs something a bit extra special, well, we can organise that too, to be honest, and then it's all delivered to him in-country.

Doesn't matter if its Singapore or Peru, we've got people everywhere who can get equipment in for us covertly."

Grant raised an eyebrow at that. The *Karasu* must have paid informants and people on the payroll in several large airlines and shipping companies, not to mention people taking bribes in numerous customs ports.

"The contractor gets himself to the location at the allotted time, and plans the fine details out for himself. Gets near to the target and takes care of business. How does that sound?" concluded Trench.

"It sounds like business as usual to me, not a lot different than how we used to fuck people up when we were working for SIS," Grant grumbled.

Trench nodded and laughed. "Except the bloody money's better."

Gorilla followed suit and returned the laugh, playing along. "It sounds like you fell on your feet with this gig, Frank. How many contractors are on the payroll? Any that I'll be working with?"

Trench paused for a moment and Grant thought for one horrifying second that he'd pushed too hard and too soon for information. But then the moment passed and Trench winked at him conspiratorially.

"You'll be working with some of them soon, so it's only right that you know who else is on the team. There was a guy named Reierson, but he bought it recently. Suicide by all accounts, but there you go, it happens. He was good with a shooter, not in your league though. You're his replacement. A couple of mercenaries that worked the Congo, Billy Richardson and Taffy Davies, take care of jobs for us in Africa, they're based out of Antwerp. Ex-Welsh Guards, good soldiers. We've a couple of ex-IRA men who had been a little careless back in paddy land, Declan Sheehan and Seamus Corcoran. They toe the line, good for getting jobs done in America. New York, Chicago, that type of thing."

"Any intelligence guys?" asked Grant.

Trench nodded. "Yeah, a couple of hitters from Saigon, experts at torture, they were a part of the old security apparatus. Oh, and an old former copper on the intelligence staff from Malaya, still does the odd job for us. Name of Jasper Milburn. You know any of them?"

Gorilla shook his head. He didn't know any of them by reputation, but he was bloody well mentally logging their names, so that he could pass the information back to Penn and Masterman. "What about the Japanese contingent? Surely Hokku and his superiors must have indigenous personnel?"

But it was here that Trench clammed up. Grant sensed they'd entered forbidden territory, an area that Trench was hesitant to enter. "Well now, Jack, I'm sure they do, but it's not within my employment contract to start asking damned impertinent questions from a well-funded and organised bunch of killers. There's a demarcation line; I deal with the European contractors and the top man, the Raven, deals exclusively with his Japanese throat slitters."

"Sorry, Frank," Grant said apologetically. "I didn't mean to pry. Just like to know who everyone is and where my line ends?"

Trench shrugged as if it was a question he'd thought long and hard about himself. "They hire out killers to the wealthy and powerful, Jack old boy, doesn't matter if they're English, Japanese or from the planet Mars, it's what they do! They pay us and pay us well to do dangerous and illegal jobs, and if we're clever we do said jobs, take their fucking money and pray to God that we don't get caught. Frankly, I'd prefer a lifetime in jail over having to deal with some of the Raven's Japanese killers… those boyos don't follow the rules and don't know when to stop."

Chapter Eleven

The Raven sat as still as a stone in the darkness of his pagoda. The pagoda was his sanctuary, the place where he was strongest and most secure. It was the place where he could train and test himself in the killing arts. It was the domain of the Karasu-Tengu and his followers.

He felt the heat engulf him, the humidity encasing him. He still didn't move. His eyes were closed and his breathing was calm. But inside, his hard muscles and tendons were fixed, ready to spring at a moment's notice. He shifted subtly in his crossed leg position, barely more than a whisper against the wooden floor, as his arms reached up to fix the black hood of his Shinobi Shozoko, *the traditional clothing of his assassins, into place. The hardness of his face was lost in the blackness of the mask, only one soulless eye peered out. The other he had lost many years ago in combat, and all that remained of it now was a milky white orb.*

Lying resplendent on the floor in front of him was his Ninjato, *his favoured sword which had been forged by one of the most revered sword makers in Japan. It was a shorter version of the Samurai's* Katana, *no more than nineteen inches in length along the blade and perfect for close-quarter assassination work. The handle was bound tightly with cord and the scabbard, normally shiny and lacquered, was dulled with oil in case it should reflect light and give away his position of stealth. The first time he'd used it was when he was a boy, after he'd completed several years of training in the art of the sword by his late uncle, a legendary clan Shinobi. The last time he'd used it was three months ago, when he taken the Englishman's head in the forest in England.*

He grasped the handle confidently and silently pulled the sword from the scabbard. The blade was coated black, again to avoid reflecting any light. He silently rose to his feet and at the same time moved the Ninjato into a stealth position behind his back, tip down but ready to slash and thrust at a moment's notice. He stood motionless, waiting for the targets to come for him. They were not skilled warriors, but instead hired thugs from a nearby village who had been paid to test him. He knew they would never leave his pagoda alive. Not many did. They were merely targets to be cut down. He could hear them breathing, rasping in some cases, with fear. They would come for him soon and he would be ready. They would come, swords and knives at the ready and try to kill him, the Karasu, the Raven...

* * *

Yoshida Nakata had been born fifty-five years earlier in the province of Iga, Japan and his family lineage had been that of the Iga Clan. He'd been taught from a young age the skills and traditions of *Shinobi*, the honourable mercenary art of stealth and assassination. His father, and *his* father before him, going back six generations, had been employed as professional spies and assassins and had even survived the 'purge' by the Samurai warlord Oda Nobunanga, before fleeing to the mountains and rising again into a once more secret society. Secrets and stealth had been a fundamental part of the life and career of Nakata. He'd taken his first contract at the age of twenty, when he'd been given the task of assassinating the heir to a Yakuza family by the clan leader, his uncle. The young man himself had done nothing wrong, he was only sixteen, but the killing had been commissioned by a business rival as a warning, a threat, to the boy's father. Nakata had risen steadily within his clan after that first task, soon becoming a senior lieutenant and one of their most versatile assassins.

But Yoshida Nakata held a secret close to his heart, something which would see him killed by both his friends and enemies alike. He was a spy. He'd allowed himself to be recruited as an agent of the British Secret Intelligence Service in the 1930's. His recruiter and case officer had been working as a shipping manager for one of the British firms in Tokyo. The recruiter was a young man known to Nakata only by his cover name of 'White'. How they'd met was unusual, even by espionage standards.

Nakata had been captured during an aborted assassination contract, and was imprisoned by the target's hired thugs. He'd misjudged the level of security greatly and he'd quickly been detained and tortured. His weapon – a blowgun with poisoned darts – had swiftly been removed and Nakata had been hung upside down, blindfolded and beaten. He was aware of his torturers standing around him. He could smell them; their eagerness, their bloodlust. He knew that once they'd had their fun, the target would give the order for him to be executed. The leader of the group had stepped forward, ready to slaughter the failed assassin. Nakata had steeled himself, ready to accept his fate… then from somewhere behind him, in the distance, he heard a voice asking "Gentlemen, what is going on?" That question was followed by five popping sounds, low calibre gunshots he'd guessed, and then the noise of heavy bodies slumping onto the stone floor. Nakata remained motionless, hanging upside down and completely vulnerable. He was sure the unknown killer was going to finish him off, too. He heard slow footsteps clacking across the floor, drawing ever closer until finally, they stopped before him. He sensed the killer kneeling beside him, and he heard the man's breathing, mere inches from his face. He was surprised when the killer spoke, his accent English. "Are you injured? Can you walk?"

Yoshida Nakata had responded simply. "I can walk." In truth, he had no idea if his response was accurate; the punishing beating he'd taken could have done no end of damage, but he was desperate.

"Hang on, old boy, while I lower you down," said the Englishman, before cranking the lever holding the rope. His body had gently dropped to the floor and the rest was a disjointed blur. The Englishman wrapped one arm around him and held a semi-automatic pistol out in front of him with the other, ready to gun down any more threats. After that, Nakata must have passed out, because the next thing he remembered was being propped up in the back seat of a car and being driven at high speed out of the city and into the provinces. "Where are you taking me?" he'd asked, pain wracking his entire body. He'd turned and examined the Englishman's features through one badly swollen eye. He was young, handsome, confident, and smartly dressed.

"A little safe house we have set aside, we'll patch you up, eventually get word to your people where they can find you," his English rescuer said. "Don't worry about that now; we'll have plenty of time to talk over the next few days." The Englishman turned his attention to the man driving the car. "Hurry up, Ferguson! Put your foot down, this poor chap is bleeding all over the back seat!"

Several days later, with his wounds cleaned and bandaged by an ancient Japanese nurse, Yoshida Nakata woke up in a private room to find the young Englishman sitting at his bedside. In daylight, he looked even more youthful and handsome, but the eyes, the cold blue eyes held the stare of someone used to making harsh decisions. It was a stare that was instantly recognizable to Yoshida Nakata.

"You look better, fighting fit in fact. That training of yours has obviously paid off. Although the doctor who looked you over thinks you've lost the sight in one eye. They did rather go to town on you with the beating, I'm afraid" the man said smoothly.

Nakata stared at him, remaining non-committal and trying to read the man sitting beside him. The Englishman nodded, as if understanding his guest's reluctance to speak. "I'd like to offer you some work, separate to your clan activities; a private contract between you and me. How does that sound?"

"Work? I'm a small business trader from..." Nakata blustered.

"You are Yoshida Nakata, assassin of repute and a senior member of one of the last *Shinobi* clans remaining in Japan. You are a hired killer, an assassin who works on contract. The man you attempted to assassinate several nights ago was an underworld criminal known for his ruthless grip on the vice trade. Shame you mucked it up."

Nakata frowned, accepting that this Englishman, whoever he was, obviously knew enough about Nakata's background that there was no point in further denial. "I was too eager to complete the contract. I was foolish enough to think that my planning was exceptional. I was wrong."

"We all make mistakes, old boy, even the best of us," said the Englishman.

"But that does not mean I work for just anyone. The clan has strict rules and obligations." Nakata knew the consequences of breaching the clan's code. Execution.

The Englishman nodded. "Ahh... yes... I see. But there is the little matter of a life debt, I mean, I did rescue you from being butchered... those thugs were about an inch away from slitting your throat when I walked in and took them out. You see, I didn't just wander in there by accident, Yoshida, oh, dear me, no. I've had my eye on you for quite some time and I like what I see. I think we could work together quite well. My name is White. Alex White. I work for the rather nefarious bunch of creeps that make up the British Secret Service. I'm one of their lower ranking spies, to put it bluntly. But I recognise a good potential agent when I see one, and I see that in you, Nakata-San."

* * *

What followed was a fruitful and busy few years for the British Intelligence officer and his Japanese agent. After some initial suspicion, the pair soon settled into the everyday relationship of a Case Officer and his agent. Nothing was beyond White's imagination when it came to intelligence operations, and nothing was beyond Nakata's skill when it came to operating against the enemy; espionage, burglary, infiltration and even the odd lethal removal of enemy agents. They were a perfect pairing.

Regardless of his unusual recruitment, Nakata had been a willing participant in the whole process. He'd used the skills of his forefathers on many occasions, to assist the British Service in their quest for information about the war machine of Japan, or to eliminate enemy agents of various persuasions who had come into conflict with SIS. As a mercenary for hire, he could reconcile it completely and the thought of being judged a traitor had never entered his mind. His clan owed no direct allegiance to the Emperor or his minions, and considered them disposable within the context of the lineage of Japan. They were paid mercenaries, hired out to the highest bidder and the fact that the paymaster was effectively a foreign power made no difference whatsoever. Yoshida Nakata was a ruthless intelligence agent and assassin and didn't care either way.

In 1940, with the gears of war grinding onwards, Nakata had been a perfect recruit for intelligence and security work. Encouraged by his SIS case officer, he'd served in the *Kempeitai*, his country's intelligence and security police. After his initial year-long training in espionage, firearms, lock-picking and code breaking at the Kempeitai's special training school in Tokyo, Nakata had quickly risen to the rank of Captain. His first operational responsibility had been co-ordinating and recruiting Japanese chemists and scientists to be a part of the Kempeitai's Unit 731, a covert chemical and biological research facility in Japanese-controlled North East China. He'd seen first hand the atrocities which had been committed; had taken part in some himself. The torture, the rape, the vivisection, the chemical and weapons testing on human subjects; all meant to advance the Japanese military's weapons capabilities.

One of the personnel under Captain Nakata's command was a young, studious-looking chemist called Okawa Reizo. His job was to test virulent bacteria strains on the unwitting Chinese prisoners and see if the strains could be replicated and made more flexible in how they attacked their subjects. One day, Reizo requested to see his senior commander, Captain Nakata. The young chemist entered Nakata's office, bowed formally and presented the Captain with a sealed folder.

Nakata glared at this strange young man. He was thin and pasty-looking and he certainly didn't inspire confidence in one such as Yoshida Nakata. "What is this?" he asked.

"Captain, it is a file I've been preparing for you alone. It is all my own work, research that I've been completing in my own time while in the laboratory," Reizo said nervously.

Nakata eyed him coldly. "I ask again. What is *this*?"

The young chemist swallowed hard. "Captain... forgive me... part of my daytime duties are to test the resilience of certain bacteria and viruses. To see how they react against one another."

Nakata nodded in understanding. In truth, he had no idea what this idiot was talking about, these scientists spoke in a language all of their own. But he knew that to appear ignorant of what the men under his command were talking about could be viewed as a sign of weakness. And Yoshida Nakata was not weak and would never be seen that way.

Reizo continued. "I was trialling a number of different serums, some biological and some chemical, over many weeks. Most of them were failures, Captain, in fact all of them were. All except for one. One of the test subjects has shown promise."

"A human test subject?"

Reizo nodded. "A Chinese woman. She did not die, well, not immediately. In fact, for over twenty-four hours, she seemed to thrive on the virus serum I'd injected into her. The results were limited, but showed real potential."

Nakata sat forward and stared hard at the chemist. "Explain to me what you mean. What was so special about this particular serum?"

Reizo brightened and straightened his back, his confidence returning. "My Captain, it was a mixture, a cocktail if you like. I had isolated a strain of rabies and combined it with a number of other chemical compounds; drugs, in simple terms."

"What types of drugs?"

Reizo rattled off a number of names which Nakata had no knowledge of or any idea of what they did. Again, he simply nodded, feigning understanding. "And what was the result?"

The young chemist grinned. "It made the subject both violent, and unaware of her surroundings. The subject was a frail elderly Chinese woman... she weighed almost nothing. I injected her and within thirty minutes, she seemed to enter almost a trance-like state; this was followed by a brief outburst of violence against the guards who had been goading her. She wrestled one guard to the ground and started beating him. She knocked him unconscious with her bare hands!"

"Impossible," Nakata scoffed. He knew how brutal and violent the facility's guards could be – for them to be bested by a prisoner, an old woman, was unthinkable.

"I saw it with my own eyes, Captain. She picked him up and threw him against the cell wall before she attacked him. The other guard rushed in and clubbed her. Three hours later, she died from side effects of the compound I'd given her. Her body appeared to feed on itself, from the inside out."

Nakata glanced down once more at the technical folder lying in front of him. It meant nothing to him... they were details outside of his knowledge. But the idea of a serum that could do that? *That* interested him. "Why are you bringing this to me now?" he asked.

Reizo clutched his hands together anxiously. "I have gone as far as I can go on my own with this project. I would like official permission and resources to further investigate the possibilities for this particular serum. For that, I need your signature and authorisation."

Nakata thought for a moment. "Could it be improved? Could the host be kept alive for an extended period, to allow time for further refinement?"

Reizo nodded. "I believe it could, depending on the research we're able to conduct with your permission."

Nakata's mind was working swiftly, adapting to the concept, considering the possibilities. He had ideas, some uses for what this 'thing' could do. Perhaps there was potential in this project... perhaps... something for the future; a weapon, a means of attack. "Who else knows about this private research of yours?" he asked.

"Only you and I, my research assistant and the two guards who are assigned to me," Reizo answered.

"Then keep it that way. You may keep your assistant, but all your findings and the details of the project should be passed to me directly. I want no-one else involved. Do you understand?"

"I... I... of course," said Reizo, and Nakata noticed his hands were shaking when he bowed.

Nakata reached into his desk for a pen and signed his name and military number on the bottom of an authorisation document, before handing it over to Reizo. "Please keep me informed. I wish you the best of luck." The young chemist, bowed again and left, clutching his official authorisation. Nakata sat back in his chair and reflected upon what he'd just been told. An opportunity perhaps? Something that would allow Nakata to advance within the Kempeitai? He just needed to keep this project contained, especially if it proved successful. The young chemist he would need, but the assistant, well, he would need to be silenced and as for those guards who'd witnessed the effects of the virus –there were many, many battlefronts where soldiers could die in Asia.

* * *

In February 1942, Singapore had fallen to the Japanese Imperial Army. The Japanese advanced rapidly through Malaya to Singapore and took both with minimal casualties, capturing thousands of Allied troops and civilians, routing the country and bringing it to heel. Somewhere within that military might was Major Yoshida Nakata, recently transferred to the Kempeitai East District Branch, the headquarters of which was located in the old YMCA building on Stamford Road. In the months following the invasion, the Kempeitai conducted anti-Japanese purges and the massacre of civilians by the auxiliary police was commonplace. Singapore was a city enveloped in fear.

Despite having risen in rank, Nakata continued to pass vital intelligence to his British spymasters, specifically, his case officer Mr. White.

The means of communication was a secret radio set which had been buried in the forests on the outskirts of Singapore in the months before the invasion. Nakata would, on some pretext, take the staff car and go walking out in the hills. In reality, he would unearth the radio set and send coded intelligence reports about troop movements, casualties and the morale among the population. He was careful and only transmitted when he knew that the Kempeitai were overrun with an operation elsewhere. And all that had remained the same, until one fateful day in March of 1942 when the life of Yoshida Nakata, double agent and traitor to his own country, turned on its head and caused him to question his own sanity.

He'd been summoned by his senior officer, Colonel Fujimoto, on a matter of urgency. The Colonel was a fussy man, tall for a Japanese, who liked to involve himself in all kinds of areas he had no seniority in. Nakata thought he was meddlesome and a buffoon. But he was a senior officer, so it was wise to simply nod and agree in most instances. "We have identified a British subject we located hiding in the city, we believe he may be a spy. We're holding him in one of our cells. I am handling the interrogation personally; perhaps you would like to assist me," the Colonel said, marching up and down at a steady pace in his office

Major Nakata nodded, but his stomach lurched unhappily. A British spy... hiding in the city? No... please don't let it be...

* * *

The cell was dark and hot and the wretch of a man who was manacled face down on a surgical table in front of them was battered and bruised,; only a dirty loin cloth was wrapped around his hips to cover his nakedness. But even with the gloom in the interrogation cell, the dirt and sweat covering the man's face, Nakata instantly recognised his SIS case officer, the man known to him as Alex White. 'White' had been captured less than a week ago while operating undercover in

Japanese-occupied Singapore. He'd been informed against by another prisoner, who'd denounced the Englishman as an undercover spy.

Colonel Fujimoto had personally taken charge of the beatings, using an old piece of bamboo. So far, the Colonel informed him, the English-man had been completely uncooperative. What would Major Nakata suggest as an expedient means to elicit information from the prisoner?

Nakata felt beads of sweat running down the crease of his neck. Could he do this, could he assist in the interrogation, the torture of the man who was his case officer, who had once saved his life and who over the years he had come to think of as a friend?

"Major," barked the Colonel. "Suggestions?"

"Sleep deprivation?"

The Colonel shook his head. "We have done this… the man has been kept awake for almost three days."

Alex White groaned as Nakata looked down at him with both pity and remorse for what he knew was to come. In the interrogation sec-tion of his basic training phase, the rule had been that after sleep de-privation and physical assault, the next and most effective method of extracting information was by denailing the subject; the removal of both finger and toenails. However, the Japanese soldiers had improved on that barbaric method by introducing sharpened bamboo shoots and driving them up and underneath the subject's nails. Although Nakata had never personally taken part in such an extreme action, he'd heard the reports from Kempeitai officers in the field that it was effective.

"Bamboo treatment," he heard himself say, but it didn't sound like his voice. He couldn't believe he'd said the words. White moved his head up and looked directly into the eyes of the man who'd suggested the method of his latest pain. He looked into the eyes of his friend, his agent – his torturer, his captor.

"Excellent," Colonel Fujimoto shouted cheerfully. He gave the or-der for the guards outside the interrogation cells to bring him some sharpened bamboo nails. "Major, would you care to indulge?"

Nakata looked over at the tall officer and shook his head. "Unfortu-nately, I have been summoned to witness an execution organised by

Colonel Oshiro later today at the Police Station. He is personally going for his unit's execution record. One hundred heads, I understand."

The Colonel looked disgruntled, but accepted that a prior summons by a senior officer overruled his own interrogation. "I understand, thank you Major. I will let you know how we progress with the subject."

Nakata nodded and made his way steadily out of the interrogation cell. He'd almost reached his staff vehicle when he heard the first agonizing shrieks of pain from the Englishman. It cut into him like the blade of a Katana.

* * *

Several hours later and feigning important business elsewhere in the city, Nakata dismissed his driver for the evening and drove out to the foothills of the forest where the radio set was stashed. He retrieved it, checked the signal and sent an emergency contact protocol to the SIS radio section. The communiqué told of an SIS officer who had been captured and was currently being interrogated by the Kempeitai, and of an agent in place to try for a rescue attempt. Then he waited, sitting silently in the gloom of the forest. An hour later and the return signal started to come through. The message was short and stark in its clarity:

RESCUE DENIED. ELIMINATE OFFICER BY ANY MEANS NECESSARY WITHIN NEXT 24 HOURS. OUT.

The British, thought Yoshida Nakata, *were as ruthless a bunch as his own people.* They'd handed down a death sentence on their own officer.

Nakata made his move later that night.

The easiest thing would have been to don his military uniform and order his way in. But that would expose him to his colleagues and officers and… then what? Walk out with a prisoner in tow? Besides, he had no authority to remove a prisoner, Kempeitai or not, and it would require signed documentation from his superior officer before he could get anywhere near the interrogation room. So he resorted to the practices he knew best, stealth and covert entry. Only this time, it would be against the Japanese Imperial Army. Despite having limited resources, he'd donned the dark clothes of the *Shinobi*, his old clan, smearing his face with dirt and mud and carried the *Tanto* knife used for silently eliminating sentries and targets in confined spaces. Around his waist he'd wrapped a small grappling hook with a twelve-foot length of rope. These were the only tools he'd need. The *Shinobi* were expected to be able to improvise at a moment's notice and be resourceful. He'd dressed himself and wore his weapons and laughed at the idea that he'd have to break into a prisoner of war camp to rescue the enemy. The irony was not lost upon him.

The skills he'd learned as a boy came to him as easily as a flick of his hair or a scratch of his nose. He'd moved swiftly in the darkness… approaching the twenty-foot-high perimeter wall where he knew the guards were at their weakest. He used the grappling hook to scale the wall, clambering up like a cockroach on a black curtain and slipped silently over the top. He'd crouched in the darkness, feeling the cool of the night attack his eyes through the hood over his head. From his very brief reconnaissance, he knew that the British prisoners, poor wretches that they were, were kept in a wing on the far side of the compound. To complete his mission, he would have to cross some wide open spaces and negotiate the rest of the outbuildings if he wanted to reach the Englishman. The first few hundred yards were easy, merely staying in the shadows and avoiding any light. But as he got nearer to the interrogation building, the light grew brighter and the regularity of the guards increased. The first guard he'd approached silently from the rear and taken him down with a knuckle blow to the nerve cluster behind the man's ear. The guard dropped like a puppet whose strings were cut and Nakata had been quick to drag his unconscious body out of view and dump it in the space under the nearest hut. With the intensity of the blow, the man would be out for an hour at least.

Creeping along the darkness of the compound wall it had been the guard standing directly outside the detention block who had caused him the most trouble. He'd almost made it to within killing distance when the guard spotted him from the corner of his eye. Nakata jumped at the last moment, Tanto raised and ready to slash open the man's throat, anything to silence him before he could sound the alarm. Nakata had covered the guard's mouth with his left hand and thrust the short knife up and into his throat, ripping sideways to destroy the vocal chords. The only noise emitted was a faint gurgling sound, which was barely noticeable in the quiet compound. A quick thrust with the blade up and under the ribcage and into the heart, and the guard was silenced permanently.

He removed the keys from the guard's belt pouch and let himself into the detention block. After the coolness of the night, the detention building was a hothouse. He moved silently down the darkened corridor, peering through the slides to find the Englishman. He found him in the fifth cell. He knew that he may have to carry the Englishman such was the frailty and weakness of his body. His colleagues in the Kempetai had been thorough in their torture and his body was a shadow of its former self. Death would have been a welcome release if his captors had granted it. Soldiers had it rough in the cells, but suspected spies would have had a special kind of treatment at the hands of their interrogators. Even for a killer as ruthless as Yoshida Nakata the thought made him shudder. He knew that the Kempetai had no level to which they would not sink when it came to torture and the debasement of prisoners who they viewed as beneath them. The wretched rags hung off the SIS agent's skeletal frame, his eyes were gaunt and hollow, but worst of all was the smell of decay and death that permeated his body. It clung to him like the plague.

The man known as Alex White stared up at the hooded figure in black, standing in the doorway of the cell. *He must think that death has come for him this night,* thought Nakata. Yoshida Nakata took a single, silent step forward into the cell and spoke in English. "Can you walk?"

The eyes of the Englishmen widened with shock, then recognition. He said one word, "Yoshida." He was saved.

* * *

Two hours after escaping from the Stamford Road building and being smuggled out into the countryside in the trunk of Major Nakata's staff car, the two men sat in the rain and the mud under a makeshift shelter provided by the canopy of the jungle. Between them, they had a canteen of water and a little rice that Nakata had brought with him.

"Did you tell them anything?" asked Nakata, squatting next to the ragged spy.

"No… not much… not everything… no."

"Did you tell them about me? I have to know. It is important for both our sakes."

The Englishman shook his head. "No, I swear. I gave up my shipping network, my agents from Tokyo, but not you… not the big agents… not yet. They hadn't had me long enough… but I suppose I would have done it in time."

Nakata seemed to accept this with good grace. No one could hold out against physical torture indefinitely. It seemed he'd rescued his case officer just in time. He closed his eyes and contemplated his next move. He was bound by an obligation to this man. To snuff out his life, as easy as that would be here in the vastness of the jungle, somehow did not sit right with him. The English spy had, after all, risked his own life to save him all those years ago. "I was ordered to kill you. Kill you inside the camp, if possible, find out what you'd told them and then silence you before you betrayed any more British operations," said Nakata harshly, eager to spit the venomous words out.

The wretch of an Englishman tensed and then through sheer exhaustion, his body slumped and he seemed ready to accept his suspected fate. Murdered by his own people.

"Get up. I am letting you go free." Nakata pointed. "You head in that direction. Move quickly, take as little rest as you can manage. Soon you will reach the border, keep out of sight until you are sure. Sooner or later, you'll meet an allied patrol. Make yourself known to them. Here, take this," said Nakata, handing the Englishman a pistol he'd removed from his knapsack. "Now go," he hissed. "Tell them that you knocked out a guard, killed another and escaped. It protects me, it protects you. You're weak, but you can make it if you are cautious and cunning."

Alex White seemed unsure what to do for a moment. He stood in the darkness of the jungle and stared blankly at his agent and friend. "Yoshida, I..."

"Just go. This is no time for speeches. Be safe, my friend." Nakata had watched as the Englishman ran off, heading deeper into the jungle. His case officer would either survive, or be caught and returned to the camp to resume his torture. If that was the case, then Yoshida Nakata would be a dead man; either way, he was satisfied that the life debt he owed this Englishman had been repaid in full.

* * *

It had been more than a decade before he saw the English spy again. By that time, of course, the world had moved on. The war had ended and old enemies became new trading partners.

From 1945 onwards, Nakata was hunted constantly and only survived due to his training in stealth and infiltration. For weeks he'd lived off the land, staying far away from the allied soldiers tracking down Japanese war criminals on their lists. Eventually, he'd heard of the bombs which destroyed Nagasaki and Hiroshima. The Japanese Imperial Army had been defeated by the Allies. Hirohito had surrendered and this version of his war was over.

In desperation, he'd stalked and killed a young Japanese soldier, buried his body in the reeds, and took his uniform and identity cards. The soldier was a man of no consequence. He was a soldier of almost no ranking and therefore unlikely to be hunted by either the Allies or his own people. But this young soldier did have one important thing in his favour. He was not Yoshida Nakata, traitor and assassin. His name was clean. And so for a period of a year he'd become a POW, surrendering to the American interrogators and answering their questions. He'd survived on his wits, playing the role of the poor dumb soldier whose identity he'd taken. Until eventually, he'd been seated before a British Captain with the responsibility for intelligence and told the young man, with a whisker of hair on his young lip, that he had been, for the best part of a decade, an agent of British Intelligence.

"Well of course, I shall have to verify your story," said the young Captain, casting a doubtful eye over his dubious prisoner.

Yoshida Nakata, once an enemy agent, had been granted immunity for his war crimes by his protectors within SIS and the British establishment. It hadn't taken long before SIS had scooped up their agent, whom they'd thought long dead. After that, he had been reborn with a new start and a clean record.

The rise of Yoshida Nakata had been meteoric after that. Following the death of his uncle, the clan leader Kenta Nakata, there'd been an internal war within the Nakata clan as to who should take control of this secret society. Battle lines were drawn between some of the older *Shinobi*, each determined to wait out the opposition and strike when they were at their weakest. With cunning ruthlessness, Yoshida Nakata had driven a wedge between the warring factions inside his clan and personally taken the heads of the two contenders on a bloody and brutal night. Assassin had hunted assassin. The next day, he'd called a conference for the entire clan's soldiers and presented the heads of his rivals as a gift to those who would remain loyal to him. He'd ruled supreme over his clan, gathered his closest allies and brothers to him and taken control with an iron grip.

He'd reorganized his clan, making it suitable for the melting pot of the Cold War. He embroiled himself in the world of international mercenaries, private assassins for hire and the movement of illegal arms sales in Asia. His operatives were contracted out to the Russians, the Bulgarians, even the Libyans; anyone that needed an enemy agent liquidated. But he understood that he still had to be a part of the shadows, his name could not be connected in any way with the operations he was conducting. He would need to be a shadow, a ghost, a phantom. He took the title of the *Karasu-Tengu*, the legendary monster that was half-demon and half-raven. The name was soon feared within the Yakuza underworld as the *Karasu* violently dispatched anyone that dared to challenge or threaten him. He was swift and merciless. He was now the *Oyabun*, the leader, of the *Karasu-Tengu* clan. His lieutenants never met with him personally and instead orders were issued through his trusted *Saiko-Komon*, chief advisor, the formidable Hokku. The Raven and his clan had, at their disposal, a network of couriers, agents, smugglers and assassins. All were professional, and all were ruthless. His reach stretched far and wide within the international criminal networks. He was known and respected and he dealt with traitors in the most extreme fashion. Death was his stock in trade. The wealth he'd accumulated had been wisely poured into his legitimate enterprises, most notably his flagship corporation; Nakata Industries. Through this, he was able to purchase a cutting edge research facility, laboratory, vehicles and sea and air transport vessels.

The English spy had also risen within the ranks, to become a part of the establishment that had saved Yoshida Nakata all those years ago. Both had, over the years, cultivated a veneer of respectability, but now the Englishman was a co-ordinator, rather than a field agent. He was on the ascent and climbing rapidly. So it had been a surprise to both men that on an ordinary day in the winter of 1956, they had both, accidentally, made each other's acquaintance once more. It was unplanned and unexpected. Fate it seemed, had taken a hand and it would prove to be a fruitful and dangerous rekindling of a relationship for both the spy and his long-time agent. They'd both been in Tokyo visiting the Meiji Shrine, there'd been no subterfuge involved, merely a random chance, a passing encounter. The shrine had been moderately busy and the two former colleagues had simply passed each other. They'd both paid their respects separately and had been ready to leave. Yoshida Nakata had been the first to notice the Caucasian man. He'd simply walked up calmly, bowed out of respect and said, "Hello my friend. It is so good to see you again."

The Englishman, who'd once used the working name of Alex White had turned in surprise, took a moment to register the man in front of him and then smiled that open and warm smile of his. "Nakata–San, my friend…"

* * *

Their cabal had been formed out of bitterness and opportunity. It was a mutual arrangement, borne out of the days of their secret war. What had started as a friendly meeting in a tea house between two old comrades had, over the months and with caution, developed into something more. No one had mentioned the word 'traitor' even though they both knew that treachery against their respective countries was what they were taking part in to further their own naked ambitions. In some ventures, there is almost a psychic link that connects co-conspirators and for the Englishman and the Japanese assassin this was certainly the case.

The Englishman was bitter about his betrayal by his SIS masters, the capture, the torture, the leaving him to rot in a Japanese hellhole of a camp, the order for his murder. He'd worked hard to rise within his organisation, but still... at the back of his mind, there was a persistent nagging that someone should pay for what he'd gone through and what he was still suffering now; the nightmares, the horrors, the years of mental trauma. He'd pulled himself back from the brink of suicide many a time, clawed his way back to reality and sanity. He'd bided his time and waited... waited for an opportunity to take some kind of revenge, however small, on the people, the establishment which had left him for dead. All that nonsense on the SIS new agent course, 'We always bring our people home'. Bullshit. He'd been forgotten by some fop of an SIS desk officer when the going had gotten tough... war or no war. They'd left him... and when they couldn't rescue him, they'd decided to kill him. Except they would have used an official term for it... elimination, expediency – something that hid from the sensitive souls in the War Office what they were really talking about; the assassination of one of their own officers. And he hated them for it... hated them with a passion that burned. He needed a road back and it was the reuniting with his former agent that had provided him with the opportunity he needed.

As for Yoshida Nakata, the now reborn crime lord and assassin clan leader, his motivation was what it always had been; the acquisition of wealth, power and influence. He was a man of respectability, a captain of the new Japanese industrial complex. His true self was hidden behind a veil of legitimacy. But Nakata, the Raven, had a plan, something that was far above his contract killing, arms dealing and extortion, something to be played on a bigger stage, and something which would send shockwaves throughout the Western world. A slow revenge. A joining of forces. Old comrades protecting each other's backs, helping each other along for their mutual benefit, gaining power and influence along the way. It was from this humble beginning that the Raven and the Salamander were born; one the planner and one the agent of influence, able to manipulate behind the scenes and in the corridors of power. Theirs would be a devastating partnership.

And from this embryonic pact came their long term plan, to hold control over the most powerful governments in the world and reap the financial rewards, by means of the ultimate terror weapon; the *Kyonshi*. The Raven would pick his targets wisely. For instance, he knew that to threaten the CIA or the Russians would bring about his downfall, so when he'd bankrupted the British, and Salamander had his thirst for revenge against them quenched, he would move on to the Germans, then the French, the Swiss and the Italians. Over the course of the next decade, the Raven wallowed in his invincibility. He was a man with no wife and no children. His only love was for power and domination over those who feared him. When he died, he would leave nothing of himself behind. His bones would be dust and he would go to face the lord Buddha as a lone warrior.

* * *

Ensconced in the sanctuary of his pagoda, Yoshida Nakata prepared for combat. In the darkness of his training hall, he stood motionless. His senses awake, alive and he could smell his targets approaching. He could smell the fear and desperation in all of them. They approached as a pack, foolishly thinking that numbers would protect them from the Raven. They were wrong. He watched as they came at him. They were slow, foolish, not even a challenge... even for a training session, he'd expected better fodder than this. He quickly stepped back and slashed with his sword, the blade arcing down, its steel giving a faint hiss as it cut through the warm air around him before it hit flesh. There was a silent gasp, an aroma of fresh blood and the noise of a body falling in the darkness. Yoshida Nakata's blade had barely stopped moving before it was angled horizontally and slicing through the neck of the second attacker... he too fell... as did the third and the fourth. The room was filled with the carnage of silent death and Yoshida Nakata had barely moved from his spot. He knelt down in the darkness of the room and sheathed the sword in the scabbard across his back. He breathed deeply and relaxed. Within moments, the doors to the training level of the dojo slid back and the huge bulk of Hokku entered the room. The giant Japanese looked down at the dismembered bodies strewn across the floor. He wrinkled his nose in disgust at the blood and then turned his attention to his *Oyabun*. "They were satisfactory?" he asked.

The Raven stood slowly and frowned, his one clear eye fixed on Hokku. "They were of poor quality, easy fodder."

"I will punish the recruiter in the village. The next batch will be up to standard. I will not let the skills of my master wane," Hokku replied earnestly.

The Raven shook his head. "No, my brother, you misunderstand me. It is not myself that I was training... it was my steel which required blood to quench its thirst."

Hokku stared down at his master's sword and nodded in understanding. The sword was but an extension of the man, after all.

"Come, we have much to discuss. Our time today is short," said the Raven.

Chapter Twelve

Hokku was experienced enough to know that the Raven implicitly distrusted the telephone at the best of times, and especially when important matters relating to the working of the clan needed to be discussed. It was always a meeting held in secrecy and face-to-face. The Raven was a careful man, having survived many conspiracies and plots against him. Which was why Hokku, the *Saiko-Komon*, or senior organiser, of the *Karasu-Tengu* clan, was forced to give his opinions directly to his *Oyabun* on the employment of a new *gaijin* contractor.

Not that Hokku would ever be summoned into the busy evening streets of Tokyo, to attend the high rise headquarters of Nakata Industries. Nakata Industries was a respected corporation that had been formed in the embers of Japan's defeat in 1945 and it had played a major part in giving Yoshida Nakata a veneer of respectability. Nakata was now known as one of the foremost businessmen of modern Japan, known for his stoic work ethics and determination to make the pharmaceutical branch of Nakata Industries the best in the world. Already he was developing corporate strategies to branch out into the American and European markets.

Nakata sat calm and in control at his desk on the upper level of the pagoda. He looked the very epitome of a successful Japanese Chief Executive Officer. Dark business suit, sombre tie, elegant gold watch at his wrist. He was a man who, through his legitimate business, had made many contacts in the Ministry of International Trade and Industry and various branches of the *Kokkaii*, the national Parliament. He was respected and influential. But Hokku knew that was only the outer mask of the man. In his glass office block in Tokyo, he conducted the business of Nakata Industries, but it was here in the pagoda that he would officiate his true affairs. Beneath the respectability, Yoshida Nakata's true heart lay in the world of arms dealing, terrorism-for-hire, espionage and contract assassination. It ran in his blood, had done so for generations, and it was what drove him forward; the adventure, the violence and the intrigue of being the leader of one of the last of the assassin clans.

But where the other clans such as the *Iga* and the *Koga* had refused to change with the ways of modern Japan, Hokku knew that the brilliance and visionary planning of Yoshida Nakata ensured that the *Karasu* clan would continue for another hundred years. The Raven had respected the old ways of the *Shinobi*, but had been wise enough to expand and outgrow the confines of Japan. He made contacts with other organised crime families throughout the world and had, on many occasions, provided services that helped their businesses thrive. And the fact that no one was any the wiser regarding his true identity, was a testament to his skills as a prudent and careful operator.

They sat across the desk from each other and discussed the details of their business as only warriors who have fought and killed side-by-side can. They spoke in hushed tones, Hokku briefing his master and Nakata only occasionally asking a pertinent question if it was needed. There was a contract being placed by a high ranking Mafioso, who was keen to remove a rival in the Turkish heroin pipeline... job currently being organised. The training of a Right-Wing extremist group in Peru... job being considered. The payment of $20,000 from a senior Chinese official who wanted his mistress's Western lover murdered in Paris. The man also wanted to have the murder filmed, so that he could gloat repeatedly. The organising of a bombing campaign designed to destabilise a small African economy and thus increase the need to bring in 'foreign' corporations to manage the country's diamond mining operation. And finally the recruitment of a new *gaijin* contractor, a former spy who was reputed to be an exceptional gun-man and assassin.

The Raven nodded, satisfied that the day-to-day operations of the clan were being well attended to by his senior advisor. Now he wanted to focus on the most important of operations and the one which would gain him the most reward and power. He settled back in the leather chair and fixed Hokku with a stare of authority. "And how are we progressing with the *Kyonshi* operation?"

Hokku searched for the information that was secreted away in his vast memory. Nothing would ever be committed to paper, not while Hokku was responsible for the clan's most audacious plot, a plot that had been years in the planning. "Everything is as we envisioned. The technical devices are completed and can be in place within a week at any of the target countries and locations that you choose."

"And the conduit responsible for the transfer of monies, once the British decide to pay again?" asked the Raven. His one good eye fixed on his clan brother.

"It is all in order, *Oyabun*. The money transfer route is impeccable and untraceable. Salamander will deal with any last minute problems, if the British government decide to stall. He will exert a small amount of pressure here or there; he is perfectly placed to bend them to our bidding."

"And the architects? They are still unaware of their impending fate?"

Hokku nodded. The 'architects' were the two technical experts who had been vital in helping the *Kyonshi* operation come to fruition. One was an expert in bio-toxins who had helped develop the virus under the cover of the legitimate Nakata Industries chemical division, while the other was an engineer and explosives expert who had been given the task of developing several small devices to help deliver the toxin into the wider populace. Both had outlived their usefulness and would soon need to be eliminated. The less people that knew of the operation, the better.

"They are both still in Brazil, living the good life and keeping a low profile until the operation has been completed… or that is what they have been led to believe," said Hokku.

The Raven mused on the information. His mind was working rapidly, bringing all the threads together, and then merging them into one. Surely, that was the sign of a great leader, having that ability to take the abstract and make it co-ordinated. "Perhaps there is a way that we can combine these separate operations, temporarily," he said, staring down in deep thought at his powerful hands. "The *gaijin*, the one that Trench is so enamoured with… the new contractor…"

"Grant – his cryptonym is Gorilla," explained Hokku.

"Has he been tested?"

Hokku knew that the Raven expected the best from his contractors. Before they were given anything of value to do, they were first tested to see if they could live up to the standards of the clan. If not, they usually disappeared. "Trench had some Chinese gung-fu thugs try to attack him in Hong Kong."

"How did he respond?"

"He killed one and seriously disabled the other… blinded him and left him with broken hands, so I am informed. Grant only received a few cuts and bruises," replied Hokku honestly.

The Raven raised an eyebrow at that. A *gaijin* besting two martial artists in hand-to-hand combat! "So, not just skills with a firearm then? Although protocol dictates he should have killed them both!"

"Perhaps he let the other man live to send a message," countered Hokku. That comment brought the full gaze of the Raven upon him.

"You admire him, like him even? Share your thoughts with me as my senior advisor," said the Raven.

Hokku considered his response before replying. "For a *gaijin* of little culture, I did like him, yes. The man was honest, directly so sometimes, and he is undoubtedly a skilled killer of men. I think he would work well under the control of Trench, perhaps even taking over from Trench at some point in the future and running our European contractors."

The Raven nodded, having made up his mind. "Send him to Brazil to eliminate the two architects. Their time has come. He can take over from that fool, Reierson. The one that committed *seppuku.*"

"I shall see to it at once," said Hokku.

"I want this contract completed as soon as possible. He is to have minimal back-up and a short window to carry out the executions. Do not give him the best equipment we have, give him something… basic. Something that will make the contract that much more challenging," ordered the Raven.

"You mean to have him fail, *Oyabun*?"

"No, never! I merely wish to see how a man of this Gorilla's reputation can cope when he has the odds working against him."

Hokku thought that was an understatement – minimal back up, poor equipment, a solo contractor doing both hits and all within a short time frame? "And if he should fail?"

"Then he will have been tested and found wanting. I fully expect that he won't make it out of Brazil alive. Make sure that Police Captain we have on the payroll is standing by, ready to gun him down if we need to remove him. Of course, if this Gorilla succeeds, well then…"

"Yes *Oyabun*?"

The Raven smiled and stood ready to leave, his car waiting to whisk him to his legitimate life in the business world of Tokyo. "Then bring him to me. I would have him stand before me, as I would wish to look into his soul and see a kindred spirit. I would wish to see my best man face-to-face."

Chapter Thirteen

HONG KONG – OCTOBER 1967

The first real intelligence provided to the Sentinel team, from their undercover agent inside the Raven clan, was delivered to a pre-arranged dead letter box which was actually behind the cistern of a toilet in one of the many anonymous restaurants in Kowloon. Gorilla had filled the dead letter box on the Saturday morning, as soon as he'd arrived back from Vientiane, and then followed it up with a call to the safe contact number which directed him straight to his case officer, Penn.

When it was opened and the numbers were decoded, it sent a shockwave of excitement through the team. They were ready, primed and keen to get into the action on an operation which had, thus far, been slow going. But all that changed when the coded message turned up at their ad hoc base in Hong Kong, an apartment they'd rented for several weeks, through a front company that Penn had access to. They had names; they had targets, now they could launch into action.

"We've hit a goldmine! And Gorilla went in behind enemy lines to get it!" cheered Penn, ever the loyal agent runner. "We've got the names of several black operators, already on various criminal wanted lists!"

"And once we have names, we can soon find out locations," added Masterman, thinking of his unofficial source inside SIS. His little dormouse who had access to the secret liaison files of SIS, the Security

Service and by default, numerous friendly intelligence and enforcement agencies across the world. His little dormouse would be able to
track down the locations of these people and then it would be game
over for them.

"We take out the Irishmen, the mercenaries and that old bruiser
from Malaya," Masterman had decreed.

"But what about the rest of them, boss?" asked Penn. "Don't we get
to take a pot shot at them, too?"

But Masterman had firmly put his foot down on this option. "We
target our own traitors and rogue operators only; the others can be
left alone… for now."

After deliberating on the pros and cons of this for several minutes,
Penn had quickly seen the wisdom of Masterman's train of thought.
Taking out a few home grown mercenaries would certainly reduce
the amount of opposition they would have to deal with later on, when
things reached an inevitable climax. And to completely eliminate a
whole team of the Raven's people would put Grant at even more risk
as the possible leak inside the organisation. They knew Trench wasn't
stupid and they'd guessed correctly that his suspicious mind would
initially go to his new boy, Gorilla, as the source of the leak. But with
only some of the contractors dead, the Sentinel team hoped Trench
would have some reservations, some doubts about his conclusions.
Maybe the contractors were just in the wrong places at the wrong
time; maybe they'd been killed by rivals of the Raven as a warning.
Maybe it was to do with each killer's own private 'contracts'? Whatever the doubt was, Masterman hoped it would buy Gorilla a bit more
time to discover the Raven's location and track him to his lair. The
next step was to give the names to his little dormouse, see what she
could discover and then… wait.

Finally, with the fresh information incorporated into their operational planning, Masterman gave the order to Penn to issue the alerts.
"Get the rest of the team back here, Jordie, bring my boys and girls
home. Send them the code word. Let's get them into the game and
earning their money. It's time to get them armed!"

* * *

MANCHESTER, ENGLAND

It was nearly time to down tools. Tommy Crane stood up and stretched, hearing his back click ominously. He'd been at it for the past eight hours, back-breaking work in the cold and wet. General labourer, moving rubbish, lifting bricks, digging foundations. It was the best he could get at short notice; cash in hand, off the foreman's books and no questions asked. He'd told them he was ex-army and needed a bit of work. They hadn't bothered asking what regiment, and he doubted they'd have known what he was talking about anyway, even if he'd mention Special Forces – nobody in civvie life knew the Hereford boys existed.

He took off the work gloves he'd been using for the past hour of digging and tucked them into his overalls. The rest of the lads on this shift at the housing development site were mostly tradesmen; bricklayers, carpenters, plasterers, sparks, plumbers. Crane and the few of his fellow labourers where on the bottom of the pile – the shit shovellers, the lackeys capable of lifting wood and bags of cement.

He trudged through the muddy track that would be someone's front lawn in six months' time. He was halfway to the site toilet, ready to wait in the queue in the pissin rain when he heard his name being called from the foreman's Portakabin across the width of the building site.

"Crane! Phone call for yeh!" The huge foreman's harsh Ulster bark cut through the air, catching everyone's attention in the vicinity.

Crane changed direction and headed towards the Portakabin. When he entered the office, his boss grumbled. "I've better things to do than to be your messenger, Crane. Personal calls aren't allowed on site, so make it quick and get back to work." The Irishman stomped out of the office and into the rain.

Crane picked up the phone and spoke. "This is Tommy Crane."

He recognised the voice at once; it was Jordie Penn. "This is Sentinel Funeral Directors of Lympstone," Penn said down the line. "I'm so sorry to bother you at work, Mr. Crane. Sadly, your great Aunt has passed away and we wondered if you could arrange to travel to Lympstone and take care of the burial arrangements, at your earliest convenience."

The call was disconnected abruptly and Crane settled the receiver back into the cradle. He was glad to get the call – no more working on a building site for a while. He'd received the SENTINEL activation code. He was back in play.

* * *

CROYDON, LONDON

"And don't come back, you bloody drunkard!"

Andy Lang landed in the gutter, the stench of stale beer, fags and fresh blood from his cut lip in his nostrils. The landlord, a big bruiser brought in by the Brewery to sort out 'trouble' in one of the pubs in the South London area, had personally done the dirty work and ejected him. He'd been thrown out of the 'Crown and Roses' for making a nuisance of himself twice over the past month. Tonight, he'd knocked a tray load of beer flying, started a fight, and his crowning glory had been grabbing the arse of the landlady and giving it a none-too-gentle squeeze. The inevitable shouting and punches had followed... before he'd left the boozer horizontally and landed in the street.

He rolled over in the gutter; his head swimming from the amount of alcohol he'd consumed, as well as the punch he'd just received. His once-new suit, which he'd bought for himself when he signed out of the army, was covered in blood, piss and rain. He was a mess. Not the first time, probably not the last. He staggered to his feet and the cold night air hit him like a sharp slap. He breathed in and exhaled, letting the night's events wash over him. From inside the pub, he could hear the sound of laughter and drinking.

His lodgings where along the Croydon High Street, a flat above a launderette. It was nothing startling, just two rooms and a toilet. Barely worth the money he paid for it out of his severance pay from the army, but it would do him fine… for now. For the past month he'd lived a life of boredom and inactivity, which for someone with his background and experiences was a hard road to travel. He'd hunted terrorists in jungles and on mountains, he was one of the elite of the British army, and now here he was… a drunk, a layabout and a troublemaker. It was killing him.

But it was the best cover story he'd ever had.

Why had he thrown away, or at least made it look as if he had thrown away, a promising career in his country's elite forces? Why was he taking part in what was to all intents and purposes, an illegal operation without the direct knowledge of his own government?

It was simple. He'd lost several of his brothers-in-arms to this Raven and his terror organisation. Taffy Jones and Dave Shackley had been part of the bodyguard team protecting Colonel Masterman, in the aborted agent handover on the docks in Australia. Both Taff and Dave had saved his neck more than once on operations with the Regiment. He was doing this for probably the same reason that his pal Tommy Crane was; he felt he owed them.

He trudged home, feeling low and dejected. When he finally made it to the front door, he was violently ill, puked his guts up all over the pavement. Taking in a deep breath, he let the cold air fill his lungs. God, that felt better. He fumbled the key from his pocket and went through the rigmarole of trying to aim the key at the lock. On the sixth attempt, he got it and let himself into the damp hallway.

A leaflet for a local nightclub had been pushed under the front door. Nothing remarkable, a place he wouldn't be seen dead in – full of ponces with long hair and weird clothes. But it was only when he turned the leaflet over and saw the words 'Sentinel Promotions' written in the top right hand corner that he knew tonight would be his last drinking session for a while.

* * *

GOLDERS GREEN, LONDON

Mori Goldman stared down at the heavy stones in his hand and knew he could get twice as much as what he was going to pay for them. On this deal, he would make a huge profit.

Not that Hodges would know how much – oh sure, he would know they were worth something – just not exactly how much in the internal workings of the London diamond trade. Hodges was, after all, just a thief.

Mori Goldman had used Bill Hodges several times over the years, as a courier to smuggle diamonds of dubious reputation to his contacts in Europe. He knew the ex-soldier – something top secret in the jungle wars, apparently – was tough and resourceful. He also knew Hodges was a thief in his black heart, through and through. But they'd formed a mutual trading agreement based not on trust, per se, but more realistically, on mutual greed. It was a case of better the devil you know.

Mori stared down at the diamond necklace Hodges had liberated from somewhere. "I'll give you three hundred, best I can do at the moment," he said

He saw Hodges' face darken; anger spreading across it.

"Piss off, Mori. Don't even try to play me for a fool. That's at least five hundred quid's worth of swag lying there in your sweaty little mitts," countered Hodges. The swag had been liberated from a safe at an exclusive address in Mayfair, some Arab who was a flunky to one of the royal families out there. It had been a piece of cake – watch until the owners went away, back door entrance and then a bit of 'jelly' to take care of the safe. Bingo! And when Bill Hodges had a nice little tickle from his thievery, he always brought the booty to Mori Goldman's little jewellery shop in Golders Green. Mori was, after all, one of the best 'fences' in the business. He could move stuff quickly, had the right contacts, and knew enough to be discreet.

"Alright, seeing as it's you Bill, four hundred. Any more than that and I'm cutting my own throat," said Goldman, running a finger across his throat.

Hodges let the moment hang, let Mori Goldman swing in the wind for a few seconds more and then nodded in agreement. Moments later, the deal was done with a handshake.

"Oh, by the way... I almost forgot. A message turned up for you last week."

Hodges looked up from counting his cash payment. Mori Goldman was one of several 'faces' who was happy, for a small fee, to take in unofficial messages for Bill Hodges, professional criminal. The fat diamond merchant rummaged in his desk drawer and pulled out a postcard with scenes of Margate on the front, handing it across. Hodges took in the scene on the front of a bawdy strongman at a local fair before turning it over. Aside from the address of Mori Goldman's little shop, it bore only a few more words. It was signed 'Mr. Sentinel'.

The game is on, thought Hodges. Tonight, he would rip open the emergency pack hidden inside the mattress in his bedsit and recover the false passport and cash. Soon he would be back to his old life, and back to the action.

* * *

PARIS, FRANCE.

"And over to the left, we have the Arc de Triomphe, which is one of the most famous landmarks in Paris. It honours those who fought and died for France in the French Revolution and the Napoleonic wars..."

Miko had her tour group following her like a bunch of lost puppies. They clung to her every word and over the course of the past half a day, she had educated, informed, and amused them with her well-rehearsed patter. She was their leader for the day. They had travelled along the Seine in the coach, up past the Eiffel Tower, enjoyed a long visit to the Louvre, and spent considerable time gazing at the Sacré-

Cœur. It was the same old routine, same old dialogue, same old route for Miko Arato, tour guide to wealthy Japanese tourists.

Later that day, when the coach had dropped off her party at their hotel, Miko took a cab to her own hotel, a little place on the Rue Lecluse where she always stayed when she was on the Paris tour guide job. She collected her room key from Reception and was just about to head towards the lift when she heard the receptionist call out. *"Excusez-moi , mademoiselle , vous avez un message."*

Miko turned and smiled sweetly as the middle aged lady dashed around the counter and handed her an envelope. Miko's hand trembled as she took it. She knew what it was instantly, could somehow sense the gravity of the information this envelope concealed. She thanked the receptionist and hurriedly made her way up to her room on the third floor. Letting herself in, she checked around the room closed the curtains and flicked on the bedside lamp. She took a long breath and gently slit open the envelope with one manicured fingernail. Inside she found a single piece of paper with a single word written in the centre. It said simply, '*Senchineru*', which in English, translated into Sentinel.

* * *

They flew in separately to Hong Kong, all using false documentation and all arriving from countries outside of their homelands. Though Miko was not taking part in the 'Redactions' on the mercenaries – she had, after all, only vowed to go after the killers of her father and had no interest in the elimination of British traitors – it was felt by all concerned that for team cohesion she should be in on *all* parts of the operational planning.

"We're going to take these buggers down," said Penn at the safe house. "One at a time, like chopping down trees in a forest."

"Think of it as a warm up for the big target," warned Masterman, leaning heavily on his cane.

"So, who fancies what?" asked Penn.

The team had all swapped glances, seeing who would jump first.

"I'll take the Micks," said Hodges. "I've a couple of ideas on how to deal with them."

Penn nodded in acceptance.

"Me and Tommy will take the mercenaries," said Lang. "Only seems right, Brits taking on other Brits don't it?"

Masterman nodded with pride at the two members of his old Regiment. "I agree lads, something I whole heartedly approve of. We take care of our own – good and bad! Which is why I'll be taking a little trip to Singapore, to take care of that slimy bastard Milburn. Something I'm greatly looking forward to, I might add."

* * *

MADRID – NOVEMBER 1967

The two Irishmen, Declan Sheehan and Seamus Corcoran left their apartment building on the Calle de Caracas and walked to their car, a new Fiat. They were up for a night out, a few beers, talk through their options and decide whether to stay in Madrid or move location. They'd spent the day hunting around for work and so far, they'd drawn a blank. There was a possibility of some 'heavy hitter' work for a Madrid-based illegal arms dealer... taking out business rivals, warning off the opposition, but nothing concrete at the minute. The arms dealer had remained non-committal, but promised to give the former Irish terrorists a call if anything pressing came up.

They knew they would always have the contract work from the Japanese organisation they were employed by, but for men like these, there always seemed to be a 'grass is always greener on the other side' mentality. They'd actually been toying with the prospect of breaking free from the Raven group for the past few months. The work paid well, but was strictly limited... maybe twice a year, if they were lucky and requiring the odd trip to America. They both agreed they needed something of their own, work they could pick and choose from. Not that they were ungrateful, after hot footing it out of Ireland with Special Branch on their tails, and being wanted men for terrorist offences against the Crown, Sheehan and Corcoran had been bloody lucky to be contracted to the Japanese killers.

"Seamus, do us a favour," said the tall, red-headed Sheehan, tossing the other man the car keys. "You drive; my head is banging after listening to that fecking Spaniard all afternoon. I need a drink."

The black-haired and black-hearted 'Derry gunman, Corcoran, caught the keys one-handed, opened the door to the little Fiat and settled himself into the driver's seat. He reached across and flicked up the passenger door lock, letting Sheehan settle into his seat before he spoke. "Where are we bloody well going for a drink then?" asked Corcoran.

"Not Franco's! That piss he serves, I wouldn't feed it to the Proddy's! No, we'll go to that place over on—"

Sheehan never got to finish his sentence, because in that same split-second, Corcoran shoved the key into the ignition and turned it with a forceful motion, something he'd done numerous times before. The turning of the key set off a chain reaction, sparking an electrical current down through the vehicle and into the detonator buried deep inside blocks of plastic explosive which had been secured to the underside of the vehicle in the wheel arches.

The blast lifted the vehicle fifteen feet into the air, nose first, and then ripped apart the undercarriage, along with the two human beings inside. By the time the remains of the vehicle landed, it had exploded into a fireball. Of the two Irishmen inside, there was very little left to positively identify the bodies.

* * *

ANTWERP – NOVEMBER 1967

The party had been good, bloody good. Beer, hookers and pills. It had been a wild night alright. Richardson and Davies, ex-Welsh

Guards, former good soldiers were spent, both physically and financially. But that was okay... there was always new work and new money coming in for them.

They'd started partying early the previous day, celebrating the completion of a contract in Sierra Leone for the Raven organisation. The Japanese group were their most prestigious employers, always ready with the big contracts and the most dangerous jobs. Not that Richardson and Davies were scared of a little danger. No, far from it. They were professional soldiers who'd made the shift to the mercenary trade quite easily. They'd worked all over Africa, bits of South America and lots of Asia before being recruited into the private assassins-for-hire business the Raven oversaw.

With the job over, the boys drank and danced, fucked and blew their minds with whatever drugs they could score from their dealers. It was a way for them to unwind, let off steam. Unfortunately for them, it also made them distracted, sloppy, and careless and they'd both missed the surveillance placed on them by the two hard-faced men who'd been watching them for the past two days.

So it took the two mercenaries completely by surprise when the door to their apartment overlooking the Scheldt estuary was booted in and two shadows burst in, one moving left into the lounge and the other to the right. Richardson, to his credit, made a fumbled attempt to reach for the .45 pistol hidden underneath the cushions where he'd been sleeping. He never made it.

The sub-machine gun fire ripped apart the naked bodies of the two men and the women who lay strewn across them. Modern munitions are very unforgiving on human flesh and the barrage of 9mm from the MP40's shredded them all in seconds. Blood, tissue and bone mingled with sofa stuffing and shattered glass, giving the room, if only for a few seconds, an almost ethereal quality. Within seconds, the noise had abated and the shadows were gone, as quickly as they'd entered. Their final touch was to lob a couple of M42 grenades into the blood soaked room, just to be sure.

* * *

SINGAPORE – NOVEMBER 1967

"I believe that with the right personnel behind this little operation of yours, you could have quite a lucrative result by the end of the year," said Milburn. He was on his third gin and tonic, happy and confident that he'd talked this potential 'client' into hiring him. The client was paying for the drinks and lunch, and Milburn was happy to let him.

They were in the Long Bar of the Raffles Hotel, had been since lunch time. They'd met and appraised each other and then settled into a quiet corner of the bar. "Away from prying eyes and ears, what old boy," said the client. *Obviously, discretion was the order of the day,* thought Milburn. So they'd chatted casually. The client, a tall, middle-aged gentleman, sporting a scar on his face, a limp and a walking stick, was wearing a summer suit, and a Panama hat and he'd led the conversation. And Milburn, renegade and killer, had lapped it up. Talk of a long term contract, training opportunities, teaching insurgents, maybe a bit of personal throat-slitting on the side. Somewhere in Latin America… somewhere that needed some covert personnel to help out the poor local security forces. The client had dug about in Asia and come across the name of Jasper Milburn, mercenary for hire. The client was the money man; Milburn, he hoped, would be the operational controller on the ground. Several rounds of drinks later and Milburn excused himself to visit the toilet. The client nodded graciously and said "No problem, old boy, take your time. If you need to pee, you need to pee, what!"

The Raffles really was an exceptional hotel, world famous in fact, Milburn thought. It was beautiful to walk through. So good of the client to cover his expenses flying into Singapore and then buying him lunch and drinks. Maybe if this contract panned out, he could tell those Japanese butchers to bugger off once and for all. They paid well but… they sent shivers down the spine of Jasper Milburn. They were just *too* ruthless.

The toilets were empty and he found a cubicle at the far end of the row and settled himself down. Too much good food and over-imbibing, especially all those G&T's the client had poured down his neck, had taken a toll on his bladder. *And let's face it,* he thought, *you're in the middle of negotiating a business contract –an illegal and deadly business contract for sure, but a business contract nonetheless.* He needed to keep a relatively clear head. Minutes later, he'd finished in the small cubicle, opened the door and was surprised to see the client, Panama hat and all, standing directly outside the lavatory door. Confusion passed across Milburn's face, then fear as the client reached out one deceptively strong hand, covered Milburn's mouth and pushed him back forcefully into the cubicle. Milburn landed hard on the cistern, the wind knocked out of him, but before he had time to react, he became aware of the client's other hand, holding a long thin stiletto knife in a firm grip. The knife moved forward at speed, aimed at Milburn's heart, and plunged in once, twice, three times… the pain sharp and powerful, intense and all-consuming. Milburn stopped counting the number of times the blade entered his body at thirteen. He stopped counting, because he was dead.

The client stood back to admire his handy work. Knifing was always a messy business, but then, Masterman had received plenty of practical experience in killing people with a knife during his wartime operations, silencing sentries on guard duty, mostly. He wiped the stiletto clean on the dead man's suit jacket before slipping it back into the sheath which made up the handle of his walking cane. A small 'click' and it was back in place, to the entire world appearing to be nothing more than an ornamental stick. He kicked Milburn's legs into the toilet cubicle and gently closed the door after him. It would be hours before the body was discovered.

Masterman checked himself in the mirror: no blood, tie straight and hat pulled down to cover his features. On his way out he removed the 'OUT OF ORDER' sign he'd stuck to the door before he'd Redacted Milburn. Within minutes, he'd left the hotel and was being whisked toward the airport in a taxi.

Two hours later, a cleaner discovered the body of a former veteran of the Malaya campaign, brutally stabbed to death. Witnesses remembered the victim talking to a tall Englishman earlier that evening. The tall Englishman had been wearing a Panama hat, suffered a pronounced limp and carried a walking stick... but what happened to him, nobody could say.

International news agencies around the world would later report on these seemingly random acts of violence. The murders would forever remain unsolved and the police knew they had little chance of finding the people responsible. No one connected the separate incidents in any way. Men of violence usually did something to earn such a ruthless end, and in truth, no one really cared.

Chapter Fourteen

The meeting of the unofficially named 'Berserkers' took place on a wet Friday afternoon in London. Officially, it was known as the Biological Warfare Crisis Management Committee and its regular meeting place during this sensitive period was an obscure room on the upper floor of 70 Whitehall. It had been created as a direct result of the threat from the Raven Organisation.

In attendance, as they had been for the previous meetings during the crisis, were the Prime Minister, his Foreign Secretary, the Home Secretary and the Chief of the Defence Staff. Representing the covert arm of the British Government were the Director Generals of both the Security Service (MI5) and the Government Code and Communications Headquarters (GCHQ) as well as Sir John Hart, a career diplomat who had been given the role of Chief of the Secret Intelligence Service, as well as the Chairman (Acting) of the Joint Intelligence Committee, the official overseer of all the intelligence and security apparatus for Her Majesty's Government. The last member of the committee was a small bird of a man, wearing a tweed suit. His name was Professor Maurice Barking and he was one of the leading biological and germ warfare experts from the Microbiological Research Unit at Porton Down in Wiltshire.

The meeting had been in full flow for twenty minutes, and had been mainly concerned with what new strategy was going to be used to counter this current threat. So far, none of the members of the committee had come up with a tangible solution.

"We need, Prime Minister, to throw an aggressive operation at these killers! We should not be demeaning ourselves by bartering with them!" said C.

"I thought this committee had decided the risk was too great," replied the Foreign Secretary.

"Especially if the threat is real… and not a… umm… a ploy just to extort money," cautioned the D-G of the Security Service.

"We have no evidence that this virus is real, our experts say it can't be done," C threw back in response.

"What about the footage… the boy killing that animal… feasting on it almost!" said the D-G of MI5.

"Could be a fake, designed to elicit a response," advised the Prime Minister.

"Or it could be real… and we could be laying ourselves open to a terrorist threat of apocalyptic proportions. After all, these people killed your predecessor over it," said the Home Secretary dourly, turning to look at the Chief of SIS. The mood in the room changed drastically. No one wanted dead bodies on the streets of London, Birmingham or Liverpool.

"Can I just interject for a moment, Prime Minister?" The voice was calm, soothing to listen to, and yet it held a clear authority. Its owner was Sir Marcus Thorne, the Deputy Chairman of the Joint Intelligence Committee. He was tall, his sandy hair greying at the temples, and his manner was one of respectable seniority. He was a man who was comfortable within the corridors of power. For the purposes of this meeting, he was acting Chairman of the JIC, following the recent heart attack of Sir Bernard Cowley, the official Chairman. It had been Thorne who'd stepped into the breach and helped re-organise SIS, following the sad death of Sir Richard Crosby, the 'old' C.

"Please do, Sir Marcus," said the Prime Minister.

"Thank you. It seems to me that we have much to lose and not a lot to gain from blundering in with limited intelligence," said Thorne.

"Sir Marcus, I believe a covert operation is not beyond the realms of possibility," suggested C.

Thorne looked across at his protégé. In the chaos following the old 'C's' murder, it had been Thorne who'd championed the cause of Sir John Hart, to take over the position as chief spy of Her Majesty's Secret Service. He only hoped his faith hadn't been misplaced. "Really? Do you have, perhaps, some unseen intelligence information that we are not privy to, C? I hope not, because that would go against our working rules. As an old SIS hand myself, I understand the need to keep actionable intelligence limited, but not to this committee, surely."

"I... um... er ... of course not," floundered C.

"So *do* you have some new information?" asked the Prime Minister

"Or perhaps a source for that information?" countered Thorne.

Sir John Hart knew instantly that he'd been caught in a trap, a trap he'd had a hand in himself, bloody fool that he was sometimes. His bravado had gotten the better of him and he knew it. "There is the possibility that we may have a useable source on the fringes of this terrorist group. It's still early days, but my officers are currently assessing his reliability."

"An agent... an agent that SIS has actively recruited?" asked the Prime Minister, sitting up straighter.

"A walk-in agent, Prime Minister... he approached our man in Tokyo, offering information about a group he'd been contracted to," muttered C.

"So who is he, this source?" asked the Foreign Secretary. He was keen to know if a diplomatic incident was in the offing and how he could avoid it! Bloody spies were always buggering about on his bailiwick.

"Well, no names obviously, Minister. All I can say is that he's connected to the Japanese underworld and he was recently part of a security detail transporting a high value cargo from one part of Japan to another," said C.

"What was the cargo?"asked the Foreign Secretary

"The details, thus far, are imprecise. But it was shipped in a truck resembling what we would use for moving dangerous substances such as chemicals."

"The Beserker virus, you think? What they call the *Kyonshi*, 'the living dead', if my Japanese serves me correctly," asked Thorne.

"As I say, it's too early to say. All we know is that his security team were only responsible for the security for part of the journey, after that it was handed over to another group. Therefore, I suggest we put together a strike force, led by officers from my service," said C.

This last comment was directed at the General representing the Chief of the Defence Staff. He was a sturdily built professional soldier, who'd seen action in every theatre of war for the past thirty years. He frowned. He didn't like the way that 'his' men were being cornered into a power play by these civil servants; men who, to the best of his knowledge, had never had to spill blood on a battlefield.

"Would that be possible, General?" asked the Prime Minister. "To put together a unit capable of launching a rapid attack?"

The General knew that when dealing with politicians, it was best to keep the answers vague until they'd made a decision. Many a soldier had died due to an abundance of enthusiasm on behalf of a back room boy. "It is certainly possible, Prime Minister; the Special Forces people up in Hereford for example are more geared towards this type of work... as are the Royal Marines and the Paratroop Regiment. But again, it would depend on the target and the level of intelligence we would be provided with." *The ball is back in your side of the court, sunshine,* thought the General, glancing over at C.

"Well let's make this happen, move the ball along," shouted the Prime Minister. He did so with enthusiasm at having found a positive action they could take; it made him feel as if he was in control of situations that were beyond his borders.

"My officers hope to gain access to this potential source sometime over the next week. Communication in this trade is always slow," said C, cautiously.

"And I can alert the Commanding Officer at Hereford, get him to come up with some basic plans, get his teams ready," said the General.

Thorne suddenly had the impression the meeting was being taken over by madmen. It was spiralling out of control and he needed to bring them all back to reality with an explosive bump. "Prime Minister, I do think we need to take a pause, take a step back before we launch into anything too hastily."

"You have concerns, Sir Marcus?" said the Prime Minister, frowning. He did so hate it when a good plan was frowned upon by his people, even one as talented as Thorne.

Thorne nodded. "There seem to be an awful lot of 'ifs' and 'buts' being bandied about, but nothing concrete, no information of any substance. Until the time comes when SIS can give us something tangible, something definitive, I would urge caution once again. To close down negotiations with these terrorists, or even worse to renege on the terms that we'd already agreed to could prove fatal!"

"Surely you don't agree with paying these terrorists a ransom; they're common criminals," C rebuked.

"They are common criminals, with a highly lethal and state-of-the-art bio-weapon," corrected Thorne. This new C was beginning to irritate him. The man was so dense and short-sighted, especially in comparison to his predecessor who had been the epitome of a modern intelligence professional and always saw the bigger picture. "And in my book, that makes them worth listening to. What do you think, Professor? Is it feasible that they would be able to create such a bio-weapon?"

Professor Barking leaned forward and opened the folder sitting in front of him. His spectacles were perched precariously on the end of his nose as he looked over at the acting Chairman of the JIC. "Well, theoretically it's possible, of course it is. But if what they have is real and active, it's unlike anything we've come up with, or even the Germans before us, during the war. And they were the defacto experts in this field."

"But what is it, Professor? How would they produce it? Where would they produce it?" asked the Prime Minister.

The scientist glanced down at his notes. For the first time in his career, he was unsure of the notes and information he'd amassed over his life. He was heading into uncharted territory. "They would need research and test facilities comparable to what we have at Porton Down; I would say that worldwide, there are only a handful of legitimate locations like that. Then they would need the best minds available, to create and produce whatever it is, not to mention a delivery mechanism of some kind."

"Like a bomb?" asked the Security Service's Director-General.

Barking shook his head. "Not necessarily. An explosive device would more than likely vaporise the toxin instantly, nullifying it. No, it could more likely be something as simple as an aerosol can or a squirt from a perfume bottle, anything that was small, up close and personal."

"And what would be the result of any planned attack, based upon what little we know of this Berseker toxin?" asked Thorne.

Barking shrugged. "Our best estimates are that anywhere from between one hundred to a thousand individuals could be infected by one perfume bottle alone. Within an hour of first contact, it could conceivably infect a small town. I'm not counting the collateral damage in this. The infection will certainly cause numerous deaths, but what about the people the Berserkers' actually kill once they've become infected? That number could rise into the thousands? You've seen how the infected turn violent and murder. Half of London could come under attack. We also need to take into account that if an uninfected person is attacked by an infected one, will that person automatically become infected and 'turn' also? These are all things to consider, and unfortunately, we don't have enough information to confirm either way."

"And we're sure they have the wherewithal to pull this off, Professor?" asked the Prime Minister.

Professor Barking nodded. "So *could* they do all that? Yes, quite possibly, definitely in fact. Have they, is the main question though, and that, as of yet, remains to be seen. Until we have a live sample of the bio-agent or a dead host we can study and examine, you might as well say they've invented fairy dust. There's just no proof."

"So in your opinion, Professor, "said Thorne. "Is it better to play along and pay for the moment, until we have more conclusive proof or information?"

"You're damned if you do and damned if you don't I'm afraid, Sir Marcus. You don't pay and they release the virus, well, at least we'll have plenty of dead hosts to use, to examine the virus and perhaps create an antidote. You do pay, and they still have you over a barrel indefinitely," explained Barking.

"But what if the press gets wind of the news that we're dealing with terrorists – or worse, that we were kowtowing to them and paying them off," murmured the Foreign Secretary.

"It would be a gamble, especially with an election coming up," said the Home Secretary.

The Prime Minster sat back in his chair, inspecting the ceiling above him, lost in thought. He knew he needed to make a decision and soon. His government's life might depend upon it, not to mention his own political career. "Umm… I think we need to appear strong. We've already made one payment and these butchers have come back for more. This has to end. Sir John, please do everything in SIS's power to find and interrogate this source, offer him whatever you think is reasonable to make him talk. The time for us being on the back foot is over. Today, we close the negotiating links with the Raven and his murderers. General, organise a military quick reaction strike force to act on SIS's actionable intelligence. The next time I want to hear about this Raven, is when he's dead on a slab."

"Prime Minister, I think you're making a mistake, we should…" Thorne began, attempting one last time to let wiser heads prevail. But the Prime Minister was adamant. There could be no backing down from his decision.

"Your objections are duly noted, Sir Marcus, but I've made my decision. Thank you, gentlemen. This meeting is adjourned," said the Prime Minister. The members of the committee stood to leave, gathering up their papers and starting to head back to their respective departments. On the way out, Thorne saw the Prime Minister give C an encouraging pat on the back, a headmaster praising a school prefect for good work. Sir Marcus Thorne shook his head at the wonderment of the world he lived in, a world where a man of power would risk the lives of the people of his nation for a political advantage, and where a lethal toxin could be released onto the streets of the capital and they had no way of stopping the bloodshed and violence which would follow. Thorne just hoped it would be a decision the Prime Minister wouldn't live to regret. But he was afraid he knew better

* * *

The Raven's response to the closing of the communication channels was both swift and violent, as befitted a man of his reputation and cunning.

The actions of the British Prime Minister and his minions was both naive and stupid. They were behaving like children playing outside of their safe environment, foolish and ignorant about the repercussions of their actions. The Raven would temper them, teach them and finally, he would have them submit and bowing down before him.

He called his killers to heel and gave the order to unleash death. A week later, several seemingly unconnected incidents took place in different parts of the globe. The first was the bombing of a BOAC passenger airliner travelling from London Airport to St. Helier, Jersey in the Channel Islands. The flight 767 attack was later judged by counter-terrorism experts to be one of the first cases of air terrorism in the post-war era. The flight came down fifteen minutes after take-off, with wreckage being strewn far and wide along the coast of Dover. There were no survivors.

Several days later, the body of a baggage handler who'd worked at London airport was found stabbed to death in his flat in Bermondsey. His uniform and security identification were missing. They too were later found, discarded in a dustbin a mile away from the airport, the bomber having dumped them during his escape.

That same day in Panama City, several well-dressed young men carrying concealed automatic rifles entered the Global Tower Bank on the Via Espana. The bank was part-British owned and up until recently, one of its senior directors had been the British Prime Minister. The gunmen entered around mid-morning, the busiest part of the day, when the customers were lined up waiting for individual tellers to serve them. The killers stood in a small, tight circle in the centre of the room and opened fire. Bullets penetrated both glass and flesh. When the gunmen's magazines were emptied, they each took out a handgun and set about executing any wounded survivors before they casually walked out of the bank to several waiting escape vehicles. The whole hit had taken no more than three minutes. Police would be baffled as to why no money had been stolen during the attack.

A day later in Tokyo, several bodies were fished out of the Sumida River. They were all men in their early thirties and all had connections to several organisations within the Japanese underworld. Most recently, the victims had worked together as part of a security detail to transport a high-value shipment across land from Tokyo to an undisclosed location. The men had been rounded up and all had their throats slit. It was assumed that one of them had been an informant for the police, or a rival gang, perhaps an intelligence service – who knew? The fact that all the men were executed only confirmed the killers were both thorough and cautious. After all, why take the risk that you'd killed the wrong man? Better to kill all involved to make absolutely sure.

At the end of this week of violence, a letter was hand delivered to the British Embassy in Berlin. It was addressed personally to the SIS Head of Station. On the paper were several short handwritten lines:

Flight 767 – 150 people
Panama – 35 people
Kyonshi Virus – Estimated: 400,000 people

Remuneration Price is now doubled.

There was no signature on the letter, only a small sketch, drawn in black ink. It was a picture of a Raven.

Book Two: Redaction

Chapter One

Jack Grant had been taking it easy in his hotel suite when Trench burst in. Their rooms had almost become ad hoc offices for both of them over the past few months, and Grant was quickly tiring of being kept on the hook waiting for something to happen. At times, the paranoia of the undercover man would kick in and he would expect a bullet in the back of the head, or a knife between his ribs when he was asleep. So far, that hadn't happened and assuming that no news was good news, he would settle back into a routine of constant boredom. His only contact was Trench and even he was only there sporadically, usually jetting off at a moment's notice to deal with some unspecified piece of 'business' before returning unannounced. Just like now.

"Got a job for you," Trench said. "A chance to lose your virginity, so to speak."

Grant put down the glass containing his second whisky of the night and took a deep breath. This was it... the entry point to the operation. Trench laid it out for him in stark detail; solo job, two targets, Brazil, all resources in place, private contract all the way from the top of the clan – from the Raven himself.

"So who are they?" asked Grant. "People in our trade. Killers?"

Trench shook his head. "Not even close. This is a private gig from the Raven himself. You have nothing to worry about, they are academics, scientists. They won't put up a fight."

"Killing scientists Frank, really?"

Trench shrugged. "The big man thinks they've outlived their usefulness and need to be removed. This has something to do with the Raven's special project. Don't ask any more Jack, it won't do you any good. In fact it would be very bad for your health."

Grant was wise enough not to press the matter. But the slip up by Trench about secret projects and scientists set his alarm bells ringing. Had he perhaps stumbled onto the fringes of the Berserker operation? Was the Raven starting to cover his tracks regarding people involved with the Kyonshi?After that, things moved quickly. Trench had briefed him and then provided a false passport and some cash for expenses and told him he would be leaving in a few days' time. Everything had been arranged – all he had to do was turn up and pull the trigger.

"And then get your arse back here and collect your spending money," purred Trench.

At the first opportunity, Gorilla Grant made contact with Penn and was ordered to get himself to an emergency meeting. Twenty-four hours later, Grant, Masterman and Penn were crammed into a small bedroom at a hotel near Kai Tak Airport. Masterman was seated on the bed, leaning heavily on his walking stick, while his two senior operations men stood tensely, checking at the window for any signs of surveillance. The Sentinel controllers had only an hour with their agent before he needed to catch his flight, and from that moment on, he would be out of their control until he returned. If he returned, thought Penn, correcting himself. They did the house-keeping first; contact numbers, safety procedures, times, dates, and last of all, emergency fall back plans. When everyone was up to speed, Masterman ran through Gorilla's forthcoming mission, giving his agent his orders regarding the Redactions. For Gorilla, it was something he'd heard the boss talk through many times in the past. Masterman's doctrine was to interrogate the targets first, if possible and then eliminate them.

"What about the justification of it all?" asked Penn, as ever the conscience of the Sentinel team. "I mean, we're effectively taking out several non-combatants, even if they are connected to this Berserker virus." Ideas were thrown about including snatching the targets off the street, incapacitating them somehow – anything and everything was considered. But the team knew that if the Raven clan were to accept Gorilla into their ranks, he would have to cross the line, and crossing the line meant killing the targets. There could be no half measures, it was all or nothing.

"They'll want to know you're serious. They won't let you get any closer unless you have blood on your hands and even then, it's only a maybe. The more you do for them, the deeper in you'll be and the more they'll own you," reasoned Masterman. "But if you don't want to go ahead with it, then now's the time to let us know."

"There's no shame in it, Jack. It's a big step. If you're not positive about this, we can get you on a plane today and you can be gone," added Penn.

But Gorilla Grant was a soldier, a specialised kind of soldier, but a soldier nonetheless. He wasn't above getting his hands dirty when the need arose and the idea of aborting the mission rather than committing himself to murder elicited a short response from the little gunman; "They're just as guilty as that maniac who took the Chief's head. Fuck 'em. Putting a bullet between their eyes is doing the world a favour."

And with that, the deal was done. Masterman and Penn, both experienced case officers, knew better than to try to convince Gorilla otherwise once he'd made his mind up. Grant picked up his bag, hefted it in his hand and made for the door. He left without looking back. The time for talking was over; the time for action was only just beginning. The next thing was the flight out of town to his new destination: Brazil.

"Will he be alright?" asked Penn.

Masterman looked at his agent-runner and shrugged. "He's beyond our reach for a while, we have to let him go and let him find his own strength, especially if we want him to survive this."

"And will he?"

"Gorilla always has before; it's what makes him the best."

Chapter Two

The BOAC flight from Hong Kong to Brazil (with an overnight stopover in Paris) landed safely almost twenty-four hours later at Galeão International Airport. On it were one hundred and thirteen passengers and one Redactor, recently out of retirement. The flight had been a nightmare. Long, uncomfortable and he'd been sitting next to a middle aged woman who snored constantly for the first part of the journey. He hadn't expected first class tickets, but anything would have been better than being stuck here in the cheap seats. He'd removed his tie and undone the top button of his shirt, which was sticking to his skin in the muggy conditions. Christ, even the air conditioning wasn't working properly, for the entire flight it had been intermittent at best.

Once the aircraft rolled to a stop at Galeão and the passengers had escaped their tubular prison cell, they all hurried down the stairs onto the tarmac and into the main terminal. Gorilla noted the number of armed soldiers scattered about, before remembering the airport also housed a contingent of the Brazilian Air force. He went through the usual eyeballing at the Customs desk, and for those few brief moments he wondered if the false passport Hokku and his people had supplied would pass the scrutiny of the pan-faced officer on duty. The security man looked down at the passport, then at the bearded face of Gorilla, then back to the passport... there was a brief tense hiatus and then he reached for the official stamp which would provide entry for this passenger. A resounding 'thump' onto the page of the passport with the stamp and Gorilla was in. Either the passport really was that good, or the Raven's people had paid enough money to the right people to grease the wheels.

The taxi he managed to flag down outside the main concourse was driven by what must have been the oldest taxi driver in existence. The man was from a bygone age, dressed in a three-piece dark suit, chauffeurs' peaked cap and an exquisitely clipped handle-bar moustache. Gorilla imagined he'd once been the driver of a wealthy family and had since fallen on hard times. But regardless of his age and formal dress, the taxi driver handled both the Mercedes and the traffic well and didn't ask too many questions. "Where to? Your first time in Brazil? You here long?"

That was the depth of his conversation and Gorilla was thankful of it, earning the driver a good tip. His destination was the Hotel Grande, located way off the main strip of Copacabana Beach and judging by its exterior of rotting window frames and faded grey walls, it was grand in name only. The aging taxi driver hefted Gorilla's small suitcase from the trunk of the car and left him to climb the steps to the main reception. The interior proved to be no better than the exterior. Gorilla thought he could practically hear the cockroaches crawling behind the thin walls. A sullen concierge in last week's shirt took his name, checked his reservation and handed him a room key. "You want a woman?" asked the concierge, seizing the opportunity to try and make a little extra cash from a tourist.

"No. Any messages for me?" asked Gorilla, already at the end of his short fuse after the long and uncomfortable flight. There was always the temptation to put his fist through the faces of people who got his back up and annoyed him. It took an effort to rein in his anger.

The concierge shrugged as if he couldn't care less. "A man left something for you. It is in your room. Everything is paid for."

Gorilla made his way up the bare wooden staircase to his allocated room on the third floor and unlocked the door. The room was at least clean and serviceable, with a stunning view of the plain concrete wall which made up the side of the building next door. He checked the closet and the bathroom, just to make sure there were no nasty surprises lurking, ready to perform a double cross and knife him to death. Once he was satisfied, he turned his attention to the 'something' that had been left for him. The Raven clan and Trench were good to their word. Lying underneath his bed was a chequered valise, sealed with a small padlock. It was the type of suitcase a travelling salesman might lug around with him from meeting to meeting, trying to sell subscriptions for encyclopaedias.

Before he'd left Hong Kong, Gorilla had been given a small key by Trench and told to keep it safe. Obviously, it fitted this padlock. He took out the key, inserted it into the small lock and turned. The clasp made a 'clunk' sound as it snapped apart and he flipped open the lid of the case. Inside, buried half way down in a variety of clothes and towels were the items Gorilla had been expecting. His tools for this job; a Beretta M1934 that had been around when Methuselah was a kid, a box of cheap 9mm Italian ammunition, and an inside the waistband holster made of poor quality vinyl. All together it was a piss poor effort from his paymasters wanting an overseas hit against two targets! There wasn't even any oil or cleaning kit for the gun! At the bottom of the case was a large, sealed envelope. Gorilla knew this would be his briefing pack, containing all the intelligence on his targets. Photographs, addresses, itinerary, surveillance logs; everything he would need. He ripped open the seal, glanced casually at the contents and then tossed them back into the case. He would read it in full later. It was still mid-afternoon and the sun was blazing in through the window; in the distance he could hear the sound of the ocean. Despite the heat, the noise and the killing he would be undertaking over the next twenty-four hours, he recognised that his body was shutting down and he needed to rest. He closed the blinds, stripped naked and lay down on the bed. Within minutes, he was asleep.

Chapter Three

The next morning, Gorilla was due to meet his driver outside the small post office on the *Rua Tonelero* which was ten minutes' walk from his hotel. He was dressed in light coloured slacks and a jacket, a white short sleeved shirt and a pair of wraparound sunglasses. The shirt was untucked and covered his belt area. It also covered the Beretta, tucked inside the waistband holster in the appendix carry position to the right of his belt buckle. He'd checked himself in the mirror before leaving his hotel room, twisting in different angles to see if there were any signs of the gun. Satisfied that it was as good as it was going to be, he exited the room and made his way out onto the street. It took him less than ten minutes to make his way along the beachfront and into the side streets to reach his meeting point. There were only a few people lingering about and no obvious signs of surveillance. The Brazilian security services weren't noted for subtlety, or for being invisible. Gorilla thought he'd be able to pick them out instantly, but there was nothing that was setting off alarm bells to his trained eye.

The car was a black, dust-laden Volkswagen Beetle, one of hundreds that toured the streets of Rio on a regular basis. It was exactly where it was meant to be, parked half on and half off the pavement on the street corner. That was a good sign. At least his driver was professional enough to be punctual. He knocked on the roof with his knuckles as per his instructions and almost instantly the passenger door flew open, followed by a female voice that said "Get in." Surprised, he bent down to clamber past the front seat and into the rear. The front seat flipped back up into position and the passenger door was pulled shut by one brown, slender arm.

"I like your beard. It suits you," said the girl. Gorilla stared into her deep brown eyes as she studied him in the rear-view mirror.

She told him her name was Maria and she was proud to be one of the few women drivers operating in Rio de Janeiro. So far, he'd only seen her eyes in the mirror and the back of her thick black hair, which was tied in a ponytail and fell down onto her slim shoulders. She wore a cloth cap, perched on her head at a jaunty angle which made her look like a revolutionary and also managed to give her an air of vulnerability. It was only when she turned around to look at him and asked "Where are we going, Señor?" that he finally got to see her completely. She looked to be no more than twenty, maybe twenty-two at the most and she had that lithe, beautiful quality of many young Latin American women. Gorilla thought she should be modelling the latest fashions in Paris or Milan, rather than driving hired killers around the streets of Rio.

Gorilla drew his eyes away from her face and studied the address he'd been given and which he'd copied onto a small sheet of paper from his hotel room. "What did they tell you about this job?" he asked. Her eyes met his in the rear-view mirror again. Gorilla thought they resembled pools of dark chocolate.

"That I was to take you wherever you wanted to go and then take you back to where I picked you up this morning," she said.

"Is that all? Nothing about what I'm going to be doing?"

She shook her head and remained silent. Then as an afterthought she said, "I will not sleep with you, Señor. It is not who I am."

Gorilla smiled sadly. "The thought never crossed my mind."

"And you are not going to hurt me?"

He heard the tension in her voice and he shook his head. "You have my word that I will treat you with respect."

She considered this for a second or two. "Then I believe you, I have the word of an English gentleman. So where would you like me to drive you to?"

* * *

Enzo Marcello, the technician, sat at a pavement bar in the 'City of God' *favela,* enjoying a cool glass of the local beer and watching the world go by. It was his usual seat in his usual part of the bar. He came here once or twice a week, to meet up with his contact, the emissary of the Raven.

The locals had come to know the face of this swarthy Italian, knew his ways of leering at the young girls was harmless enough, and had come to accept that he wasn't a police spy or a threat to them. He kept to himself and always tipped well. In truth, the technician hated being stuck in this cesspit of a country and hated having to come to this bar just to be given his expenses like a peasant worker. But when the Raven says that you keep a low profile for a couple of months, you do as you're told. He was resigned to his fate... for now.

Sometimes his contact showed, and sometimes he didn't. Today was obviously going to be a day when he was otherwise engaged. No matter, Enzo Marcello was being well paid to sit in a bar in Rio and drink as much as he could manage. He had just enough time for one more drink, before he made his way back to his apartment for the evening. Back to counting off another day in exile, another day nearer to his return to Europe where he could spend the reward the Raven would give him for his services.

It was when he was taking his last swig from the bottle that he heard the beep of a car horn. He looked up to see what the commotion was and saw a short, stocky, blond-haired and bearded man heading straight for him from across the street. *He looks so angry,* thought Marcello. *Who has upset him!* He looked around and not seeing anyone else paying attention to the furious man, Enzo Marcello came to the very rapid conclusion that it was he who the blond man was on a direct course for. He saw the man's hands move – one lifted up the flap of his shirt and the other dug deep into the waistband where the handle of a gun could just be seen jutting out. Enzo Marcello didn't know how he knew the gun was meant for him. He just did. It was as much information as he needed. He'd worked for the Raven long enough to know how these things worked, so he pushed himself away from the bar, hurled his half empty bottle of beer at the angry man, and ran as if the devil was on his tail.

* * *

Gorilla had the technician in his sights for a good ten minutes before he made his move. He'd left the girl, Maria, at a junction about five hundred feet away. The last time he saw her she was happily lazing back and listening to the radio as he walked toward his target location.

He'd stood at a similar bar across the small street from his target, biding his time, sipping at a small glass of rum, watching for an opportunity and blending into the crowd of men who were standing around, talking noisily. From his basic smattering of Portuguese, he could make out bits of the conversation around him; talk of working in a factory, this man's bloody wife cheating on him, the kids, the bills. They were working class people with real life problems. It was background noise for Gorilla, whose eyes flicked regularly across the street to the stick thin Italian slouched against the bar.

Then he was off in a straight line, a direct attack. It was Gorilla's way. He knew what to do; get there fast, pull the weapon and one shot to drop the target then melt back into the crowd. It was nothing difficult and he'd done similar hits dozens of times before. He knew once the gun had been fired, the noise would send the busy street into chaos and the locals would scatter like cockroaches when a light shone on them. He would scatter as well; 'shoot and scoot' the old timers called it. He was halfway across the road when he started to access the gun tucked in the waistband holster. He dodged an old truck which blared its horn at him impatiently, and then the gun was in his hand, kept low, still concealed beneath his palms. A quick flick of the safety with his thumb and the Beretta was live and ready.

He locked eyes with the target. The man, seeming confused, looked around to see what Gorilla was focused on. And then the inevitable happened, the Italian realised that it was a hit and he did what anybody with survival instincts did – he bolted! Gorilla tracked him as the lanky Italian pushed his way past the other barflies and was away. He picked up his own pace, first as a fast walk and then, as he cleared the edge of the bar area he broke into a trot and finally, by the time he'd reached the corner he was sprinting. Gorilla was no runner, had never claimed to be, so if he had any chance of catching this racing snake of an Italian he would have to work bloody hard! He had the target's back in his sights, about twenty feet away. Not any great distance really, but in this type of enclosed environment full of right angles, hidden doorways and alleyways, it might as well have been a mile. He knew where the target was heading. He was running towards the maze-like alleys of the *favella*, the infamous slums of Rio. The walkways, already packed closely together, were getting smaller and smaller, with sharp turns and steps leading ever upwards. Gorilla's feet pounded on the stone steps as he struggled to keep up with his target.

They reached the base of a road which led steeply upwards and at the end of it was a wall. A wall that the lanky Italian could probably scale comfortably, but Gorilla, for all his strength, would struggle. The track up was hard going and both men's legs were growing weary. There was a gap of over ten feet between them… enough to matter between the hunter and the hunted and the Italian had almost reached the wall. He jumped, desperately groping with his hand for the lip which would have assured his escape. But there was no escaping on this day. The jump was far short of what was needed and Enzo Marcello fell back into the road, landing on his back, utterly exhausted. It was all Gorilla needed. He pushed himself those extra few feet and when he was within range, he launched a vicious kick which connected with the Italian's jaw. He saw teeth and blood explode outwards in a spray of white and crimson.

Gorilla grabbed the target one handed, by the scruff of his shirt collar and pulled him up to a kneeling position. A quick look to ensure no one was nearby and then he pushed the muzzle of the gun against the technician's temple, pressing it hard so that it wouldn't skid off the man's skull when he fired. He took up the pressure on the trigger, leaned into the shot and pulled. Nothing. Just a dead man's click. Fuck! *A misfire,* thought Gorilla. What could he expect, it was a poor version of a Beretta and appalling ammunition. He knew he needed to clear the jam from the weapon quickly, but first… he tightened his grip on the man's collar and swung his knee around to strike him in the face, busting his nose and stunning him. Then he moved the inert weapon down to his waist and hooked the rear sight onto the rim of his leather belt, furiously pushing down once, twice, three times, causing the slide to move and retract and clearing the jam in the process. He watched as a dud bullet flipped out and onto the ground, rolling down the gutter and into the drain.

He returned the gun to the technician's temple and pulled the trigger again, watched as the gun bucked, spitting out the bullet into the man's skull, shattering it. The technician dropped like a sack of potatoes into the gutter, rolling onto his back, blood flowing from the head shot. Gorilla took a step forward, levelled the gun with both hands and fired four consecutive rounds into the man's chest, splintering his torso. It looked as if someone had hacked at his silk shirt with a blunt knife. Gorilla took one final look to confirm that the bullets had done their job and then he walked away, slowly at first, but then picking up the pace. No one met his eye; the locals, such as they were, made way for him. There were no challenges and no five second heroes waiting to arrest him or take him down in a fit of bravery. He tucked the gun back into the waist band holster and walked free.

It took him another twenty minutes to backtrack down onto the main street again and a further ten before he was satisfied that he was clean. Only then did he make his way to the edge of the *favela* and locate the VW Beetle. He opened the door and climbed in, checking that the gun was concealed in his waistband. Maria was still listening to the radio when he returned, her feet up on the dashboard, tapping along to some kind of Samba music. "Was everything to your satisfaction? Is your business completed?" she asked.

Gorilla smiled, trying to calm his breathing. "You did well, thank you."

"And your business… there were no problems?"

"Everything went fine, thank you Maria," he said politely. "Can we go please?"

They drove back to his drop off point in silence. Gorilla watched the streets as the car passed through them, playing over the shooting in his head, mentally checking for anything he could have done differently. It was a messy situation and the fact that the whole planning for the hit had been taken out of his hands didn't sit easy with him. Still, too late now to worry about it. He just hoped that tomorrow went without a hitch… tomorrow was the 'important' one.

Several minutes later the car was back where they'd begun earlier that day on the *Rua Tonelero*. Maria pulled into a parking spot and turned the engine off. She took a sip of water from an old army canteen she kept at her feet. "What type of business are you in, Señor? You are a businessman? An important businessman like you must have better places to be than the *favelas*."

He thought it was better to tell her something; to say nothing would arouse her suspicions even more. "I work in the construction business. I sort out labour problems for work gangs. The company I work for is hoping to get the contract to rebuild certain quarters here in Rio."

She met his eyes and nodded. It seemed to be answer enough for her. Whether she believed him or not, he had no idea. "So… tomorrow?" she said, raising an inquisitive eyebrow at him. "Here? Same time, same place?"

He nodded and smiled at her through their medium of communication – the rear-view mirror. He liked this girl, liked her streetwise ways and blunt and to the point conversation. "I look forward to it, Maria."

"Me too Señor, me too," he heard her say as he climbed out of the car and disappeared into the streets.

Chapter Four

Okawa Reizo, the chemist, was irritated.

The thin, grey haired and aging chemist was irritated, because his courier had failed to show at the regular time. This was most unusual and for someone like Okawa Reizo, it set off alarm bells suggesting perhaps something had gone wrong. The couriers were never late. It was the rule.

He had paced the floor of his villa, out in the affluent *Ipanema* area of the south zone of Rio. In the distance he could make out the sandy curve of *Ipanema* beach and see the tanned bodies carousing along the shoreline. He'd looked at the pool, thought about having a swim and instantly dismissed the idea. What if he missed the courier at the front door? So he'd paced some more, made some tea and sat. Sat and waited for hours… more hours than was sensible. The couriers, a different one every time but always Japanese, were his lifeline to home. They brought news, money, and letters from what was left of his family… even food from his favourite store in Tokyo. In truth, he had not taken well to living in exile in Brazil. But when the *Karasu* spoke, Okawa Reizo knew better than to complain.

The fate of the *Karasu* and Okawa Reizo had been entwined for many years. Over the years, the *Karasu* had encouraged him, protected him, and given him the power to achieve his greatest creation – the *Kyonshi*. All was fine in the world of Okawa Reizo. Except… except for the missing courier. And it was as he was about to give up for the day and do the mundane chores of his confinement here in this luxury villa when he heard the most beautiful sound he'd heard all day.

It was the doorbell.

* * *

The courier was not Japanese. Odd.

Okawa Reizo was confused. He was staring at the man through the glass window in the front door. He was a European. Stocky, bearded, sunglasses, light coloured suit, shirt open at the neck. Not the *Karasu*'s usual type of employee. For a moment, there was an impasse as both regarded each other through the glass. The bearded European just stood there impassively, not moving, merely watching. Finally, he'd apparently had enough and raised one fist and rapped directly on the glass in front of Okawa Reizo's face. "Open up. I'm your new courier!" he shouted.

Reizo flinched, taking a step back from the glass. His hand nervously snaked out and reached for the handle and turned the lock. He pulled back the door and was in the process of saying "What is your name? Where is Saburo?" Unfortunately, he only got the first part of the sentence out when the angry, bearded man pushed his way in and punched Reizo in the face with one meaty fist. The man watched as Reizo crumpled and hit the floor, blood pouring from his nose.

Gorilla closed the door behind him and drew the gun from the holster. The Japanese man tried to get back up and Gorilla hit him again, this time with his left fist. Not as good a punch as the first, but it got the message across and Reizo went down onto the floor once more.

Gorilla grabbed Reizo by his shirt collar, dragging and pulling him into the lounge area, before he shoved him onto a leather sofa, smearing blood from his busted nose along one of the cushions. It was a fantastic place with modern furnishings and decor and Gorilla quickly closed the blinds, in case anyone from the adjacent villas happened to catch a glimpse of what was going on. He reached into his back pocket, removed the newspaper clipping that he'd ripped out of that morning's paper and handed it to the bleeding Japanese man on the floor. Gorilla's gun never wavered an inch. "Read it," he said. He watched as the man glanced down at the face in the picture and the secondary photo of the dead body lying sprawled in a gutter. "You know this man?"

"Yes, I know him," stammered Reizo, his eyes drinking in the picture of the bullet-riddled corpse of the Italian Marcello.

"I thought so. I put five rounds into him yesterday. He's very dead," said Gorilla.

"And are you going to do the same to me?"

Gorilla shook his head. "I'm going to offer you a deal, a once in a lifetime deal, so listen to me carefully. You give me the information I want and I let you walk out of here. You will be met by a man; he can get you out of the country, get you false papers, make you disappear and reappear anywhere in the world that you want to be."

"What is it that you—"

"Information about the Raven," Gorilla interrupted. "Who he really is and what you've been doing for him."

The Japanese man suddenly became wary and a sly smile passed across his face. "This is a test, a test of my loyalty. But no, the *Karasu* and I, we have been through too much. He has no need to test me!"

Gorilla shook his head sadly. "This is no test. You saw the picture of the man you knew and what I did to him. The Raven has decreed that you'll go the same way before the day ends... that's what I've been sent here to do, to kill you and tie up any loose ends. This is no test, no game; it's about your survival now."

The Japanese chemist stared at the gunman in horror and shook his head. "No, I would be found and killed... the *Karasu* would find me anywhere I went."

Gorilla growled under his breath. "He already fucking has you, idiot... I'm here! At least this way you have a chance of surviving. You help me, you go free. You don't and I end you right here, right now! My people can give you a head start. You run fast enough, he'll never get to you."

Reizo stared at the gun held inches from his face and then at the furious bearded man behind it. He breathed in deeply once – he was a man of logic, and understood the need for pragmatism. He looked one more time from the gun to his would-be assassin and spoke clearly.

"His name is Yoshida Nakata. He is the Raven."

* * *

The chemist told him everything. Gorilla suspected it was the man cleansing his soul, unloading all the guilt he'd brought upon himself over the years. He was a mass murderer, a torturer and sadist. He told of his work with the Kempeitai, his meeting with Nakata during the war, his life in exile and finally, his recruitment to the Raven clan. He'd effectively become a mercenary, selling his knowledge to the highest bidder. Then of course, there was the Raven's greatest secret, the thing he kept buried above all else and the thing that he, the chemist, had helped bring to fruition... the *Kyonshi* – the 'living dead' – the ultimate weapon of terror for the modern age which was the Raven's doomsday device.

"It began during the war, when I was part of a team conducting experiments for the Japanese Secret Police, the Kempeitai. My area of expertise was in the promotion of nerve agents and biological warfare. I'd been placed in charge of a department known as *Konbājensu*... convergence. Its aim was to bring together several sciences to create new viruses for warfare. We would integrate various serums, experimenting to see what we could achieve. Then we would test them on our live subjects in the camps. Many of the serums were of no use and would quite often kill or deform the hosts. There were a lot of failures..."

Gorilla could well imagine the poor souls, tied to chairs and tables before being injected with a vile cocktail of who knew what. It had been the same for the Nazis in the camps and so it seemed for the Japanese secret police who had a reputation for barbarity.

Reizo continued. "But then, purely by random, we came across something interesting... a combination of various drugs. Together, they created a powerful serum designed to make the subject both un-aware of what they were doing, as well as extremely aggressive. We were well into our project trials when something happened—"

"What?" asked Gorilla.

"The defeat of Japan in 1945. I was captured and placed in prison. All my research notes for all of my projects were confiscated. The Allies were very thorough. All except for my work on the *Kyonshi* project – that was all in my head, nothing written down. Those were the orders of the *Karasu* — I mean, Captain Nakata."

"So what happened to you next?"

"I was eventually released and after the war, I went to work in a small laboratory for the government, testing bacteria samples. For someone of my calibre, it was a menial position. Many years later, I was approached by a man, he offered me a job, an opportunity to come and work for a private pharmaceutical company. He told me that my salary would be tripled and I would be offered a full team of assistants. He did not mention the specifics of my contract, only that it was for Nakata Industries in their secret research and development program."

"And you took it? Without questioning what you had to do?" asked Gorilla.

Reizo shook his head. "Oh no, I knew exactly what I was doing. I had done much worse in the past; it was my duty. But the *Karasu* was offering me so much more, the chance to live again – wealth, influence, freedom… plus the chance to complete what I'd failed to finish during the war; the *Kyonshi* project."

"So a drug that causes violent outbursts? Tell me about it… tell me everything," demanded Gorilla, pointing the gun at the cowering man.

Reizo nodded. "I was given free rein to bring my wartime project back to life. I had facilities, assistants, the latest technology and of course, money. My orders were to take the original idea and improve upon it. The *Karasu* wanted me to design a synthetic drug, a serum, which would turn the subject delusional and violent, capable of attack-ing anything in its path, increasing strength and allowing the subject to experience limited pain. His vision was for this high strength serum to work on two levels. Firstly, as an enhanced aggression drug and secondly, as a conduit for infecting the civilian population. The *Kyonshi* would attack, bite, and scratch their targets and within hours, those targets would be infected and become debilitated."

"What was the virus you used?" asked Gorilla, trying to fathom where this was going.

"It was something we had been working on for years, part of the original projects for the Kempeitai, a combination of virulent spreadable diseases. We trialled many, but the combination that worked best was the convergence of some strains of tetanus, tuberculosis and herpes simplex virus. These worked extremely well together. They affected the nervous and muscular systems and caused chronic pain, vomiting, nausea, fatigue, usually death. It was particularly nasty."

"What was the Raven planning to do with it?"

Reizo wiped the blood from his nose. "I do not know what he planned to do with it. I heard details of it being used as a weapon of terror, to be used in a revolutionary coup. This makes the most sense to me. The Tier One hosts... the *Kyonshi* ... spread fear and panic with their violence. The infection they spread through bites to the Tier Two hosts causes a drain on the country's medical and emergency resources. Within a day, the *Kyonshi* would die, if they hadn't already been killed, but the fallout from the 'infected' hosts would have far-reaching consequences for the country it was to be used against. I would surmise it would be at that point when a ruthless coup plotter could take over the mantel of power and seize control of the country."

"So you obviously got the *Kyonshi* virus working at some point?" asked Gorilla.

Reizo smiled. "Oh yes... we achieved what we wanted to do, quite quickly. The technology and the science behind it had moved on since the war. Plus, we had the facilities to make it state of the art. Once we had the basic elements in place, the project proceeded rapidly. The *Karasu* is a man who you don't disappoint... ever. He procured dozens of test subjects for our trials. They were mainly vagrants and low-life scum from all over Asia. Many of them died in the trials, but once we had manipulated the fundamentals of the virus, we began to achieve quantifiable successes. We would gas them and monitor their violent behaviour to see how long it lasted, the level of aggression and that sort of thing."

"And then what would you do with them?"

"Oh, we would have a weapons team ready to eliminate them in their cells. We could take no chances, the *Kyonshi* were extremely strong and extremely violent. Even the guards wouldn't enter their cells. They would simply poke the barrels of their weapons through the grill in the door and fire. I once saw a guard empty an entire magazine into one of the *Kyonshi* subjects – a teenage boy – before he died," explained Reizo.

"And there was no cure? Nothing?" asked Gorilla. He could already imagine the chaos that something like this terror weapon would cause on the streets of most civilised countries. It was almost designer terrorism, a low-risk, high reward operation for the plotters involved in releasing the *Kyonshi* virus.

Reizo shook his head. "Not initially. Eventually someone would have found the correct level of medication to treat the infected. But by that time, the damage would have been done. My guess was that the *Karasu* was planning to sell it to the highest bidder. I spent many months working with Marcello, the Italian – he was an expert in making improvised explosive devices, probably as a delivery method for the virus, but we were never allowed to know the details of what we were doing. We were watched at all our meetings, watched by the *Karasu's* people. It was on a need-to-know basis."

Gorilla considered this. "What about the supplies of this drug, the vials? Where does he keep them? At Nakata Industries headquarters, perhaps?"

"No, not there."

Gorilla didn't believe him and stepped forward, ready to pistol whip and start kneecapping this mass-murderer-in-waiting if he had to. He was tired of pissing about with these people.

"Wait! Let me explain… I do not know, I only suspect!" shouted Reizo.

Gorilla growled. "Start talking fast, before I start shooting out your joints… I can make you feel pain like you've never imagined! Not everyone gets to die straight away."

Reizo sat up and began to sing. "Okay… okay… Once the *Kyonshi* virus was completed and tested, all of the vials were taken off-site and transported to a secure and secret location." Gorilla lifted the gun a little higher, ready to pistolwhip the Japanese man and Reizo shook his head frantically holding his hands up in front of his face. "Wait, wait! I do not know where this facility is… but I once heard the *Karasu's* advisor, the big man…"

"Hokku," Gorilla supplied.

"Yes, the giant sumo that is the *Karasu's* clan brother – I overheard him giving instructions to his people, thugs and criminals, responsible for the security on the transport. All I heard was that they would be travelling to the *pagoda*, that is what he called it, the *Karasu's* private *Dojo*. It is said to be the *Karasu's* sanctuary and most secret facility. I had to countersign the manifest, authorising the release of the shipment. There was a map on the dashboard of the truck with a route through to Matsumoto, in the Nagano Prefecture. Within the hour, the full consignment of vials left in a Nakata Industries refrigerated truck."

"When was this?"

"Less than three months ago. Not long after, I was told that I would be travelling to Brazil and told to keep a low profile. They said I would be protected. I was given this villa and I have a maid and everything I need. *Sake*, women, money… I was told that I would be contacted by couriers and they would tell me when it was safe to return to Japan. When the courier didn't show today I was worried, I did not know what to think, and then you came," Reizo said hurriedly.

Gorilla took it all in, trying to decipher if this little monster of a man was telling the truth. In the end, he had no way of knowing, but at the very least he had some fresh intelligence which could blow the hidden parts of the operation wide open. Information that Masterman and Penn could trace back, back to the secrets that C had taken with him to the grave. The problem now was, although he had answers to his questions, he still had a living target and witness who should be dead as a pigeon by now. The chemist had outlived his usefulness in all sorts of ways and to keep him alive, despite Gorilla's promises of protective custody, was just too much of a risk. A risk to the operation certainly, but also a risk to Gorilla's own chances of survival. If he went back without a body being found shot to death, then the chances were that he wouldn't make it through until sundown. Trench and his team of cut-throats would see to that.

"Get up... get yourself dressed. Pack an overnight bag, just a few things; you'll be travelling light... change of clothes, toothbrush, that type of thing. My people will sort the rest out," ordered Gorilla. He watched as Reizo quickly flitted around the villa, grabbing clothes, socks, money and stuffing them into a small leather holdall. Gorilla knew what he was going to do and when he was going to do it. He was just waiting for the right moment. The bathroom, he would do it there when the target went into the bathroom to collect his wash-bag.

Reizo stepped through the bathroom door and leaned over the large bath to pick up a razor and shaving brush and it was then when Gorilla stepped up behind him, raised the pistol and fired once behind the chemist's right ear. The report echoed around the small tiled room and the body of the Japanese chemist flopped forward into the bath, his body convulsing on the way down. He landed almost in a foetal position, his body curled up, with one leg casually hanging over the side of the bath. Gorilla pointed the pistol down and fired three more shots into the man's chest. He knew from experience it wasn't really necessary; the shot to the head had finished him off already. But when the Raven's people came by to make sure the job had been completed, Gorilla wanted as much blood and gore on show as possible, to make it look as if the chemist had been gunned down ruthlessly.

* * *

"Not too quick this time," said Maria, a hint of playfulness in her voice. They'd been driving for only a few moments, winding along the coast road. "So where to now?" she asked.

"Back to where you picked me up yesterday, thank you," said Gorilla pleasantly.

"So we are finished for the day, your business is done, yes?"

"Yes. All complete."

She drove for a few seconds more and then slowly pulled the car to a stop in a lay-by. She cranked on the handbrake and turned in her seat to look at him. Her cap was still cocked at an angle, making her look even more youthful. "When the job was over, I was told to give you this," she said. She turned back and pulled an envelope out from underneath her seat, passing it to him.

Gorilla stared at it. The envelope was sealed. He quickly slit the lip with his finger and pulled out the small note inside. Written on it were three words:

KILL THE GIRL

Now it made sense. While the hits were definitely genuine jobs, contracts that the Raven wanted carried out, they were also a test of how good Gorilla was as a contractor. They wanted to see if he had mettle, was adaptable and versatile, but above all, they wanted to see how ruthless he was. The shoddy weapon, poor ammo, no suppressor to keep the noise down, terrible holster, spotty intelligence and now, using an amateur to drive the contractor around – it all smacked of Hokku and his master giving their new recruit a rough ride. But that was okay. Gorilla had been in far worse situations than this and survived.

Kill the girl. It would be oh so easy... just pull the gun from the concealed holster, and one shot would finish it all. She wouldn't even know what had happened. He could shoot her and walk away. He drummed his leg with his fingers as he toyed with what to do.

The moment of indecision passed. He'd decided and he was operational again. Gorilla took one last look at the girl's jet black hair. He reached inside his jacket, one-handed, and withdrew the item which would seal the girl's fate. He leaned forward and whispered into her ear. "Take this money and go, get out of here. Don't go back to the people who gave you this job. I was meant to kill you, once I'd finished. If you go back to your contact, they'll kill you for sure. Get out of Rio, start again somewhere else. Drive and drive fast!"

He'd done what had to be done, what he could live with, and then he left the car for the final time. He stood by the side of the road and watched as she drove away. When the car was nothing but a shimmer in the distance, he began to walk towards the city.

Chapter Five

In the days when he'd been an employee of the Redaction Unit for the Secret Intelligence Service, Frank Trench's cryptonym had been *Iago*. It was a name which fitted him perfectly, for like the character from the Shakespearean play, he was always plotting, scheming and involved in any number of double crosses. He was a man who thrived on the art of conspiracy and secrets and this, he was sure, gave him the perfect mindset and practical experience to solve the mystery of what had happened to his team of contractors.

He was sitting on the bed in his Bangkok apartment, naked except for a loose sarong tied around his waist. He had all his toys around him. The bottle of half-finished Chivas Regal, the young – probably too young – Thai girl he'd bought for the night and the opium he was saving until last, saving until he'd untangled the mystery that was hammering at his head. The opium was his reward, his gift to himself when he'd sorted all the evidence in his mind. But not yet, that was for later, for now, he needed to dissect what he knew about the deaths of his men.

Trench knew his men. Knew how they thought, worked and operated. What's more, he knew that all of his European contractors did jobs on the side – a little extra income – of course he did. This was despite the rules laid down by the clan, demanding they were be the sole employers unless otherwise agreed. Trench had argued against this with Taru Hokku, but the Japanese man had been rigid in his commands.

Trench knew it was easier just to go along with it in the long run, tell the clan what they wanted to hear and turn a blind eye to his men's 'alternative' short term employment contracts. After all, you couldn't expect to have the quality of men he'd recruited, and not let them chase their own private contracts when they thought the boss wasn't looking. *The question was,* he thought, *was that the reason for their recent mass demise?* Work for the Raven clan, or work for their extra-curricular employers?

If it had just been one of them, Trench might have put it down to a random accident, a one-off. But there was too much happening too fast. First Reierson had seemingly blown his own brains out in Amsterdam, then the assassination of the two Irish gunmen in Madrid, followed by the shooting of his two top soldiers in Antwerp, and now the news that Milburn had been found dead, stabbed to death, in the toilets of a hotel in Singapore. Nearly half his contractors wiped out in the last few months!

He knew where it led back to, or at least, what his gut was telling him. Gorilla Grant.

Up until Gorilla arrived, Trench was running a nice little operation for his employers. No leaks, no compromise, nothing. Gorilla Grant was on the scene for five minutes and all his top hitters were suddenly riding a helter-skelter down to hell. Was Grant still in league with SIS? Had it all just been a long term operation – getting fired, living the life of a down-and-out before trailing his coat in Hong Kong, hoping that Trench would scoop him up? It had to be the new guy on the team... but still... there was one tiny, but significant problem in his theory, and that was the men Gorilla had killed along the way. First the two leg breakers in Hong Kong and now the 'hits' he'd performed for the Raven in Brazil...

Trench was sure – no, he was positive, that SIS in its current form would never sanction such an operation. Getting an SIS undercover man in place was one thing, but having him murdering for the enemy... never! SIS just didn't have the balls for that anymore. They'd been effectively neutered operationally over the past year or so. Thanks partly to his hunting down and decimation of his old colleagues in Redaction, but more importantly because Salamander had set about destroying SIS's covert action capability from within. It was all part of the Raven's long term master plan, whatever that was...

He knew he would never make it as high up as the Raven, but Hokku would give him what he needed to help him get to the bottom of this mystery. He knew what it would involve. It meant going back into his old stomping ground. For him personally, it was a risk, he was now classed as an enemy agent, even if he had faked his own death and been officially declared dead. There was still the chance that someone might recognise him.

Still, he would manage; a bit of a disguise, false papers – the Raven had some excellent forgers on the payroll. He would manage to get into the UK, conduct his investigation and get out without any of his old colleagues being made aware of his presence. But if his theory of what had happened with Gorilla Grant was correct, then he'd need access to the highest level of intelligence information the British government had on secret operations. And for that, Trench would need the help of the Raven's most closely guarded secret – the Salamander.

Chapter Six

A week later the man known as the Salamander sat staring out at the River Thames, waiting for his contact to make the approach. He'd never met this man, Trench, but he knew everything about him; had in fact, co-ordinated his successful recruitment as a freelance killer into the Raven clan's organisation. He knew the man's face, his quirks, his tastes and his weaknesses. Especially his weaknesses…

Salamander was seated on a cast iron bench, a little way out from Westminster, near Blackfriars Bridge. He glanced lazily at that day's edition of The Times. Hidden inside the pages of the newspaper and held in place by a small strip of Sellotape, was the envelope containing the information Trench had requested. It had taken Salamander's 'people' – trusted sources all of them – several days of digging to find what he wanted. It was a risk, but a worthwhile one, especially if it plugged the leak and kept him protected. The Salamander had it all; influence, wealth and respect – and all supported by his wife of good breeding and his extensive array of mistresses. His facade was that of a man who yearned for nothing more than to be respectable and a servant, albeit a secret one, of the country he claimed to love.

But Salamander was that rarest of political animals, in that he was completely honest – to himself, if not to the rest of the intelligence community and Whitehall – about the fact that he craved nothing but power. He'd manoeuvred himself up through the ranks of the post-war intelligence machine, circumventing rivals, removing fools who were out of their depth and attaching himself to noted power players of influence whom he could use and later discard. He'd risen and risen fast and had in fact, come a long way from his humble beginnings as a foot soldier of the intelligence war, to become one of the most influential executives in the secret espionage world. Not that he'd yet achieved the zenith in his ambitions; there was still some distance to go. But he was at least secreted high up; not at the top, but an inch or two behind the man with the power. Salamander was a king maker and judged it the safest place to be, to feed his ambitions and remain hidden.

His relationship with the Raven was a symbiotic one. They'd helped and protected each other over many decades. What had started out as a classic agent/case officer agreement had quickly developed into the Salamander becoming a willing accomplice and partner in the Raven clan's operations. Salamander provided information which would help the clan carry out an operation – move a shipment of arms, or conduct a terrorist attack – and in return, the Raven would give his source a share of the profits and dispose of any of Salamander's political rivals. Many an old agent, government appointee or even on one occasion, a love rival, had been 'hit' by the Raven's assassins. This was something the Raven encouraged because he knew it would benefit the survival of the clan for years to come. The Raven would do anything to keep the Salamander protected and safe.

The last person to challenge the dual power of the Raven and the Salamander had been the Chief of the Secret Intelligence Service, Sir Richard Crosby. C, with his usual cunning, had started to have his suspicions about who was behind the *Kyonshi* operation and who the masterminds and architects were. The old spy was just too damned clever for his own good and he had gotten far too close for comfort. It would only have taken one more leak or slip up, and the whole house of cards would fall. So he had to be silenced. Partly to plug the leak, but also to send a message to others who might want to challenge both the Raven and his partner, the Salamander. The message was simple; 'face us and face death'.

Salamander glanced at his watch, it was eleven-thirty in the morning. The hustle and bustle of the busy London rush hour had receded several hours earlier and now, there was a serene calm. He folded the newspaper and placed it carefully on the seat next to him. Then he stretched out his long legs and waited. Only a few more moments before the brush past was due to take place. Then, to the moment exactly, there was the contact. The man looked like any other businessman in London on a working day. A smart suit, hair perhaps a little too long for the Salamander's liking, and a briefcase. He sat down, ignoring his fellow bench dweller and watched the small boats moving stoically along the river for a few moments.

"The paper?" asked Trench, muttering out of the side of his mouth and staring straight ahead.

Salamander nodded. "Yes, the paper."

Trench coughed, picked up his briefcase and his newly acquired copy of The Times and set off on his way, walking briskly against the chill in the air.

Nicely done, thought Salamander as he watched his contact walk away. Natural and no one had noticed anything. Why would they? To the rest of the world, they were just two businessmen taking a breath of fresh air before returning to offices and meetings and the day-to-day grind of official life. When instead, what they really were, was a traitor and a killer working in tandem.

* * *

An hour later, Trench was sitting in his small hotel room, flicking through the information provided in Salamander's letter.

Trench had caught a brief glimpse of the man's features. He'd been tall, well-groomed – quite unremarkable, really. He could have been any one of a hundred Whitehall mandarins. Trench was none the wiser as to who he actually was, even now. But whoever Salamander was, he must have had excellent sources. The information could only have originated from one location – inside the Secret Intelligence Service.

The files gave all the details they had on his dead contractors and what SIS and the Security Service knew about them. They'd been flagged as having recently been requested from the Registry; nothing recent for some of them, but several had the same access code of 'RSI', which Trench knew stood for 'Research/Secret Intelligence' and could only have come from the Archives Section in Century House, SIS's headquarters.

So someone in Archives?

The second sheet of paper gave a listing of several possible Personnel in the RSI Section. Two had their names highlighted. One man and one woman. Good – that narrowed down the possibilities.

Trench flicked down to the conclusion which had been typed, he assumed, by Salamander himself. The man was a possible, certainly had the access and opportunity on the days when the files had been removed from the Archives. But it was the woman who interested Salamander. He'd checked her background and her tours of duty stretching back over many, many years.

Palestine, injured in the King David Hotel bombing in 1946. Her fiancé had been killed during the initial explosion. After that, she had several overseas tours at various stations, always in the backroom, administration or research, before being given a promotion and becoming part of the Registry Team at Broadway, before SIS had moved to its current location of Century House. But then, several years ago, she'd been part of a team attached to the now-defunct Redaction Unit, under the control of Stephen Masterman. The operational commander had been one Jack 'Gorilla' Grant. By all accounts, the investigation team had been first rate and discovered some exceptional intelligence that had helped the Redaction team to bring down the enemy they were hunting. *Yes,* remembered Trench. *Like that little shoot-out we had in that whorehouse in Marseilles.* But more telling was that in the intervening years, Masterman had personally requested this particular Archivist from RSI to be attached to Redaction for several other operations he was conducting.

It wasn't concrete and he knew it wouldn't stand up in a court of law, good intelligence never does, but at least he had a possible link from his dead contractors, to Grant, to Masterman, to this Archivist possibly acting as a source of information inside SIS. Someone was feeding a hit-team intelligence to take out his men and this was the best lead he had at the moment.

Trench closed the folder and sat in the darkness for a few more moments, thinking. Next he would have to talk to this Archivist and ask her some hard questions. And Frank Trench was good at asking unwilling people hard questions, very good indeed.

Chapter Seven

Nora Birch hurried, pushing her head down against the driving rain, clutching the net shopping bag closer to her body in case the contents – her tea of sausages and eggs for this evening – should spill out onto the cold and wet street. The streets were poorly lit in this part of the city and she increased her pace, keen to be home safely. She'd already missed the bus to her lonely flat in Ealing, and decided to walk to the next bus stop along. Better that than standing in the freezing cold of a dark night; at least by moving, she was keeping warm and getting nearer to home.

Every day she got up and went to the new office block that was the Secret Intelligence Service's headquarters. She would lock herself away with her equally bland colleagues in the Research/Secret Intelligence Section. The section was lost in the maze-like corridors of Century House. It had no windows and the doors were deadlocked and bolted from the inside. Access was granted by means of a buzzer. It had been many years since she'd been a part of any operations of value for SIS. That was when her talents as a researcher and a finder of vague clues had been her forte. She had helped, in those heady days, to catch spies, hunt down terrorists and avert assassination. She'd been valued and respected. In the old days... before the murder of C and the decimation of the operational arms of the Service by the politicians and back-room deal makers.

These days, she was just another file clerk and paper pusher. There to dot the 'I's' and cross the 'T's'. In the space of a few short years' things had changed at SIS. It had once been a place of beauty and hope for her. Now, it was like living inside the rotting remains of a long dead corpse. Her life had become a routine of boredom and drudgery, each day as bland as the next.

So her recruitment by Colonel Masterman for a private operation had been an easy one. The Colonel was such a charmer when he wanted to be. He knew the right buttons to press to keep people loyal to him. She would be fed names, dates, places and for the Colonel, she would ferret about deep into the darkest secrets of SIS and their liaison departments within a host of friendly intelligence services worldwide. So far, she guessed she'd been foot perfect, no Special Branch officers had been beating her door down, dragging her off to be charged with leaking top secret information, and as far as she was aware, she wasn't under hostile surveillance from either SIS's Hawkeye teams or the Security Service's spy catchers. She was Nora Birch, the Dormouse, and Sentinel's spy inside SIS, the woman who no one looked at twice, who the male officers pitied because of her scarred face. A nobody, a nothing. A perfect spy.

But that had only been part of her mission. The other part, far more valuable and dangerous, was to seek out leads about the ultimate devil, the traitor, the Raven's man inside the Whitehall intelligence machine who had long been suspected but never found. It had been a long road, littered with many false starts and blind alleys. She'd had doubts about her role, effectively being an informant for someone now classed as outside the Service, but her moral fortitude had kept her committed. They all owed that to the memory of their murdered Chief. Once the information gained from Gorilla Grant had come through, about the real identity of the Raven, the rest had been easy. Tracking files, old field reports, case notes until she had whittled it down to five possible officers, then three... then another discounted... until finally, there had been only one man left... the Raven's spy. And his identity was located, in written code for Sentinel's Eyes Only, inside the small cigarette carton she had in her coat pocket.

She'd barely made it through the door of her basement flat when the leather-gloved punch hit her directly on the jaw. The force sent her falling into the darkness of the room, dizzy and uncoordinated; she landed on her side and immediately experienced another sharp pain as a heavy shoe was kicked, with force, into her side.

"Get up, you little bitch, get up," said the voice in the most calm and reflective way. It was as if in her dizzy state, the voice, its gentle manner and the violence, were coming from two separate people. But Nora was canny enough to know that they weren't. Then the man grabbed her by her hair and lifted her up and she felt the scream rising from deep in her throat...

* * *

Frank Trench had everything he wanted. The woman had folded easily. Of course she had, she wasn't a field agent or particularly tough. She was just a sad, middle-aged spinster, scarred and deformed and lonely. It hadn't taken much to break her.

He'd started with the rough stuff, beatings and kickings. Then he'd calmed her down and talked to her. She'd been good, held out for a little while until he'd grown tired of her stalling. Then he'd produced the knife, a long, thin filleting knife he'd purchased from a department store. He'd threatened to chop off her fingers – she'd screamed – and it was only when he took her thumbs by crunching down through the bone with the blade, that she told him, through tears, the whole story. He'd held her hand in the sink of her small and neat bathroom and cut away at her. She'd fought at first but then submitted. Through sobs of shame and pain, he'd barked questions at her and occasionally smacked her face when she didn't answer fast enough.

She spilled her guts fast. Masterman recruiting her... working inside SIS as their informant... a private operation to get close to the Raven organisation... Redact the top man, the Raven...

"But who?" he'd cooed gently in her ear moments after torturing her with the knife. "Who is going to get close to us?"

"O-o-ne of M-m-masterman's men... retired, on the outside," she stammered, her left eye almost closed over from the punches she'd suffered.

"Does he have a name?"

"O-o-only a... c-codename... Gorilla! His name was Gorilla..."

Trench believed her. "And then what? What happens after this man, Gorilla, gets inside?"

"I... I...think the plan was to destroy the organisation... they had some kind of terror weapon... some kind of hold over the government... they had to be Redacted... all of them... killed."

"But not by SIS?"

She shook her head and the sweat from her face and in her hair flicked out across the bathroom. Trench thought that he could have fried an egg on her skin at that moment, such was the level of fear in her. "Redaction was dismantled. Masterman had taken it upon himself to fight back for C. The mainstream didn't want to know, made a half-hearted attempt to start some kind of... investigation... but it faltered and died." The last part had seen her wincing as blood poured from her wounds.

"So how do you know Masterman?" asked Trench.

"We worked together, years back, an operation in Europe. I was part of the intelligence team. The Colonel had remembered me, he said, said I was good at tracking down leads... said he needed my help... that it was important."

Trench laughed. "Ha! And that didn't bother you, selling out your employers on a bit of a private mission?"

She glared at him, the fire returning to her eyes. "Never seemed to bother you, Trench... I know who you are and what you did. You were on the rogue agents list I helped to compile."

That snippet had earned her another lost finger and she'd passed out after that. Trench had gone to the kitchen to find a saucepan and then filled it to the brim with cold water. So, it was a private operation organised by that cripple, Masterman. No wonder Salamander hadn't been alerted to it – it had fallen through the cracks in the British intelligence community. The clever bastard. And of course, who else would Masterman pick but that little killer who had watched his back for years and done his Redacting for him – Gorilla Grant. He returned to the bathroom to find her slumped on the tile floor, blood everywhere. Disgusted, he pitched the cold water into her face to bring her round again.

"So this Gorilla chap gets inside, then what. *Then what!*" he barked.

"A t-team… an unofficial team… storm their way in and kill the top men," she spluttered

"Who are they?"

"I don't—"

"*Who are they!*"

"I don't *bloody know!*"

Trench believed her. Operational security would dictate that the spy on the inside would be on the wrong end of the flow of information and anything she did know would only be on the periphery of the operation. He stared down at her; Christ, she was feeble and pathetic. His hand tightened around the handle of the knife, he felt it twist in his grip. He grabbed her head, forced it back onto the floor and moved the knife blade closer to his target.

She knew what was coming, had seen and felt the knife. More importantly, she'd seen Trench's face and she knew the way it worked. She'd seen him, knew he was alive and consequently, she would have to die. So when Trench grabbed her head and forced it sideways against the cold floor, she knew it was happening now. There would be no hero storming in to rescue Nora Birch. No fanfare, no medal, she would die a cruel and lonely death… and yet she still smiled. She smiled, because she knew that even though her end would be brutal and painful, she had still won. Oh, maybe not the battle between Trench and herself, but certainly the war. She'd given him the slimmest of details, nothing really, regarding what she knew of Masterman's operation. Really, she couldn't handle the torture and the violence against her… would do anything to make him stop… and she'd known that not talking was never going to be an option. Everyone talks.

But the little dormouse, the spy, kept the most precious thing hidden inside and deep away from sight… not the name of the agents on the ground, not the plan of attack, not the fact that Masterman was on a private operation. No, she kept hidden deep in her heart the information she'd left at the dead letter box at the bus shelter, for Jordie Penn, her case officer. The information in the little packet of cigarettes, left between two bricks in a crumbling wall next to the bus shelter, had been found earlier that day in some obscure SIS Registry file she'd unearthed, holding the details of the only man in the British Intelligence community to have intimate knowledge of Yoshida Nakata, the Raven. This man had been the Raven's wartime SIS case officer, who had eventually been rescued by the Raven from a Japanese interrogation camp in Singapore… but of course, Trench would never know that now because he'd taken the bait and thought he had the gold seam, when all he really had were a few titbits'. *Checkmate, Mr. Trench,* she thought. *I've outplayed you and your murderous mob.*

Nora felt the cold tip of the blade brace itself against her neck, just behind her ear. Then she felt an explosion of light and pain as the blade was inserted quickly and violently, felt her body tense and then go limp and then she rolled onto her back and slipped away.

* * *

Trench stared down at the body.

The mad cow, why was she smiling like that, he thought. Even in the throes of death, she still had that stupid grin on her face. Almost as if she knew something more – had he killed her too soon? He didn't know, didn't care really. He'd managed to get some useful information for his employers, well, with the help of Salamander, of course. Information that would see that little bastard Grant nailed to a tree and that fucker Masterman dead in a ditch somewhere. Masterman. *Maybe he should pay his old boss a visit here in London,* thought Trench. Visit him and finish what he'd started on the docks in Australia over a year ago.

Trench looked at the body of the dead woman one last time. Something was not quite right. He reached down and ripped open her blouse, exposing her bra and then he gently scooped one perfect breast out and let it hang. Next he lifted up her skirt and pulled down her knickers. When the body was eventually found, the Police would think they were looking for a sex attacker, rather than it having anything to do with her job. A small detail, maybe, but it might just buy him some time.

But still, that smile on her face... Yes, that smile worried him.

Chapter Eight

Five days after the killing of Nora Birch, Salamander and Trench met again, this time the venue was the Royal Botanic Gardens in Kew. It was far enough out of mainstream London that they could consider themselves reasonably safe. It would also be the last time they would have contact. They walked side by side, Salamander tapping his tightly-bound umbrella on the stone pathway and Trench, with his hands pushed deep into his coat, walking in the Salamander's wake as they admired the fauna on the route

"Did you get everything you needed from the woman?" asked the Salamander.

Trench nodded. "It was perfect. She gave everything up without too much trouble. She was playing games she had no right to be meddling in."

Salamander grimaced. He'd seen the newspaper clippings regarding the discovery of the woman and read the press reports, revealing what Trench had done to her. Most distasteful, but necessary. "So what was it?"

Trench shrugged. "It's a hit, what else could it be? They're nothing, if not predictable. They plan to take down the Raven. They evidently have a location and they think they're up to the challenge."

"Ambitious fellows, then," Salamander remarked.

"Indeed they are. Remember I used to work with these people, I know what they're capable of carrying out," cautioned Trench.

"So what will the Raven do? Fight or flight?"

"Not my department, I'm afraid," said Trench. "I just take care of the dirty work and pass the messages upstairs. But if I was in his shoes, knowing what we know now, I'd give them just enough rope to hang themselves. Draw them in and finish them off."

Salamander knew the Raven was a brilliant tactician. He would expect nothing less of his long-time friend and partner. God help Masterman, Grant and whoever else was engaged in this stupid operation. Which reminded him. "Here, have this," he said to Trench, handing him a sealed envelope.

Trench, confused, frowned. "I don't need your money. I'm well taken care of."

"No, you bloody fool, it's not a payment," growled Salamander. Was this man stupid? "Call it an extra insurance policy, in case the worst happens to the Raven or to me. In that eventuality, you can personally strike back."

Trench ripped open the envelope and looked at the two addresses handwritten on a card inside it. He smiled, a sense of euphoria overcoming him. The first was the address in Chelsea of Mrs. Elsa Masterman, wife of the retired Colonel Stephen Masterman. The second was the address of a small house in Arisaig, Scotland which belonged to one Willie McHugh, local fisherman, and brother-in-law to Jack Grant.

Chapter Nine

Barney Upwright had once been one of the best Security Service surveillance watchers in the business. That had been in his heyday during the Second World War, looking out for enemy agents and Fifth Columnists, and then during the early days of the Cold War in London, trailing Soviet agents to and fro from meeting some source or other.

Now he was a broken down private detective who occasionally did 'funny' jobs for those boys across the river in Lambeth and his old mob at the Security Service. Most of his day-to-day work was the mundane jobs; process serving court papers, following cheating spouses ('Matrimonials' they called it these days) and tracking down people that owed money. But occasionally, just every now and then, he'd get a call from his old firm or their sister service, asking if Barney Upwright wouldn't mind taking on the odd 'unofficial' and very discreet job.

Take today's number for example. Barney had received a phone call in his dingy office above an Italian restaurant in Battersea. The caller was Colonel Stephen Masterman, recently retired SIS officer who was known to Barney from the old days. How did Barney fancy a three-day surveillance job? Expenses up front, low risk, easy, just a little snooping around to see where a particular 'gentleman' was going. Well, Barney fancied it very much thank you Colonel! The Colonel was always a charmer, a decent gent, and within the hour, Barney was planning out his newly acquired surveillance job for the next day.

The following morning he'd loaded up his little Lambretta scooter with his kit for the job; map, binoculars, camera with detachable long range lenses, note pad and pencil.

Barney looked like a librarian. Small, slender, neat, non-descript. He could get lost in a crowd of two, which was why he'd been one of the best surveillance watchers the Security Service had ever had, so he had no doubts he would blend into whatever environment the target was visiting. That first morning, he'd laid up along the street from the target's known address, an exclusive property in Mayfair. He'd watched as the target exited and made his way to his car, a Mercedes Coupe, and drove off. The description he'd been given was perfect; tall, patrician, confident, greying hair. Barney thought the target looked like a man in control of himself. He also thought that he looked like an operator. He would have to be cautious following this man.

The first two days had been humdrum, with nothing out of the ordinary. The target was out of his house at 7.30am, into the car, and off to an anonymous building in Whitehall, a walk to a nearby restaurant at lunch time and then an hour later a walk back to the office. The working day finished for him at 6.30pm and then the target drove to his private club for, Barney assumed, a few drinks before heading home. Barney had hung around, but the target made no attempt to leave the property again. But it was on the third day when the target showed out and did something completely out of the ordinary. On that Wednesday morning, the target left his property slightly later, an hour later in fact, headed to his Mercedes and drove off with Barney on his little scooter in close, but discreet, pursuit. Things took a stranger turn when the Mercedes headed away from the usual Whitehall route and went in a westerly direction, leaving the urban sprawl of central London behind and heading out to suburbia.

Barney's biggest concern was that the Mercedes would just floor it and leave his little scooter behind, but thankfully, his target seemed to be intent on taking a leisurely amble to wherever his destination turned out to be. This was both good and bad for the lone surveillance operator. Good, because at least he could keep a decent 'follow' on his target vehicle, but bad because it meant that Barney would have to be a bit canny, hanging back three vehicles behind, especially if he didn't want to be spotted.

It was when they entered the Borough of Richmond and took a turning leading towards Kew that Barney started to think today was going to be interesting. The big Mercedes turned left down the main high street and headed toward Kew Botanical Gardens, all the while with Barney at full throttle, attempting to keep in sight. When he saw the car turn into the car park, he slowed the scooter down and hung back, pulling over to the kerbside. He counted to fifty in his head then started the engine and set off towards the Botanic Garden's Lion Gate entrance.

After parking the scooter in the small gravel car park, he set off in search of his quarry with camera in hand. To the casual observer he would look like just another horticulturalist, here to take a pho-tographic record of his favourite bushes, shrubs and plants. *Shouldn't be too hard to find,* thought Barney. A tall, distinguished civil servant walking around the gardens mid-week couldn't be too hard to spot. Barney figured his target had a five-minute head start on him and somewhere within the maze of the gardens, he knew he would find him. The trick was, to avoid being spotted. It was as he approached the main grounds that he saw them, sitting next to each other on a bench, admiring the perennials and talking, clearly, but not looking directly at each other. *Like a couple of bloody spies if ever I saw them,* thought Barney. He moved backwards until he was concealed behind some kind of evergreen hedge and changed the standard lens on his camera to the long range one. The target and his pal were thirty feet away and with this lens at this range, he would be able to I.D. them in detail.

Barney brought the camera up to his eye and clicked, heard the whir of the fast motor shutter as it peeled off a couple of shots. A good few snaps of both the targets together, the older one doing the talk-ing and the slightly younger one nodding his head in understanding. Then the passing of some kind of an envelope from his main target to the younger man... snap... snap... snap... before he ripped it open and stared at the piece of paper inside. Snap... snap... snap... Barney clicked off a few more shots and watched as the two men went their separate ways, one to the north and one, his target, back the way he had originally come. Barney didn't know, could only guess, that this was exactly what the Colonel was after.

Barney reckoned that those few photos had probably earned him a lovely bonus.

* * *

Less than twenty-four hours later, Masterman stared at the series of black and white surveillance photos. He knew both men. Trench, he certainly recognised, despite the longer hair and different style. But it was the other man. This was the confirmation of the Raven's traitor inside British Intelligence.

Gorilla had managed to get word to one of their agents, a hooker by the name of Nancy Lo in Hong Kong, about what he'd discovered in Brazil from the chemist, Okawa Reizo. They had a name – the respected businessman, Yoshida Nakata. Penn had set the little dormouse to work, running a trace to see who Nakata had been affiliated with during the war. The day after Nora disappeared, Penn had emptied the dead letter box and read the intelligence hidden there. It was mind blowing, to say the least. The Sentinel team already had a 'possible' confirmation from the information Nora had traced about Yoshida Nakata, regarding who the spy was. But this... this surveillance photograph definitely confirmed it.

"So that's him?" asked Penn.

Masterman nodded. "Most definitely."

Penn ran a hand through his hair and whistled. "Bloody hell, boss... that's who we've been competing against all along *and* we have evidence of him consorting with a known enemy agent – bloody Trench! Well... what do we do now?"

Masterman thought for a moment and then, as he'd done numerous times before in his life he made the right decision for the mission at hand. "We do nothing."

"Nothing! But he's there! We could do... something!"

"And we will, in time. But for now, we keep the status quo. He may know bits about us, especially after what happened to Nora, but we know a hell of a lot more about him. We know who he is, who he's met and what he's involved in. What we don't know about him, yet, is just how far he's connected and who else is on his payroll. Going after him is a luxury at the moment; our main priority is getting the Sentinel team close to the Raven and destroying his chances of setting loose a bio-weapon of apocalyptic proportions. I think that's enough in anyone's book."

"And then later?" said Penn.

Masterman smiled and crunched his walking stick down onto the floor. "Then we find him and squash the little bastard, like a bug."

Chapter Ten

THE PAGODA – FEBRUARY 1968

"We should execute him straight away," said Toshi Goto. Goto was the Raven's top *Shinobi* assassin, a small, lithe man, and a personal student of the *Oyabun* himself. He longed for the honour of killing this infiltrator personally. There were murmurs of agreement around the circle they'd formed. The secret meeting of the Raven's master assassins took place in a darkened dojo, lit only by lanterns, on the third floor of the pagoda that was their sanctuary. Only the trusted *Shinobi* of the clan were allowed to be present and the doors were guarded by the apprentice shadow warriors. They would die defending the *Oyaban* and this meeting's security.

"Oyaban, let me travel to dispatch this gaijin. His body will be sleeping at the bottom of the river that same day," Toshi Goto continued, his head bowed low in honour of his superior.

Hokku sat away from the barrage of anger, on the fringes, and let the *Shinobi* fight it out about who was going to be the one to complete the kill for the *Oyaban*. They would all battle it out for the honour, to see who would be chosen by the *Karasu*! The chosen assassin would be raised high in the pecking order. They'd received the word from Trench in England about the covert operation being planned against the Raven and his people. How deep they had been infiltrated by an enemy agent and what his true purpose was. Things were becoming complicated, mused Hokku.

"And where would this killing lead us?" The voice that cut through the rabble of noise was that of the Raven. It stilled the atmosphere in the room Instantly. "It would lead us nowhere, a dead assassin, a dead spy. Then what? Why destroy one snake when we can take the whole nest of them? If we leave them alone, they will keep coming back again and again and again... but this way, if we draw them in, we can eliminate them all," continued the Raven.

The rest of the *Shinobi* all bowed their heads in shame. The Raven, ever the brilliant strategist, had shown them the true path of seeking out an enemy.

"Where is he now, this ... British gunman?" asked the Raven.

"He is at a safe house in Hong Kong, *Oyabun*. Following the killings in Brazil, we have kept him under surveillance and containment. At least, until the murder investigation has blown over," said Hokku.

"Good. Then bring him to me. We will draw these killers out."

"Here to Japan?" asked Hokku.

The Raven shook his head. "Not just to Japan, but here to the pagoda, to the sanctuary. Let him know that I will meet him here, in my most secret location. He will alert his fellow mercenaries... we open the gates, let them enter and then..."

"Then they never leave," said Hokku, nodding.

"Tell that *gaijin* Trench to find the controllers of this team. He will know what to do. They are his people, after all. We will pit Japanese steel and cunning against western firepower and base stupidity. We will send their heads back to the British. I laugh at their feeble attempts at assassination. They are dogs," growled the Raven.

"And then?" asked Hokku.

The Raven fixed him with a glare, his milky white damaged eye staring straight ahead. When he spoke, it was with the conviction of a man who knows his years of planning are about to come to fruition. "And then, when the assassins have been killed, the British have paid and they have been thoroughly disgraced, we will release the *Kyonshi* onto the streets of Europe as a warning for those who might try to challenge me again."

Chapter Eleven

VICTORIA PEAK, HONG KONG – FEBRUARY 1968

Jack Grant lay back on the bed and stared vacantly at the cracks in the ceiling of his bedroom. He'd been that way for the best part of an hour, tracing the spider's web of broken plaster with his eyes. He was frustrated, angry and ready to punch someone's lights out.

As soon as he'd stepped off the plane from Brazil, he'd been met by Trench and handed a bag full of cash and the keys to an apartment with a magnificent view of Victoria Peak. The bag had contained his first bonus payment of $5000 in cash. The apartment was clean and sparse: a bed, a sofa, a dining table, some books, some magazines and a radio, but nothing more. But it was the view out of the bedroom window which compensated for its emptiness.

He was told by Trench to "Dig in and keep a low profile until Hokku and his people have declared you fit for work again," which was Trench's way of saying he was to remain persona non grata operationally, until the heat had died down about the executions in Rio. So he did as he'd been told, staying close to the apartment, occasionally taking a taxi into town to get out and breathe some fresh air, have a meal, have a drink, go to a club. But he was always the lone man in the shadows at the far table, or at the dark booth in a bar. He stayed hidden. Occasionally, he would get a call from an anonymous male voice to see if he needed anything: booze, drugs… women? Mostly he'd tell the voice on the other end of the line to bugger off. Occasionally, he'd ask for a woman and a bottle of Black Label. The booze was usually of good quality and the girls were pretty and willing. So he did what he always did when he was bored; screwed and drank.

It was at the end of the first day of confinement when he found the bug.

He'd been pacing the apartment, bored, after spending the previous hour working out with some shadow boxing drills. He'd needed to burn off some energy, bleed off the anxiety of the previous few weeks. It was an old routine, one that he practised when he was locked in hotel rooms all over the world. An hour's worth of stretching, footwork, jabs, crosses and hooks on any number of imaginary opponents at least kept him in shape and helped sweat out the alcohol which had been burrowing into his body over the past week. With that out of his system, he'd done what all males do when effectively trapped inside a strange apartment – he'd searched and rummaged to see what he could discover. He'd started with the basics; the phone, the headboard in the bedroom, the light fittings, the usual places where the electronic eavesdropping people tended to fit their devices. He knew they were there somewhere and somebody was no doubt getting an earful of his snoring, pissing in the morning and the noises from the bedroom when the hookers came to visit him.

It was behind the bedroom wall mirror where he confirmed what he suspected had been there all along. A small, penny-sized device, very slim with two short wires jutting out and sending a signal… to where? Not far away, he guessed. Probably the listening team were safely ensconced in an apartment above him, there to monitor his actions and see if he did anything that would be deemed suspicious by his paymasters inside the Raven organisation. So he did the wise thing and left it where it was. Now that he knew where at least one of them was, he could play them at their own game.

Being out of circulation for a while, he knew that he desperately needed to make contact with his case officer. Just to let them know he was alive and still in play. The sooner he could arrange a brush past, the better... he needed to get away from his watchers for an hour or so and write down everything the Japanese chemist had told him, before he'd blown his brains out. The opportunity came the next day, when a thunderstorm knocked out the power to the whole apartment complex. One minute he'd been staring out of the window at the ominous black clouds and lightning sparking out in the distance... the next, the lights had gone out and the gentle hum of the fridge stopped. He'd quickly jumped up and tried the switches, sockets and lights. Nothing. All dead. He knew from experience that reconnecting the power would be a long process, and he also knew that with the power gone, any bugging equipment and covert cameras would be knocked out too. It was an opportunity too good to waste.

He grabbed his jacket and a pen and paper from the desk and ran out of the apartment. He figured he had maybe an hour, at the most. He ran for the stairwell, jumping from landing to landing, pushing himself off from the railings and hitting the floor with a thud. On the ground level he rushed past the reception/security desk and out into the street. The wind and rain hit him at once and started to soak through his summer suit. Moving down the main road, he hit the corner and found a waiting *dik si* driver sitting in an old Humber. Grant pushed a wad of notes through the driver's window and climbed in. The man looked shocked that this soaking wet man had given him so much money.

"Wan Chai! And fast!" Grant barked at the driver, throwing himself into the back seat and waiting for the driver to gun the engine.

The driver knew a good deal when he saw one. Who cared what this angry foreign devil was up to, as long as he paid well? Maybe there would even be a tip at the end of it? The car skidded and pushed its way through the empty, rain-slicked streets, increasing speed in the long straight stretches. In the back seat, Grant was furiously writing down everything he could remember as concisely as he could from what he'd learned over the past few weeks. *It was a bloody mess,* he thought. Trying to write down Grade 'A' intelligence with a blunt pencil on two sheets of paper in the back of a dilapidated taxi in the dark. But try he did... he just hoped Penn would be able to decipher it in time.

He gave them as much as he could... the two men whom he'd killed in Brazil... the details of the *Kyonshi* virus... and the possible location of the pagoda, the Raven's sanctuary and safe zone...

They'd just passed Happy Valley Racecourse when the driver asked, "Where in Wan Chai you want?" His brow furrowed in concentration as he hurled the car around bends, dodging pedestrians.

"The Pussycat Club. You know it?"

"Ha! Everyone knows the Pussycat, mister," grinned the driver. "Hang on!"

The journey took them about fifteen minutes and soon main roads gave way to the bustling and lively area of Wan Chai, filled with bars, hookers and sailors looking for a good time. The Pussycat Club sat on the corner of Lockhart Road and was a first floor den of iniquity. Its sign hanging outside displayed a topless woman bending down to stroke a Siamese cat. It was one of a myriad of identical bars in the Wan Chai red light district. Grant jumped out of the taxi and watched as it moved off into the traffic before he climbed the narrow stairs to the first floor reception. He could hear the beat of the music even from half way up. At the top stair, there was a smiling Chinese bouncer who directed him to the reception desk. A pretty young Chinese girl served him.

"Is Nancy about tonight?" Grant asked.

"At the bar... she's with a guy, I think," said the receptionist, nodding toward the interior of the club.

The club itself was busy. The small dance floor already full with a melee of sailors, drunken businessmen and girls all eager to make a quick dollar. He spotted her straight away. It was hard not to. She had femme fatale written all over her. Gorilla thought she modelled her look on the old film noir heroines of the 1940's. She was small and slim and looked ten years younger than her true age. She would never see forty again, but she carried herself well and with grace. She wore a red, figure hugging dress, coiffed black hair and striking red lipstick. She had one foot balanced on the rung of her stool, which allowed her to reveal a touch of her slim thighs.

Jack Grant slid up next to her at the bar, where she was listening to her 'date' for the night, who by the look of it, had drunk too much of the cheap, knock-off champagne the club served to their clients. Her back was to him but he made a point of speaking loudly when the barman came over to take his order. "You serve any Sentinel Vodka here?"

The barman, to his credit, didn't look confused – he just shook his head and pointed to the house brand in the optics. "That will do instead," said Gorilla and watched as the barman poured him a shot glass full. The stuff was foul... but it had served its purpose. It had caught the attention of the indomitable Nancy Lo, who cast a glance over her beautiful shoulder at the man who'd spoken her activation code word. Gorilla heard her say to her date, "Excuse me, darling, I won't keep you one moment," before turning to fully face him.

"Hi Nancy, so good to see you! It's been a while," said Grant, to the complete stranger in front of him. "I see they stopped serving that Sentinel Vodka I liked."

Nancy Lo regarded the man in front of her with a critical eye. She was a street-wise, no-nonsense hooker of the old school, so she trusted no man at face value. She'd been an old SIS asset who had, on more than one occasion, coerced a businessman or diplomat into giving her a few titbits after her efforts between the sheets with them. She'd thought her spying days were behind her, until she'd been approached by a Major Meadows of the British Secret Service, offering her a cash in hand, no risk job. Listen for the code word and pass messages, nothing that she hadn't done a thousand times before, for one spy or another. They were mostly smartly dressed elderly men, 'prim and proper', her *amah* would have called them. Occasionally, one of them would make a feeble effort to seduce her, but she always kept them at a distance... after all, business was business. But this stocky, bearded man in front of her didn't look like her usual contact. He looked like a thug, like some of the rougher sailors who came into the club, except that he was wearing a suit of good quality and style.

"Sentinel?" she asked. "Sentinel Vodka... I haven't heard of that brand in a while."

"I hope the company is still trading. I'd like to write to their head office. Maybe I could give them some customer advice. I don't suppose you have their address?" asked Grant. He was keen to move the trade on, eager to get back to The Peak before his absence was noticed.

"I can always be persuaded to pass on a message for my friends," she said, opening her purse discreetly. Grant quickly reached into his inside jacket pocket for the envelope and slipped it into the purse. She clicked it shut with a discernible *snap*. Grant looked her directly in the eye. He was trusting this bloody woman, not only with the success of this operation, but with his fucking survival. He leaned forward to offer her a kiss on the cheek and whispered, "Nancy, love, I know you're a busy lady, but this message needs to get to my people quick... as fast as you can."

She accepted the brush of his beard against her cheek and smiled back at him. "My darling... I always look after my friends. You have nothing to worry about. You are in safe hands... maybe when you have some free time, you can come back and buy Nancy a drink?"

Grant nodded and walked away. He just hoped that Nancy Lo was good to her word and she would get the message back to Penn and Sentinel before the next round of bullets started to fly. He found a taxi cab outside and was back at the apartment complex thirty minutes later, happy to discover that the power was still out. The Raven surveillance operators secreted somewhere in the floors above him would be pacing furiously, waiting for the power to come back on to kick start their live feed. *Yeah well, fuck them,* he thought. He'd slipped out of the net, right from under their noses and for those few hours he'd been one lucky son of a bitch.

* * *

By the end of the second week he was bouncing off the walls, not so much because of his isolation in the apartment, but because he was tied to Hong Kong. He wanted to get out and find his own place...

anywhere, where eyes and ears didn't have him under surveillance. It was like being smothered and he was sick of it.

He trashed the apartment, upended the sofa, smashed the crockery in the kitchen and generally went on a violent spree. That would give them something to listen to, the bastards. It was by the end of the third week, when the surveillance listeners thought that the 'Gorilla' was going to go on another one of his rampages when a visitor arrived. There was no fanfare, no VIP reception. The big man simply walked into the apartment, his bulk filling the doorframe, walked up to Jack Grant who was laying naked on the bed, half-drunk from the night before, and stared down at the little Redactor.

"So Mr. Grant, I hear you've been busy," said Hokku, looking his most fearsome. "We need to talk. We have some serious questions that we need you to answer."

"Go away," snarled Grant, playing the part of angry drunk. He propped himself up on his elbow and glared at the huge Japanese man at the end of the bed.

Hokku smiled slowly and Grant knew he'd gotten under his skin. Hokku wasn't used to having subordinates talk to him like that, especially 'foreign devils' like this. "Mr. Grant, forgive me, but if you don't get up, get dressed and tell me what I need to know, I am going to lift you from that bed and take your head in my hands and I'm going to crush your skull until your eyes pop."

Grant looked at the giant's hands and knew that would be the least those hands were capable of. "Where the fuck is Trench," he barked, determined to regain some initiative.

"Trench is away for a while, a little job he is doing for us. You can deal with me for the time being."

"I work for Trench. I'll talk to him," growled Grant.

Hokku shook his head and laughed. "No, Mr. Grant you work for me, as does Trench. I pay you your fees and I make the decisions. Now we can do this the hard way or the easy way."

Grant smiled; it was the type of line he'd used himself on the unwary. So having it thrown back at him by this formidable opponent was a bit disconcerting. "Okay, let's talk," he said, lifting up the dining table and chairs that he'd thrown across the room the night before in one of his 'rages'. Both men sat by the window looking out over the bay, the early morning sun bathing the room a cloudy orange colour.

"You didn't complete the terms of the contract," said Hokku, composed once more. The giant killer had been put away and the reasonable accountant was once again in control of the negotiations.

Grant was confused. He hoped that confusion would mask, even momentarily, the fact that he knew he'd made an error by letting the girl, Maria, go in Brazil. "You've got two dead targets haven't you? Jobs complete."

"But there was a witness Mr. Grant, one whom you failed to eliminate." Hokku forced a cool glare in the little man's direction.

Gorilla Grant went with the dumb pupil look. Gave nothing back. Just silent insolence.

"The driver. The girl? You had orders to kill her after the hits were carried out," explained Hokku.

"I don't kill non-combatants. I got the targets, the two men. That was the deal, the contract."

Hokku smiled. "Mr. Grant do you think we care about non-combatants? We care about our people fulfilling the tasks they've been given. It is not complicated."

"I'd do the same again. You don't like that, then you let me walk, we go our separate ways," said Grant.

Hokku stared at him as if he'd taken leave of his senses. "Do you think that would ever happen? That we would just let you wander off, after you had been a part of something that we were involved in? No, we would kill you."

"So, why haven't you then?"

"Because I see great potential in you, Mr. Grant; you could go far in our organisation, you have a talent. Your reputation, as provided by Trench has shown me that you would be a valuable asset to us. And I don't throw away talent. I keep it close, nurture it, and guide its potential. I even admire your stance on not killing innocent bystanders, it is to be commended. We are after all, civilised and not barbarians," replied Hokku cautiously.

Grant inclined his head, acknowledging the compliment.

"Of course, it didn't change anything – you not killing the driver," Hokku said smoothly.

"What do you mean?" asked Grant, dreading what he suspected was coming.

Hokku smiled. "One of our people picked up the girl, about an hour after she left you. They killed her and dumped her by the roadside out in the country somewhere. It was for the best. She would have been a danger to you."

Grant's face held, he betrayed no emotion, but his stomach churned with revulsion and rage.

"But that is the past... now to the future," said Hokku. "Sufficient time has passed and the investigation in Brazil has been stalled, thanks to our contacts hindering police procedures. Two small-time criminals have been arrested for the crimes. Both were shot while trying to evade arrest. So you are in the clear, Mr. Grant."

"Great." It was all Jack Grant could manage by way of gratitude. He could feel bitterness and bile rising in his throat and swallowed heavily against it.

Hokku stood to leave. "Get yourself cleaned up. I will send a car for you in one week's time."

"Why? Am I going somewhere?" Grant asked, confused.

Hokku turned and straightened his suit jacket fussily. "You are to be honoured with an audience from our *Oyabun*. He has expressed a desire to meet the man who has resolved our recent problems. Your work has impressed him greatly."

"What? The Raven, here? Here in Hong Kong?" Grant was astounded. Maybe this hit was going to be easier than he'd thought.

Hokku laughed loudly. "No, the Raven rarely leaves the safety of his homeland. All the arrangements have been made. You are to travel to Japan. To the pagoda."

* * *

The next evening, Grant took a stroll into town. He felt free, as if there had been a weight lifted off his shoulders and the long walk helped him to relax. He had no proof, but he suspected that following Hokku's arrival, the surveillance in the apartment had been called off. Nothing concrete... just a feeling, a gut instinct. He didn't know how much longer he would be in Hong Kong – could be hours, could be days, but he guessed no more than a week. Grant was heading to a little bar he knew near Kowloon bay to celebrate. He was going anywhere except to Wan Chai, just on the off chance that there was still some kind of street surveillance on him. So while the walk was a good way of stretching his legs and bleeding off the confines of the past few weeks, it was also a crafty way of him running some counter-surveillance on the off chance that Hokku had set some local leg-men onto him.

He dined at a *Dim Sum* place off the Kowloon Road, downed a couple of expensive scotches and made a couple of phone calls from the restaurant's private phone. The first was to the Pussycat Club, where he asked to speak to Miss Nancy Lo, regular hostess on the evening shift. The rest were just random numbers... tailors, a shoe shop, a taxi rank... anything to hide the Pussycat Club's number in a forest of numbers and anything to slow down any trackers running traces or surveillance.

"Nancy, it's Jack... from the other week... likes a tipple of Sentinel Vodka when you have it at the bar... how are you? Sorry I won't be able to make our date next week... going on a little business trip... Japan, yes, really! So don't worry, but please feel free to let the lads over at Sentinel Vodka know that I'm away... maybe they could get the old team together and we could meet up. Yes, if you could pass the message on word-for-word, I'm sure the bosses will give you some free samples... maybe the Pagoda brand that they carry?"

And that had been the end of the call. He'd placed the phone down gently, paid his bill and jumped in the first cab he found. He was drunk and ready to crash. But the moment he thought of Japan and what it might entail, the alcohol in his system seemed to dissipate. He just had to trust, again, that Nancy Lo, hooker and spy extraordinaire would be his lifeline once more and get the message through.

Book Three: Ronin

Chapter One

It was the middle of the night when the team finally received the code sign that was to bring them back to life. Following the 'hits' on the Raven players they'd reconvened to a safe house in Paris, a large apartment on the Rue de la Paix. They'd lived frugally, quietly, as if mentally preparing themselves for what was about to come. The men had shared the main bedroom, the 'barracks' as Hodges called it, whilst Miko had exclusivity over the second bedroom. The phone had rung and Masterman barked down the line. "Sentinel is a go!" They had a location: Matsumoto, Japan. They had a rough time frame: within the week.

A day later, Jordie Penn was standing on their doorstep to confirm the details. They set about abandoning the lives they'd known over recent months and readied their false papers, money and whatever else they might need. The team headed East, drawn into the killing zone like a fly into a spider's trap. The question was, who the spider was and who was the fly? Now that they'd been given the green light, they were ready for whatever waited in Japan.

With the team on the move, the other important part was the transfer of their weapons for the operation. The guns would be coming in from Macau to Japan, via a former Borneo veteran by the name of Roper. Roper was larcenous and did a little gun-running on the side, usually small shipments, discreet stuff, deniable. Roper knew every-one and where to get hardware. But most importantly, he could get the weapons in and out of most countries in Asia. Boats, planes, even donkeys had been used in the past. Roper had been on standby for weeks, the shipment ready, only waiting for a 'delivery' address to complete the arrangement. Now that the operation was a 'go' Roper would be smuggling the kit into the country at this very minute. They were to be collected from the Port of Tokyo docks and shipped to a safe house by a contact of Hodges, a young man named Takai. Takai did jobs for Roper and could be trusted to ask no questions. He was as trustworthy as they could get at short notice and would be the team's driver, general factotum, interpreter and man on the ground while the shooting was going on.

"And it's enough is it?" asked Penn. They were sitting around the table in the Hong Kong safe house apartment, prior to Crane, Lang, Hodges and Miko leaving to fly into Japan. Penn had looked at the list; shotguns, sub-machine guns, explosives, timers and grenades, plus enough ammunition to light up the sky.

Crane and Lang nodded. "For the size of the target we're dealing with and the fact that they aren't expecting us at all, yeah, that will be more than enough."

"What about you, Bill? The whizz-bangs enough?" Penn queried. Hodges looked up from his newspaper where he lounged on the sofa. "Oh, don't you worry your head, Mr. Penn, with all that I could flatten the Kremlin. So a little wooden hut out in the sticks is going to be no problem at all."

Penn doubted the magnificent pagoda he'd spent the last few days researching could be classed as a 'little wooden hut', but he chose not to question his demolition man. Penn had read Hodge's file and knew the old timer was an expert in destroying all kinds of structures and people with explosive.

"What about Grant?" asked Lang. "What will he be using?"

"Ah, the Colonel has included a little something special for him in the inventory. Something Gorilla will appreciate, something from the old days," said Penn enigmatically. "And what about you, Miss Arato? Are you still certain that we can't order you something more... modern?"

Miko smiled sweetly at him from her seat across the table. "Mr. Penn, believe me when I say that there is only one weapon for me. It is the right weapon; it is my weapon. It might be old, but it is deadly accurate."

Chapter Two

The day after the final Sentinel meeting, Miko Arato hired a car and drove to visit her sole remaining relative in the entire world. She drove north west out of Tokyo, to Ishikawa Prefecture.

Farmer Hiro Arato had been out in the fields, tending to his crops of sweet potatoes, vegetables and dry rice in the spring months, when he'd seen the car approaching. He slowly walked up to the dirt track dissecting his fields, curious to see who'd driven all this way to see him on his farm. By the time the car reached the track, he could see the silhouette of the driver and he knew instantly who it was. It was the girl he'd helped raise; his niece, Miko. They embraced, as close family do, and Hiro Arato stood back to admire his beautiful niece. "You should have warned me that you were coming. You drove all this way?"

Miko nodded and gazed lovingly on her uncle. *He looks tired,* she thought. *Old. Beaten.* They walked inside together and sat in the kitchen of his small house overlooking the hectares of his farmland. It was his greatest achievement, working these fields. It was all he had left, except for this young woman who came to visit him only occasionally.

"You were always different, Miko, always headstrong. Wilful. You remind me very much of your mother. You have your mother's wildness and your father's western ways," he said. He was speaking of her job as a foreign tour guide, her travel to parts of the world he knew he would never see, and her westernised ways and manners. "How is Europe, the tourists?"

"The job is fine, Uncle. Thank you," she said politely.

"That is good, I am so—"

"I need the rifle, Uncle."

There was that bluntness he hated. She was such a modern young woman or maybe, he was just an old relic who was too set in his ways. "What for, Miko? Why do you need the Arisaka?" he asked. She had not used the rifle for several months, not since her last visit, before she left for England to attend the funeral of the Englishman who'd been her father.

She put down her small cup of tea and looked him squarely in the eye. In truth, she needed the rifle because it was easier to use her favourite weapon, than to have Masterman and the team try to smuggle a 'clean' weapon into Japan. Besides, the weapon was almost an extension of her; she'd trained on it and knew it well. But she knew her uncle would require more information than that; he would need a reason to give it to her, not just an excuse. So, she played up to his sense of honour. "There is honour to be upheld. I'm hunting beasts and when one hunts a wild animal, it is best to have a trusty weapon."

"Is this your dark quest, Miko? The quest for the man who killed your father?" he questioned sadly. Her long moment of silence confirmed it.

"*Giri*," she finally said, firmly.

"Yes, your obligation; the vow you have made to honour your father and to avenge his death. I understand. But I offer you this warning, Miko, from one who is older and wiser. You should be wary of seeking out death. I have seen it close at hand; I have felt its taste. It always leaves a trace and it lingers on your spirit. No amount of washing can cleanse this."

She stared at him, not revealing her thoughts in any way.

Hiro inhaled deeply before he continued. "Miko, you are the new generation, a generation of our people who should and must learn from the mistakes of our fathers. You cannot take on the burden of your father's death. He was a man of secrets. You should concern your-self with living, not taking revenge for a ghost." He looked hard at her, this young woman who not so very long ago, he'd trained in the use of the rifle, when she had been just an adolescent. He'd spoken his mind and he could only hope that for one last time, she would listen to the wisdom of her uncle. He hoped to dissuade her from whatever she had decided to do.

She reached forward and in a very western way, kissed him lovingly on both cheeks, a favoured niece to her family patriarch. Then she looked once more into his eyes, held out her hands and spoke bluntly. "The rifle, Uncle. Give it to me."

"And if I refuse?" he asked gruffly, but without much conviction. The conviction in her voice had shocked him and he suddenly felt every year of his age.

She smiled, the sweet smile which told him she could still twist him around her little finger. She'd always had that skill, as had her mother before her. He sighed heavily, resigned to defeat, and beckoned for her to follow him. She knew where he kept the rifle, where he'd always kept it. It had been locked in a crate in the cellar of the farmhouse, for as long as she could remember. She followed him down the musty and cracked steps. The cellar was much the same as had been the last time she'd been down here. Neat, compact, everything stored away in chests and boxes. Then she spied what she was after. The crate. The old man stepped past her, rummaged in his pocket for a set of keys and knelt to open up the old crate where he stored the rifle. It lay resplendent on a bed of cotton sheets. Locked away, forgotten about, like a photograph of a long dead lover. Still pristine, but discarded. Miko thought it looked both beautiful, and deadly.

The Type 97 rifle had once been the favoured weapon of marks-men within the Japanese Imperial Army. Designed for snipers hid-den in the reeds, bushes and forests, the weapon had taken the heads of many of the enemy, from long range shooting on the islands, to the close-quarter street fighting in Singapore itself. A member of the Arisaka family of weapons, the Type 97 rifle came with a fixed scope, which bizarrely enough couldn't be altered or tweaked. Hiro Arato had smuggled the weapon home when he returned to Japan for convalescence in the months before the Allied occupation. It had remained hidden, buried out in the forest, safe and protected from the elements and the searching eyes of the American and British soldiers hunting war criminals. More than two years passed before he'd summoned up the courage to go out into the forest and retrieve the rifle. He'd cleaned it, oiled it and test fired it in the fields surrounding his farm. At first, he'd struggled to hit his targets, but slowly, over the course of many months, the skills he'd learned during the war came flooding back; the field craft, the breathing, the control of the weapon and the feeling of power when the target was hit. He'd hunted with it over many years and bagged many trophies for his cooking pot. Then had come the arrival of the girl, and he'd taught her so well that she could now outshoot him easily.

"Have you used it recently?" she asked.

He shook his head. Corporal Hiro Arato had sat in the hills, jungles, reeds and foxholes with the Arisaka during the war. If he never held it again it would be his pleasure. "It is no longer a thing I wish to hold. I have killed enough men with weapons of war. Instruments of death no longer interest me. I am a humble farmer. It is yours now. It has been for a very long time."

She bowed in respect and gratitude. He was quietly pleased to see she could adapt to her heritage when she needed to, when it served her needs. Maybe all was not lost with her. But now after all these years of learning, studying and shooting she was here to take the rifle away. "Do you wish to practice?" he asked.

"Yes please, Uncle, for old times' sake."

He frowned. "How much ammunition shall we take? There is not much left in the box."

She held up her handbag and patted it. "I have brought my own."

* * *

They reached the small hillock overlooking the farm. Her uncle had completed his usual trick of placing an old milk churn on a piece of wasteland. It was their old training routine. Uncle Hiro set up the target, walked the three hundred yards back and acted as her spotter as Miko began to zero in on the metal churn. It was something they'd done together since she was a child, on summer days, winter days, hunting with the rifle, practising lying up and sniping at makeshift targets. She'd started small; rabbits and vermin, before moving up to deer and boar.

Hiro had known within a few sessions that the girl had talent. It was unmistakable and also of concern to him. A child, a girl-child who was a half-breed *gaijin* which was even worse, because that kind of talent would attract attention. He would have to hide it, he knew, so it didn't become known among the other villagers. Over the years, the child had come shooting with him whenever she visited the old farm, until eventually, she'd become a young woman and started surpassing him with her skills. It had been inevitable. Hiro Arato had been a first rate soldier and sniper, out of the necessity of wartime combat. But his niece could easily out shoot him with his old rifle, she was a natural talent.

Miko settled herself down, the bag of rice she'd carried up onto the hill she used as a rest for the rifle, its weight forming a groove into the bag. She began to slow her breathing down, breathing in and out, slower each time until she could feel her heartbeat grow more relaxed. She gently moved her eye to the scope; she knew how it worked, had taken this shot hundreds of times before.

The metal of the churn appeared large through the scope, and she saw that it was already peppered and riddled with bullet wounds from years gone by. Miko knew that, because of the placement of the scope on the rifle, she would have to compensate, knowing it would pull to the right. She centred the rifle, breathed out slowly, nothing more than a whisper of air, and gently pulled the trigger. Miko heard the crack of the bullet as it left the weapon, felt the buck of the rifle as it pushed into her shoulder, instantly reacted to control it. Then the distant clang as the bullet 'zinged' off the metal of the churn. Even at this distance, through the scope Miko could see she was mere inches off the centre. But inches mattered. Every inch away from dead centre was classed as a miss. She pulled back the bolt and chambered another round. From the side, she heard Uncle Hiro, his old binoculars still fixed to his eyes, say, "Too far to the right, you need to move left."

Miko nodded, settling herself back and breathed slowly and shallowly. She made the most imperceptible of movements with the rifle and fired. Again, she felt the buck of the weapon, heard the crack of the bullet. She heard Uncle Hiro snort with laughter. "*Hai*, perfect. You have your zero!"

She fired again… and hit.

Again… and hit.

Three, four times. All hits. All kill shots.

Hiro Arato looked over at his niece and saw the confidence and determination in the set of her face. She was ready. Whatever it was she was ready for, he did not know exactly, nor did he wish to. Tomorrow, she would return to the big city from where she had come. He just hoped he would one day be able to look into the face of his beloved niece again and see the fire of revenge in her eyes had been doused forever.

Chapter Three

Jack Grant had been in Tokyo for less than a day.

He'd been collected from the airport by a chauffeur and driven to the exclusive Hilton Hotel, where a suite had been booked for him. Once he'd checked in and inspected the room, he immediately went out onto the street and found a taxi. With a smattering of Japanese from a phrasebook he'd bought, he managed, in mangled Japanese, to ask the taxi driver to take him to another hotel. He would use the Hilton to check in for messages from Hokku's people, and the alternate hotel as his base to sleep and connect to Penn safely.

The new hotel belonged to a western chain, the Osaka. It was pleasant enough, serviceable, and not ostentatious. It catered for the ever-increasing western business market. Grant thought he would blend in perfectly here, among the senior executives from Germany, Brussels and Australia. His first task was to make phone contact with Penn and let him know he was in country and still in play. He called the Hong Kong contact number in his head, remembered from all those months ago. He heard the click from the other end of the line.

"2308. Hotel Osaka. Still active. I'm clear," said Grant.

He heard Penn murmur back, "Phone back in one hour." Then he heard the phone set back in its cradle.

So he walked, exploring the city streets. He mostly stuck to the shadows and the darkness, not wanting to attract unnecessary attention. To the average Japanese, he was sure that with his beard, his rolling swagger and his glare he would be the very epitome of a European, a Gorilla, an animal, a brute, a killer – memorable. He also knew that despite its outwardly friendly atmosphere, there was a good chance that within the next few days, Tokyo could turn into a very dangerous place for him, hunted by both the police and the Raven's people. He didn't want to attract anyone's interest.

An hour later, he returned to the Osaka and used the booth in the hotel lobby to call the contact number. Penn must have been waiting, hovering over the telephone, because he picked up on the first ring. "How's the weather," asked Penn.

"Bloody cold. Thought this was meant to be Asia?" growled Grant.

"There seems to be a winter storm heading your way, old boy, at least according to the weather reports," said Penn.

"You don't say," said Grant, aware of the double meaning. "We have any more intelligence about this pagoda?"

"Only that it's in the middle of the countryside, isolated and protected. Downside is that you may have a bit of a fight, a few guards to deal with."

"And the upside?"

"They aren't expecting you, so you can hit them while they're at their weakest and because of its isolated location, you can cause as much havoc as you like without attracting too much attention," said Penn.

I wish it was that simple, thought Grant. "How's the team, they ready?"

"They're fine Jack, everything is in place. They're in country. They know what they have to do and they'll be close behind you all the way. Just be ready for them to scoop you up. They won't be far away."

"Good," said Grant. "The Raven's people haven't been in touch yet, probably keeping me warm ready for the big man's visitation. As soon as I know, you'll know. Okay?"

"Understood. Oh, and by the way, expect a visit from one of our representatives tonight. We'll get someone to make contact with you at the Osaka, just to brief you on any last minute details," finished Penn, before ending the call.

So Grant had returned to his hotel and waited. He was expecting… someone. From the moment he'd switched hotels and given his new location to his contact number, he knew the promised contact would happen soon. His ghost family were forever watching from the sidelines.

He was unpacking when there was a knock on the door and a voice called "Room Service". He hadn't expected it to be her. Although, on thinking about it, she was perfect for the role of a room service maid: she spoke fluent English, and was just as western in culture as she was Asian. She blended into a western hotel perfectly.

"Your order," she announced. Miko was dressed in the standard uniform for hotel staff – blouse, short skirt, flat shoes, and name badge – and she was pushing a food trolley. The perfect cover. No one looks twice at a waitress doing a room service run.

He let her enter the room and then closed the door behind her. She turned to him and smiled, all the while removing a slim file from beneath the silver cloche on the trolley before handing it to him. From under the linen cloth covering the trolley, she removed a small bag. It held several pieces of equipment that Penn thought his agent might need.

"That's everything we have on where we think they'll take you," said Miko.

Grant opened it up and flicked through the contents; maps, routes in and routes out, a weapons lists for the rest of the team as well as an operational plan on how the attack would happen and in what order. He skimmed through it all. It sounded feasible on an initial glance; he would study it later when the girl was gone. Then he would burn it, inside the hotel bathroom.

"How is everyone?" he asked.

She nodded. "They are ready, I think. Men… they are always so impatient to start causing death and destruction."

"And you?"

She smiled sadly. "I am ready too. The hardest part has been the waiting."

Grant nodded. He understood that, too well. It was always the hardest part… the waiting for that call to action. The fear, the doubts, the paranoia. Just hard.

"Was it hard for you, Mr. Grant?" asked Miko. "Being out of reach for so long?"

He placed the briefing file on the bed next to him and sat down. He rubbed his hands through his beard and over his hair, as if he was trying to scrape away the stress of the past few months living inside an enemy camp. "It was difficult, but not impossible."

"But was it worth it?"

He shrugged. "We'll soon see, won't we Miss Arato?" he said, looking up at her in her uniform, her disguise. He thought she resembled a doll – so tiny and fragile. Their eyes locked for a moment – not long – but long enough for both of them to sense something between them. She took a step towards him and gently caressed his face.

"Thank you for all of this, Mr. Grant," she said and then quickly turned, collected the hostess trolley and left the room without saying another word.

* * *

An hour later he was in bed, his mind turning over the information in the intelligence file Miko had delivered to him. The location, the history, the expected number of targets. But it was the girl who held court over his mind the most. The complexity and contrast of her. A beautiful, fragile woman who was willing to give up her life, liberty and freedom to walk into hell with a bunch of trained killers on a possible suicide mission. And all to avenge the man she'd barely known as a father. Most of the women he knew would have simply thrown a wreath on the grave and moved on with their lives. But this young woman, well, she was something unique.

He was on the point of drifting off to sleep when he heard the click of the door as it was eased open in the darkness. A hotel pass key, he guessed. Instantly he was alert, old habits and old training die hard. Grant raised himself up on one elbow and with his other hand, he reached for the straight razor he kept beneath the pillow. He was naked beneath the sheets; the heat inside the hotel had forced him to sleep that way.

"You won't need the razor," said Miko.

He said nothing and watched as she quietly entered the room and closed the door behind her. The ambient light from the street cast a neon sheen of blue over her. She stepped to the side and out of its haze, blending into the blackness of the room. He heard the shuffling of material as she quickly removed her clothes and then the sheets on the bed were pulled back and her lithe body was resting against his.

"Did you forget something?" he asked, trying to locate her eyes in the darkness.

For an answer she placed one slender finger on his lips to silence him and then she rolled her body over his torso so that she was straddling him. She was in control, and despite his inbred reluctance to relinquish physical power, he willingly submitted. Her hands splayed across his chest as she leaned forward, her hair dropping downwards as their lips met. The kiss was tender, soft and both embraced it fully. He worked his hands up to her breasts and his fingers found her nipples; she moaned as they hardened beneath his thumbs. She reached down between her thighs to discover him as hard as stone and gently guided him into her wetness. She trembled at first, eager to take all of him into her and then slowly, she relaxed. She rode him gently, her hips moving forwards and back in a fluid motion, bringing him on. Grant held her up with his strong arms, thrusting himself upwards into her again and again, watching as her back arched in pleasure, her breasts thrust outwards. The intensity increased, their eyes locked, and they moved together as one until they both climaxed, both crying out in pleasure. Miko bent her head down, her black hair falling onto his chest, tears falling from her eyes.

They lay silent in the darkness, listening to the noise of Tokyo's nightlife outside, each unsure what to talk about or how to say it. For both of them, the love making had been nothing but a physical release, a salve to ease the stress and tension before tomorrow began. It was the coupling of two people who might die tomorrow. Finally, Grant broke the silence. "Are you sure you want to go through with this? The hit, the killing tomorrow?" he asked in a low voice.

Miko lay silent for a while longer, as if he'd managed to read her thoughts and she was considering her options. Would she back out at the last minute? Everybody said that it would be fine, but really, they meant the opposite. You could never back out, never walk away, never quit the mission. She propped herself up on one elbow and looked down at him. She gently caressed his face. "I have an obligation; my concerns do not matter. I have the chance to avenge my father and I have to protect my team," she said simply. "I have made a choice and there can be no turning back now."

He understood; he'd been there himself, many times, had forced himself to see through operations that lesser men would quake at. It wasn't for everyone, it changed people, sometimes for the worse, sometimes for the better, but it changed them nevertheless. "So what was all this," he asked, indicating the bed where they'd made love moments before. "Condemned man's last request?"

She smiled. "It might be the last time for both of us. There is no one else who would understand here, tonight, in this situation."

He nodded and turned over to face her. He ran his hand gently down the curve of her breast. As if sensing his conflict, she spoke. "Can I tell you a story, a story about my father?"

"Talk, if it will help."

She smiled at him, and quickly kissed him one final time. "The first time I met my father, was when I was just a child. My mother and I travelled to Singapore to meet him. My mother only said that we were going to meet an old friend of hers; I had no idea we would be meeting a man, let alone my father. Up until that point, the idea of a father had never even occurred to me. Family had consisted of my mother, my uncle Hiro and a few distant cousins. A father had never been mentioned. When we arrived at the hotel where he was staying, my mother and I were greeted at the door by a handsome man wearing a beautiful cream suit. I thought he looked like a movie star from a Hollywood film. He was tall and slim, tanned for a westerner and very handsome. We sat and had afternoon tea together, the three of us. I could tell that my mother loved him and he was a perfect gentleman, had impeccable manners. We talked until late into the evening about everything... he asked me about my home, my life, what I wanted to do when I grew up. I told him I wanted to be a ballet dancer. He smiled and said that I would make a wonderful dancer. The next day, we met him again and he took us shopping. He bought me a beautiful dress, one that I still have somewhere, packed away with my other childhood memories."

Grant smiled to himself. He'd never met the old C personally, only seen him in passing, but he knew the man had been a ruthless intelligence officer back in his day. So this new angle on the old spymaster had taken him by surprise. "Did you ever meet him again?"

She smiled. "Of course! Many times over the years. My father and I had a wonderful relationship, he guided me, protected me and gave me many opportunities in my career. But most of all he gave me love, a love that had been missing when I was younger. He made amends for not being there."

"And then the Raven happened," said Grant.

"Then the Raven took him from me... that is something I will not forget. My father lived that dangerous type of life, as you do, but to die old and defenceless and in that manner... that I cannot forgive," she said bitterly.

"So, we go all the way, Miko?"

"Yes Jack – me, you, those boys, we go all the way to the end and we finish this. We are *Ronin*." She saw his confusion. "You are not familiar with the term?"

He shook his head. "No."

She ran one delicate hand down the side of his face and nestled her head against his shoulder. "*Ronin* were a group of masterless Samurai in feudal Japan. They were mercenaries who would work on contract, or for the highest bidder. But occasionally, even *Ronin* can come together for a greater cause."

"A greater cause! Well, we have that alright," said Grant.

"We have revenge, which is certainly an important factor for what we're about to do. But we also have a duty as human beings, to stop the possible genocide this madman wants to inflict upon the world in the name of greed and the lust for power."

Jack thought back to the footage of the boy mauling the goat in the lab and shuddered. The image chilled him to the bone.

Miko carried on. "At times, the *Ronin* knew they may not survive in battle, quite often they were simply outnumbered. Even though they were no longer of the Samurai class, their greatest hope was that they would experience a warrior's death in combat. I think for us tomorrow; we should expect the same. To destroy evil, even if it means that we die a lonely death and the rest of the world will carry on as if nothing had happened, unaware of our sacrifice. That is a good thing."

Grant relaxed back onto the bed, one hand resting lazily on her hip, both of them enjoying the warmth of each other and the security of the darkened hotel room. Sleep took him and his dreams were fitful at first with his mind in turmoil. What had he become over the past few months, since he left his home in Arisaig? How did he define himself now? He was no longer a government agent of the Secret Intelligence Service; as far as they were concerned, he was old news and didn't exist anymore. But he also wasn't a full-on mercenary or contract killer working for the highest pay-packet either. He was a hybrid, something resting between two worlds. He'd killed people certainly, and he would be killing a lot more before this task was completed. What had he become and where would it take him? *Ronin.* He thought the word suited him perfectly now.

In the darkness it was a good sleep, deep and powerful. Gorilla was always that way before a "job". He slept the sleep of contentment and peace. When he awoke the next morning, Miko had gone, and for a few brief moments he wasn't sure if her visit had been nothing more than a wonderful dream.

Chapter Four

Gorilla could sense the end game playing out and tonight would bring the operation of the past few months to a very violent conclusion. Whether he would still be alive at the end of the night was another matter.

He was standing on a street corner in the *Nihonbashi* district, ironically enough, opposite the building which housed Nakata Industries. It was early evening and the streets of Tokyo were teeming with pedestrians. The night was crisp and cold, and he guessed there might be snow in the air before too long. He stood staring at a newspaper absently, not knowing what any of the words meant. The crowds moved around the foreigner, like water avoiding a rock in a stream.

He would never be allowed inside the legitimate arm of the clan, the big glass-fronted building that was the cover for Nakata's official profession. The clan and its facade would forever be two separate entities and in truth, he had no interest in that part of the Raven's operation. It was the *Karasu*'s sanctuary he wanted, the place where the clan leader deemed himself to be safe and secure.

He was dressed in clothes suitable for the winter's night. Dark trousers, black turtle neck sweater and a short black coat. Earlier that day, he'd visited the hotel barber and had his beard shaved off and his hair cropped short, revealing his natural white/blond coloring. With the beard gone, his face looked harder and leaner. It was as if he had removed a mask, a disguise, now that the final stages of the operation were happening, to reveal his true identity, his battle face. His shoes, a present from Penn, were heavy-soled and gripped well and were his one concession to his attire. The shoes would be good for fighting in. Good for stability in the snow and with a sole heavy enough to do some damage in a scrap. The shoes held another secret also – a small tracking device buried deep in the sole, no bigger than a coin. It was his lifeline to the rest of the team. As long as he didn't lose his shoes, they'd be able to follow and find him. He knew they would be near even now, sitting in the back of a discreet van they'd bought, watching and waiting.

An hour ago, he'd received a call from Hokku at his hotel, telling him to wait on a certain street at a certain time and he would be 'collected'. So it was no surprise when, almost exactly to the second, a dark BMW sedan pulled up. He instantly reached for the handle and climbed into the car. The interior was dark and warm and the only thing he had to look at was the neck of the driver as he pulled away into the traffic.

"Where are we going?" asked Gorilla

The young driver glanced at him. "To the pagoda," he announced curtly.

The drive, Gorilla estimated, would take them around two hours at this time of night. Out of the city and away into the vastness of the Japanese countryside. Gorilla just hoped and prayed the tracker in his shoe was doing its job and the rest of the Sentinel team were still 'on' him, in the distance, tethered to him by an invisible lifeline. They passed picture perfect countryside in the darkness, only the odd light here or there providing any hint of civilisation. In the distance, snow-covered mountains stood watch and even down here on the low ground, the gentle snowfall made the forests and plains look as if they'd been painted with white blossoms from the trees.

Gorilla lay back in the seat and closed his eyes. He knew what was about to happen and there was nothing he could do about it yet. So rest when you can, that was the golden rule. But even lying back in the deep leather seats of the car, his mind was still working out the angles and what he needed to do. Get the team together, get them focused, get past the guards and then... then was the easy part. The killing, the pulling of triggers, the aligning of the sights were all done with speed, aggression and surprise. The team would have to be both ruthless and brutal.

Somewhere on the journey, he must have nodded off for a while, probably only minutes really. But the warmth of the interior and gentle rocking of the car as it traversed the undulating country roads had an effect. He jerked awake with a start. Checking his watch, he guessed they were only another thirty minutes out from their destination. The time of rest was over; it was time for him to do what he did best.

He took one final look at the back of the driver's head, taking in his thin neck and close-cropped hair. He was no more than a kid, no doubt a junior somewhere within the clan, used for running errands and driving people to meet the *Karasu. Tough luck,* thought Gorilla. He didn't care who the driver was; how old he was or what he did. He only knew that what he was about to do had to be done quickly, violently and without mercy. With his left hand, he gripped the back of the driver's seat firmly, planted his feet hard against the floor of the car to give him grip and then twisted his short body in an arc. He watched as his hook punch blasted in slow motion into the ear of the young driver, knocking his head like a billiard ball into the glass of the driver's side window. A smear of blood spread onto the cracked glass and then Gorilla was launching more punches, once again into the same spot, the ear. He pounded the side of the man's head mercilessly three, then four times.

The car lurched, twisting in the empty country road, as the driver slipped into unconsciousness. Gorilla was thrown around in the back, bracing himself for what he knew was inevitable as the car seemed to pick a straight course and sped up, aiming for a ditch. There was a sudden, out-of-control spurt as the driver's foot floored the pedal and then a series of slow, descending bumps as it fell deeper down the embankment. Finally, there a solid thud of noise and energy as the vehicle smacked into a large tree. Then there was only stillness and silence.

Gorilla ended up wedged in the rear footwell of the car. He reached up and lifted the door lock, prising open the interior door handle and kicking out with his feet until the door swung itself open. The cold blast of air which hit him made him glad of his heavy jacket on this frosty night. Cautiously, he made his way out of the vehicle and into the night. The car was nose down in the ditch, its bonnet crumpled like a paper cup, and its rear wheels free of the ground and spinning. The driver had been tossed around like a rag doll and he was spread-eagled over the front seats. Mercifully, he was still unconscious. Gorilla made his way up the embankment until he reached the main road. He searched carefully and could see the skid marks on the snow-covered road, they twisted and turned like a snake before veering off into the fringes of the forest. The good news was that anyone finding the car would simply assume it had skidded on a patch of ice, rather than the driver being beaten unconscious.

He stood on the edge of the verge, banging his feet and keeping his hands thrust deep into the pockets of his coat. It didn't take long before the headlights of an approaching vehicle caught him in their glare; he winced and then re-focused as an old van pulled to a halt on the side of the gravel path. It was his team. The driver's window was wound down and a hard face poked out and barked something at him in what sounded like guttural Japanese. Gorilla just stared blankly and then was treated to the English translation when Hodges peered out from the dark interior of the truck's cab. "He says it's a bad night to be out in the countryside alone, especially for a *gaijin*, and especially for someone as ugly as you. Get in; we've got a lot of work to do."

Chapter Five

"You got any double nought rounds?"

"Nah, none left, I'm loaded up. Take the solid shots instead."

"I need some gaffer tape to hold down these straps. Where's the spare stuff?"

"Can you pass me that spare charge, might come in handy as a back-up."

The talk in the back of the van was whispered, muted. It was talk Gorilla had heard hundreds of times before. The talk of men preparing themselves for battle. Not loud, not bombastic, just professionals, ensuring that they had everything in place. He sat and watched them all in the back of the van, their outlines the only things visible in the darkness as they passed bits of kit back and forth and made sure they were ready. They talked, all except for the girl, Miko. She remained silent. Her head was leaning forward and her eyes were closed, as if she was indulging in some private prayer.

They drove another few hundred feet, until they found a place to pull in, somewhere quiet and discreet. Takai, the hard-faced young Japanese driver, remained in the driver's seat while the rest of them quickly left the vehicle. The Sentinel attack team – Crane, Lang, Miko and Hodges - were all outfitted in the same manner: black overalls, dark hiking boots, fingerless mittens, black knitted cap and faces smeared with black boot polish, as was the norm for all covert action teams the world over. The only thing which separated them was the different individual weapons; the deadly duo had Remington 1100 combat shotguns, Hodges carried an old Sten gun – clunky, but still operational – and Miko of course, had her specialised weapon, the Type 97 Sniper rifle which was secured in a padded rifle bag to keep the frost and snow from it.

They stood around in a semi-circle, Gorilla, their leader, in the centre. They waited on his word. The Sentinels were once more re-united. When Gorilla did speak, he kept it short. "We can't hang around long. We all know what we have to do, our roles in all of this. I'm the Trojan horse; I'll get us past the first post. As soon as I'm in, Crane and Lang fall in behind me when I give the signal. Hodges, you lay up until we're inside and when the coast is clear, you plant those explosives. Blow those buggers if we're not out within the hour, level the place." Finally, he turned to Miko. "Find your perch, somewhere high, concealed and with a good view of the grounds. Take down as many on the outside as you can, especially the guards. Getting us in and getting us out is the tricky part… while we're in there, feel free to eliminate anything that has a pulse! Okay?"

She nodded. She knew what was expected of her and was clear in her mind on what she would do. Then as an afterthought, as if she'd remembered at the last minute, she reached into her small rucksack and pulled out two parcels, each wrapped in a dark cloth and handed them to him. His eyes met hers, but they betrayed nothing of their love-making from the night before. That moment was long past for both of them. Now everything was purely business. He unfurled the first cloth and looked down at the contents. It was a Smith & Wesson Outdoorsman with a five-inch barrel; a large heavy revolver which fired six .38 special calibre bullets. Gorilla knew instantly that it was a man stopper. The revolver was sitting in a tan shoulder holster rig. He removed his coat and slipped on the rig, adjusting it slightly so that it didn't move about and remained snug against his body.

He unfurled the material concealing the next parcel and smiled, for there lying nestled in the thickness of the wool, was his old friend and talisman. It was the Smith & Wesson Model 39, contained in a belt holster and accompanied by three fully charged magazines. He'd last seen the '39 more than three years ago when he'd been forced to relinquish it following the operation in Europe. He had feared he would never see it again. Gorilla traced over the contours of the metal frame with his finger and he sighed. It was as if someone had returned a missing limb; he was whole, and he was complete. He loaded a magazine into the '39, racked the slide making the weapon 'live' and flicked on the safety. The other two magazines went into the leather pouch he wore on his hip. He had his primary weapon, the '39 and a backup gun; the Outdoorsman. He was ready.

"Is it what you wanted?" she asked.

She looks beautiful he thought, even with the boot polish camouflage covering her face and the dark hood covering her hair. He nodded. The '39 was exactly what he wanted. It was, without any sense of ceremony or pomp, a final gift from Sentinel.

* * *

Nestled deep in the heart of Japan's Mie Prefecture, far out on the vast empty plains and surrounded on all sides by mountains, stood Masakado Castle. It was one of the few original pagodas remaining in Japan and dated from the sixteenth century, when it had originally been built by an enemy of the Nakata clan, Sugitani Masakado, a *Shinobi* of some repute.

In the late 1870's, the Raven's great-grandfather had, through nefarious means, purchased the surrounding fifty hectares and gained control of the pagoda, taking stewardship of it. The old warrior had thought it amusing to dominate what his enemies had once owned and his clan had coveted. He'd celebrated well on the night the sale had been completed. He'd then set about renovating and rebuilding it to his own specifications, painting the exterior of the structure a dense black colour and changing the pagoda to be named, ironically, the *Karasu-Jo*, the Raven's Castle. In the fullness of time, the deeds to the building and all the land had been passed onto his great grandson, Yoshida Nakata, the *Karasu*, who had continued to use it as his private domain, and training grounds for those he judged worthy enough to take on the role of assassins to his clan.

The pagoda was a magnificent spectacle. It was surrounded by a ten-foot-high stone wall which covered some five kilometres of terrain and the castle was protected on two sides by mountains. It stood ninety-six feet in height, consisted of five levels rising to a peak and was surrounded by a moat – the only way across was via a thirty-foot ornamental bridge. Adjacent to the pagoda was the castle's keep, the *Tenshukaku*, as well as a recently-built guard barracks which accommodated the clan's soldiers. It was a fortress. Only the *Shinobi* of the clan had the freedom to enter. Those who were not the *Karasu's* brothers never left alive and were often dismembered in the *Tenshukaku*.

But for this one night, the *Karasu* had ordered that a *gaijin*, an assassin, should be allowed to enter unharmed and unhindered. The *Karasu's* orders were clear. The assassin should be brought to him, kneel before him in the sanctuary of his pagoda and there, the Raven – Yoshida Nakata, the *Oyabun* – would take the head of the Gorilla.

Chapter Six

Gorilla walked up the snow-covered path towards the pagoda, his hands thrust deep into the pockets of his black winter coat. His black boots crunched gently on the newly-fallen snow. There was no subterfuge in Gorilla's approach. He walked straight, true, alone and in plain view, the glare of the full moon's light reflecting off the snow-covered landscape and buildings. He was a lone soldier, defiant against the hostile glare of the pagoda behind the fortress walls and what its grandeur held inside.

In the distance, probably no more than fifty yards away, he saw the ten-foot-high wall forming the outer perimeter to the pagoda, and at its centre stood the immense wooden gates, painted a vibrant red colour. He stood before them, looking around for a rock he could use as a knocker. He breathed slowly, closed his eyes once and banged with the rock three times on the heavy wood.

THUMP!

THUMP!

THUMP!

At first there was silence and just as he was about to strike the gate again, he heard voices from inside and the withdrawing of a huge bolt from the other side of the gate. The doors retracted slowly, giving him his first proper view of the courtyard and Masakado Castle, the Raven's pagoda. It was stunning. Beyond the gates, he could see a wide wooden bridge which traversed a water-filled moat. He also saw the two armed guards on duty. They were alert, dangerous-looking Japanese men. Gorilla kept his head down and moved forward, not making eye contact with them until they were mere feet from the gate. He felt hidden eyes from within the pagoda and the guard house, watching his every move. The guards were dressed in dark, padded jackets and heavy, cold weather clothing. Each was armed with an M-16 Assault rifle. The taller of the two approached him. "You are Grant?" he said, in halting English.

"I'm Gorilla," he replied. It was said as a statement, matter of fact.

The guard looked behind Gorilla, confused. "Where is your car? Where is the driver we sent for you?"

Gorilla shrugged. "It broke down, way back on the road. I told the driver to stay with the vehicle. I walked the last part of the journey. I didn't want to be late."

The guard nodded. "We will send a man to retrieve it. We will have to search you. There are no weapons allowed inside the Castle."

Gorilla nodded and as the two guards approached to frisk him, he raised his arms in the universal tradition of someone about to be thoroughly searched for weapons. One guard approached him from the front and one from the side. He heard a distant CRACK and a sudden gust of wind passed by him, once, twice before the two guards suddenly dropped to the floor with a bullet in each of their heads. The angel on his shoulder, hidden somewhere on the hills surrounding the pagoda, had taken her first heads of the night. He doubted they would be her last. Gorilla turned to look back in the direction he'd come. He raised an arm and waved once, twice, then a third time. At first, there was nothing and then, emerging from the darkness just on the other sides of the wall, two shadows appeared, both tall, well-built and carrying Remington 1100 shotguns. It was the deadly duo; Crane and Lang.

"Where's Hodges?" asked Gorilla, opening his jacket and drawing the '39.

Crane jerked a gloved thumb behind him, indicating the woods along the private road. "He's holed up back there. Watching and waiting. As soon as he sees that we're inside, he'll fix the explosives to the structure of the pagoda. After that we have thirty minutes to get in and out before it blows. Until then, he stays put."

Gorilla understood, Hodges was the dems man. Inside his backpack, he had numerous timed explosive charges, designed to sabotage the pagoda and leave no traces of deniable bodies or bio-toxins alike. The destruction of the Raven's sanctuary was to be the final parting gift from Bill Hodges and the Sentinel team.

There was a commotion over to the left and from the corner of his eye, Gorilla saw the first of several black-clothed guards emerging from the adjacent keep, about thirty feet away. Crane and Lang immediately took off running and took up defensive positions on the near side of the bridge. They opened up with the Remingtons, blasting out rounds, picking at targets, firing and moving, slowing down the progression of the guards. Gorilla saw at least three guards drop to the ground. He turned and made his way at speed across the bridge, through the courtyard and to the entrance of the pagoda. The large black lacquered doors were imposing and he knew that behind them lay the distinct possibility of his death. But then again, he reasoned, it was also a distinct possibility if he stayed out here facing a small army. He turned and fired twice at the two guards who were trying to cut off his entrance to the main doors. The two Japanese dropped like sacks of rocks, tumbling down the steps and onto the earthen pathway. Gorilla turned and hit the door hard with his shoulder, expecting to encounter resistance, but was surprised when it gave way freely. Inside was shrouded in darkness.

"Lads, over here! Let's go," he called to the two Special Forces soldiers. He could see them pepper-potting forward, firing and moving, firing and moving. He helped them as much as he could, taking a bead on any visible targets and watching as his head shots took effect.

Finally, Crane and Lang made a dash for the entrance to the pagoda. Gorilla hurried them inside, still firing and taking down guards with the '39. All three of them slammed the great doors shut and slung the mighty bolts which ran through the middle and along the top of the doors. They were, mercifully, now sealed inside and safe, at least for the moment. The bottom level of the pagoda was sparsely decorated, no floor matting and nothing to suggest any sign of furnishings. Along one wall was a row of pegs, where someone might hang a cloak or a jacket. Light was provided by meagre candlelight, which did nothing to illuminate the large floor space. The three men took a moment to check their weapons, a quick re-load for some and then they took up their positions at the bottom of the wooden staircase. There was a quick flick of the eyes to each other and then a nod of acknowledgement as Gorilla and his team walked up the steps and through the darkened doorway, weapons ready, determined to face down the overwhelming odds. They were *Ronin,* on their way to war.

* * *

"I will not be afraid... I will conquer my fear. I will not be afraid... I will conquer my fear."

High on the hillside Miko had watched the scene with a sense of detached pleasure. She'd taken her first heads of the night. Good clean shots, no problem really. She knew that before the night was over she would take many more... but over and over in her head, she recited the litany which kept her strong, kept her focused and which distracted her from contemplating what she had now become: a killer.

"I will not be afraid... I will conquer my fear. I will not be afraid... I will conquer my fear."

She peered through the scope of her rifle. The guards were standing outside the doors, making sure that Gorilla and his men wouldn't be able to escape. The team were effectively trapped inside and would either survive or perish depending on what horrors awaited them. In the distance, coming from somewhere deep within the pagoda, she heard the roar of gunfire as it silenced the screams of dying men. While she might not be able to help the rest of her team inside the pagoda, she was more than capable of clearing an escape route for them should they be able to complete their mission. She counted the amount of guards, all armed and ready, taking up positions at the pagoda's entrance. She counted fifteen, with probably another ten on standby in the adjacent guard house.

Not an impossible number to deal with, but she would have to move quickly, more quickly than she would like under normal circumstances. But if the men inside were to have any chance of escape, she would need to take as many guards down as she could. Miko settled the rifle into her shoulder, slowed her breathing, and looked through the scope as it magnified the features of the first of twenty-five dead men who were still walking – walking, but not for much longer. Her finger took up the pressure on the trigger; she had her zero and fired...

"*I will not be afraid... I will conquer my fear. I will not be afraid... I will conquer my fear,*" said the voice of the killer inside her head.

Chapter Seven

"Hang on," whispered Lang. "Let me see if there's a light or a lamp." He lowered his weapon in the darkness, searching along the wall, groping to find something that would illuminate where they were and their position.

"Andy, don't go too far... stay near... keep your weapon up," hissed Crane in warning.

There were several more seconds of muffled movement and then they heard Lang say "Gotcha." From the corner where they'd ascended the staircase, a faint orange glow grew as an archaic oil lamp flickered into life. There was just enough time to register a black-covered figure wielding a deadly black sword coming at Lang from the corner of the room, and then Lang's head left his body, rolling across the matted flooring before finally coming to rest against a large vase in the corner of the room. Gorilla and Crane turned and fired, and shots ripped apart the *Shinobi* assassin, leaving his blood smeared over the wall when he sank slowly to the floor. The oil lamp fell to the floor and once more, the room was enveloped in darkness.

"Corners!" Gorilla shouted and both men, through years of training or perhaps due to some inbred survival system, split away from each other in the darkness. They would each have their own arc of fire within the killing room and God help anyone that came within that zone. Then the shadows of death seemed to melt away from the walls, moving outwards and forwards like ghosts in the night. Gorilla was aware of at least three that he could make out, but who knew how many more were hiding in the deepest recesses of the room. He guessed that Crane would be dealing with a similar number on his side.

He brought the '39 up, punched it straight out and fired twice at where he thought the enemy was, the flash from the muzzle momentarily illuminating the room. He had just enough time to see a black figure in a mask coming straight at him, wielding some kind of sickle, and heard the cry from a second assassin as Gorilla's bullet took him in the shoulder. He pulled the trigger again and *click*! The '39 had jammed. No time to lose, trying to reload would be a death sentence. He was aware of the assassin, mere feet away from him, almost upon him. Gorilla ducked his body, twisted like a coil and when he was sure the assassin was within range, he punched out the inactive handgun in a boxing cross. He heard the crunch, felt it ripple along his arm, as the heavy metal of the weapon smashed teeth and bone and cartilage in the Japanese killer. He heard the man crumple to the floor, but by then Gorilla was already in motion again. He stepped to the side, smacked his left hand into the butt of the '39's magazine, heard a faint click as it seated properly and then he forcefully wracked the slide once, twice, until he was satisfied a round had entered the chamber correctly. He pointed the weapon down where the injured assassin was squatting, felt the end of the barrel touch something solid and fired. The flash confirmed he'd blown off the top of the assassin's head. Over to Gorilla's left, Crane's Remington boomed again and again as it searched in the darkness, trying to slow down the hoard of assassins heading straight at them. He knew that if they managed to get within range both he and the small Redactor would be chopped. Japanese swords had a tendency to be quite unforgiving against flesh. So he turned, dropped to one knee and then fired to his rear… not at anything specific, just at where he thought a likely attack may come from. It was like fighting in deep jungle, jumping at shadows and firing at where you thought the enemy WAS and not IS. With his back clear he stood and turned to face the front, he aimed the Remington in the darkness from the hip and fired… BOOM… he heard a yell of pain and embold-

ened, he fired again… this time he heard no more cries of agony…
one down definitely, he guessed.

There was a brief whistling noise and then Crane felt an unbeliev-
able stab of pain in his right thigh causing him to cry out. It had hit
him right in the centre, the metal hitting bone. He brought his left
hand down and felt a small spiked wheel half in and half out of the
flesh… he knew from the briefing reports that it would be a *Shaken*,
the small lethal throwing stars of the *Shinobi*. His only hope now was
that it hadn't been tipped with poison, but then again, knowing the
type of enemy he was dealing with the odds were that it had been.
Which meant he may only have minutes to live…? If that was the case,
he was going to take as many of these bastards with him as possible!
Crane crouched, his body low, his wounded leg causing him to take
small steps. His finger was resting on the trigger of the shotgun ready
to take out the *Shaken* thrower… he heard a choking sound from over
on his left and then seconds later the sounds of gunshots… Gorilla
was making his '39 sing…

* * *

The boom of Crane's shotgun was sweet music to Gorilla's ears and
for those few moments while his gun was jammed, he'd thought he
was done for, until the Special Forces soldier worked the shotgun and
gave him time to get back into the fight.

Gorilla felt a whisper around his ears; material brushing against his
skin, and the touch of a cord grazed his cheeks. Then there was a 'snap'
as the cord was lowered from above him and pulled tight, encircling
his throat! He was lifted inches off the floor and the chokehold was
already starting to take effect. His left hand clawed up instinctively,
desperately trying to get his fingers underneath the assassin's cord,
anything to relieve the pressure and allow some air to get through to
his lungs. He tried and failed, found himself lifted another inch, the
toes of his shoes barely managing to keep contact with the wooden
floor. He gulped, trying to squeeze any last bits of oxygen into his

lungs... but still failing. His worry wasn't just the strangulation, it was that he was strung up here like a prize turkey, fair game for any sword-wielding assassin who happened to be near. *Move, do something, do anything, but don't just hang here waiting to be strangled or stabbed!* he thought.

The '39?

He lifted his weapon arm straight up, aiming at where he thought the assassin must be... his consciousness slowly starting to slip away. His life was measured now in seconds, fractions of seconds and it took all of his will to make his finger work the trigger. He was vaguely aware of shots firing from the '39, how many he wasn't sure, but however many it was, it seemed to be enough because he dropped to the floor, the pressure on his throat relieved. He breathed heavily, gulping air back into his lungs... and then he became aware of a body falling from above and landing on the floor in front of him. The assassin! He was still moving, wounded, but still lethal. Gorilla pushed his off-hand forward, found the man's head, jammed the '39 at an angle under where he thought his chin was and unloaded three 9mm rounds. There was a muffled boom and an unmistakable splatter of brain tissue as the bullets ripped off the top of the assassin's head. The body flopped limply aside.

Gorilla, still reeling from the strangulation, was now conscious of a new figure coming straight at him. He saw the ambient light glint off the edge of a razor sharp blade as it twirled, ready to strike at him as he crouched on the floor. With seconds to spare, Gorilla flung himself backwards, landing hard on his back, gaining some time to bring up the '39 one handed and start firing in a zipper motion, starting at the bottom of his range and working upwards in a straight line. He estimated that four of his rounds hit home, jerking the assassin back and halting his progress. The silver edge of the sword dropped but it was the final 'boom' of a Remington which took off the side of the assassin's head. In the ensuing silence, Gorilla knew that there were no more demons in the darkness left for them to kill.

* * *

They found two oil lamps in the room and lit them. What they faced brought home the vivid violence of what they'd just survived. Gorilla counted eight bodies. The room resembled an abattoir. The remains of the *Shinobi* assassins were littered across the floor, lying at unnatural angles, black robed figures awash with bullet holes and shotgun blast trauma. All manner of swords, ropes, knives and sickles were thrown around the room in an equally haphazard manner.

Crane sat down on the floor and Gorilla watched as he carefully removed a *Shaken,* the small lethal throwing stars of the *Shinobi,* out of a wound on his thigh, wincing as the small metal star eased its way out. There was no need to question whether it was poisoned or not, the shake in his hands and the unnatural pallor of his skin told Gorilla that it had been. He just hoped they would have enough time to complete the mission before death took him.

Gorilla searched the room carefully, in case there was a hidden assassin lurking somewhere, waiting, ready to strike out with a sword. He'd picked up Lang's Remington and was using it now to search the room. He used one of the assassin's cloth masks to cover up the severed head of their fallen comrade. Minutes later, he declared the room was secured. Crane limped over to where Gorilla was standing and they both looked up at the locked hatch at the top of the staircase, leading to the next level of the Pagoda.

"Why do you think no one has followed us from the lower levels?" asked Crane.

It was a good question and one Gorilla had been thinking hard about. "I think we've been lured into a bloody big trap. The guards outside, if Miko hasn't taken them out already, are to stop us from escaping, not stopping us from getting this far. Whatever is up there never wants us to leave this place."

Crane took a moment to let Gorilla's words sink in, before he spoke again. "What about getting up there?" he questioned, jerking a thumb at the padlocked hatch. Gorilla studied it. It was padlocked from the outside, so whoever was up there wanted to slow them down and not stop them completely. Almost as if this were a game and they were being toyed with.

"Do you have any solid rounds left for the Remington?" asked Gorilla. Solid slugs could easily take care of the huge padlock affixed to the hatch, as well as any hinges which might hold it in place. Three quick 'booms' from the Remington and the doorway to the next floor level would be wide open.

"Of course!" Crane replied.

Gorilla had already started loading the rest of the shotgun cartridges into the Remington and replaced his dead magazine with a fresh one. "Then load up a few more and blast off that lock, old son, we're going to kick the arse off whatever is up there waiting for us."

Chapter Eight

'Old' Bill Hodges was crouched in the bushes, the snow was falling heavily now, and he watched the scene that lay before him in amazement. It was like a scene from a movie. Actually, it was like a scene from a movie he'd seen the year before, 'Zulu', about the battle for Rorke's Drift as the horde of Zulu warriors kept attacking and attacking, no matter how many of them were shot down by the British.

That was what he was seeing now, albeit in a more vivid form. A seemingly endless line of black clad guards rushed from the adjacent building to the pagoda, some making it a few feet before they were taken down by the sniper, hidden somewhere on the hillside behind him, while others managed to find some kind of cover, possibly even firing a few shots into the surrounding wilderness, before giving away their positions and being killed by the sniper. So far, Hodges had counted eighteen bodies sprawled about the compound, the majority of them with bullet holes in their heads. He grinned. That little girl was extremely good with a rifle.

His orders were to wait until there were no more guards left, once the sniper had her kill quota, and then stand and quickly make his way across to the steps leading to the pagoda. The sniper would be his protector once he crossed open ground, covering his back. Then he would plant his explosives on each of the four corner supports of the building. The plan was to bring the whole building down and then watch it burn. All the wood that made up the structure would make the conflagration inevitable. His four devices, his 'Whizz-Bangs' as he called them, consisted of enough plastic explosives to bring down a small suburban street. All were set with a pre-programmed timer. He settled in the bushes and waited for a few moments more, before standing and running out across the snowy killing ground as fast as his aging legs would carry him. He ran, slipping in the blood-soaked snow several times, but he made it. He was still a tough old soldier, even if civilian life had softened him slightly.

He packed the first device into the support column nearest the lake surrounding the pagoda. In the distance, he could hear the occasional sound of long distance gunfire, as Miko took down any straggling targets. He carefully negotiated the perimeter of the building, always ready and alert in case a hidden enemy jumped out at him, ready to slit his throat. Ten minutes later he'd planted his charges in the remaining three support columns; on the last one he was extra cautious to ensure there weren't any assassins waiting for him by the guard house annex. With the last charge set and the timer clicked to 'On' he began to cross the killing ground again, returning to his rendezvous point in the bushes. He glanced once more at his watch before he settled himself deep into the safety of the darkened bushes. At best, the team inside the pagoda had thirty minutes to get clear and get to safety before the explosives detonated and destroyed the building. He turned in the direction of the sniper's perch up on the hillside, giving Miko a thumbs up signal. He knew she would see him through the scope and understand that he'd completed his part of the mission.

He never heard the arrow. In truth, he was still breathing heavily from all the running and the action of the past thirty minutes, so his heart was almost beating out of his body and the blood was rushing in his ears. He was only aware of the shocking impact into his chest, the thump that rocked him forward, causing him to drop his weapon onto the ground. And then he started to fall…

* * *

The *Shinobi* assassin, Toshu Goto approached his victim. In his black *Shinobi Shozoko* costume, hooded and silent, he resembled a wraith of darkness, blending into the trees. He lowered his bow, strapped it across his back and silently drew his *Ninjato* to finish off the old man.

His orders from the *Karasu* had been clear. He was to infiltrate himself into the grounds and remain silent until the British team arrived. He'd watched three of the men escape inside the pagoda. *Good, the* Karasu *and his fellow* Shinobi *could deal with them.* He would have the honour of taking this old man's head. Toshu Goto guessed that the man dying in front of him was older than his comrades, perhaps by a good twenty years. Obviously an old warrior, even *gaijin* should be afforded some respect. Goto would make this old man's death both quick and honourable.

He stepped forward and steadied his sword, reversing it so that the tip was pointing downwards. He picked a vulnerable spot on the old man in front of him; the base of the neck. Goto raised the sword straight up and then thrust downwards with all his strength. The sword buried itself to the hilt in the neck of his victim. Goto felt the flesh tremble – a shudder, nothing more – then he retracted the blade. The whole murder had taken less than five seconds. There was no need to push the man forward with his shoe; he'd simply slumped onto the snowy ground, the blood from the fatal neck wound running out onto the snow around him.

The *Shinobi* silently replaced the sword in the scabbard attached to his back and crouched down to search the body of the man he'd just killed. Perhaps there was some kind of useful intelligence? Maybe information the *Karasu* could use against his enemies? He hoped so. To gain the favour of the legendary Raven, his master, was Toshu Goto's greatest pleasure. He knew that somewhere out in the darkness – he wasn't sure where – was a sniper. Soon he would have to track and kill the man who had shot down so many soldiers of the clan this night. The sniper was obviously a man of great skill, judging by the number of bodies strewn in the courtyard of the pagoda. But here in the bushes, Toshu Goto judged that he was safe from enemy fire. He was invincible, he was deadly, and he was the Raven's master *Shinobi*.

* * *

Miko had watched as Hodges had given the signal that the explosives were in place and primed.

She'd picked her sniper's nest well. It gave her a clear view of the whole courtyard. To her best count, she'd taken twenty-five heads this night. Her uncle would have been proud of her shooting. Not of the killing, but of the marksmanship he'd instructed her in. Now her job was to protect the other members of the team until the explosives blew the pagoda apart. She returned her attention to where Hodges was sitting crouched in the bushes.

She could see him panting, out of breath. Then what appeared to be a large stick burst out of his chest and stopped, halfway along the wooden shaft. She saw the surprise on Hodges face, a wince of pain and then he fell forward onto his knees, placing his hands out in front of him, palms down, onto the snowy ground. Blood poured from his chest. She inhaled deeply to calm herself and closely scrutinised the scene of death through her scope. And... yes... there he was... a faint movement of shadow, deep in the undergrowth. Dark clothed and a glint of moonlight off something metallic, perhaps a sword. Miko knew instantly that she couldn't shoot from this angle, there was no definite shot, no clear target. She also knew the shadow killer who had taken Hodges might be gone at any second, disappearing back into the darkness from where he'd come. She glanced up from the rifle, scanning for a better shooting position... her eyes tracking to her left. She found one; a jutting promontory a dozen yards or so further up the rocky side of the hill.

Miko got up from her position, stretched out her aching muscles and ran. She ran against the clock, cradling her beloved Arisaka like a baby, her legs pumping.

"*I will not be afraid… I will conquer my fear. I will not be afraid… I will conquer my fear.*"

She ran almost blindly in the darkness, slipping twice on the snowy rocks but recovering her steps at the last second. Finally, she glanced over to her left and saw that she had a direct line of sight to where Bill Hodges' body lay. Miko dropped down to her knees, lying prone, and then settled the rifle into her shoulder again.

"*I will not be afraid… I will conquer my fear. I will not be afraid… I will conquer my fear.*"

She took a breath, determined to slow her heart rate and then looked once again through the scope and caught sight of the black clad assassin, his sword raised ready to plunge into the dying body of Bill Hodges. Through the scope, and because of the distance involved, the execution was like watching a silent movie. The killer raised the sword up, tip pointing to the ground, and thrust downwards. The sharp steel cut into Hodges like a hot knife running through butter and just as quickly, it was retracted and resheathed.

High in her perch on the hill, Miko watched as the assassin bent down and started to search Hodges' body. Now was her time, she knew that every second counted, before the killer melted back into the darkness of the forest. She eased back the bolt on the rifle and checked the bullet was seated properly. Then she centred the crosshairs of the scope on the dark mass of the man's head. She exhaled slowly, eye to the scope, rifle butt to the shoulder and finger imperceptibly touching the trigger.

"*I will not be afraid… I will conquer my fear. I will not be afraid… I will conquer my fear.*"

She paused… then fired.

There was a moment of nothingness, and for a brief second she thought she'd missed. Then… there it was! A crimson red halo of blood as the bullet smashed out the front of the assassin's face and dropped him to the ground in a lifeless lump. It was another target down. Another head for the little Japanese sniper. Another piece of her revenge.

"*I will not be afraid... I will conquer my fear. I will not be afraid... I will conquer my fear.*"

Chapter Nine

The lock came away easily, one blast with the Remington's solid rounds and it shattered. Crane took the steps first and pushed up and away at the hatch. It swung upwards and slammed onto the floor above, letting in more light. They climbed the wooden steps to the next level of the pagoda, their footsteps heavy after the horror of the attack on the previous level and they both knew combat fatigue was setting in.

The room was of a similar size, style and design as its predecessors on the lower levels, with heavy wood and traditionally-panelled windows and sliding doors. It was sparsely furnished, only a few simple vases on shelves and a curtain at the far end covered a small window which barely let in any light, giving this level an air of dark broodiness. There were wooden support columns dotted around the structure and the floor was covered in its entirety with a thick *tatami* matt, made of straw. Oil lamps gave off an eerie glow of reds and oranges and the smell of jasmine subtly filled the room. The darkness ruled the rest of the room, except for one small pocket of light in its centre, lit by a small candle illuminating the gross figure who sat staring straight at them. Taru Hokku sat in the light, resembling a resplendent Buddha. He was naked, except for his traditional white *mawashi*, the loincloth-like garment of the expert Sumo wrestler. He was alert and his muscles flexed constantly, preparing for the inevitable battle to come.

Gorilla and Crane split off and slowly, cautiously, approached the large Japanese man in a pincer movement, weapons up and ready. Lang had already paid the ultimate price for assuming they'd merely entered a darkened room on the previous level and not having his weapon ready... something which had cost him his head. *There was something not quite right about the whole scene,* thought Gorilla. It wasn't just that Hokku was relaxed and in control, nor was it the way the room was lit so that all the attention was focused upon the large Sumo wrestler, no something else... and then he sniffed, took in a deep breath and knew instantly what it was; animals. He smelled animals...

* * *

"You did well to get inside our operation. Very professional, very clever, but it will do you no good. You will never leave the *Karasu's* Dojo alive. You must know that?" asked Hokku evenly.

We'll see about that sunshine, thought Gorilla. He knew a Dojo was the name of a Japanese martial arts training hall. But this place was something different. It reeked of death and he guessed it was the place where the Raven and his assassins honed their killing skills. "Where is he, Nakata? Upstairs I guess, hiding, guarding his virus?"

"Ahhh... you are well informed about our *Oyabun* and the *Kyonshi* he intends to create! Oh, what an assassin you would have made for us, Mr. Grant, able to penetrate into the heart of the enemy and kill him. If only your calling had been true to the clan, oh, we could have accomplished great things."

"The name's Gorilla."

Hokku looked confused. "I do not understand?"

"I told you once that only my friends and enemies call me Gorilla... you've now earned that right," snarled Gorilla.

"As a friend?" asked Hokku, with wry humour.

"No," replied Gorilla coldly. Both Gorilla and Crane had their Remingtons trained on the large Japanese killer; really, they could have ended it there and then. But something held their fingers back on the triggers, something that pricked the senses of each of them. They watched as Hokku leaned forward and touched the floor before him with two hands and then jumped to his feet, landing in a crouch. He stretched out his legs and clapped his hands together in the ritual of the wrestler. His size and strength was even more impressive close up. Gorilla suspected those hands could crush bricks.

Hokku stood before them, ready in a fighting pose, his face a mask of concentration as he regarded the two gunmen before him. He smiled. "You think I am a fool, Gorilla, to stand before you unarmed and naked. I am no fool and I am not unarmed…"

It was then that they leaped from the darkness, vicious things, animals of power! They had speed and aggression, but worse than that, they had teeth…

* * *

The three Japanese Tosa fighting dogs sprang forward from the hidden depths of the room. Their teeth were bared and they were ready to attack anything that threatened their master, the giant Hokku. They were big and powerful, and in the brief moment when one ran at him, Gorilla was aware of the muscles rippling underneath the animal's fur. He managed to bring the Remington up in a snap and blasted off a round that decapitated the dog when it jumped to rip out his throat. The wet spray of its blood streaked his face and torso as the body of the dog slapped onto the floor in front of him. He risked a quick glance over to where Crane had been standing and saw that the Special Forces man had been knocked to the ground, his weapon dislodged, with one dog at his weapon arm and the other pinning him to the ground by his throat. There was a faint squelching noise, as if someone was ripping out the guts of a fish, and then blood was pumping freely from Crane's throat.

Gorilla turned the Remington and snapped out two blasts, killing both the dogs, the force of the rounds picking their bodies up and throwing them against the wall with a satisfying crunch. The whole incident had taken seconds… probably less, but it had been more than enough time for Hokku to close the distance between them and reach out with his huge killing hands, ready to pummel and crush Gorilla. Hokku knocked the Remington from his hands with an *atemi* strike, sending it scattering across the matted floor. Then, like a child picking up a teddy bear, he lifted Gorilla up in an underarm bear hug and instantly began to squeeze, squashing the smaller man's body in his powerful arms.

Gorilla felt the pressure, the power, of Hokku's arms, an exhalation of air spewed out of his lungs, and his ribs started to cave in from the pressure. And all the while, this giant killer was grinning maniacally inches from his face, which was a mask of sweat and bared teeth. Gorilla did the only thing he could – he punched. He brought his arms up and with as much power as he could muster, sent out right and left crosses, striking at the man's nose, jaw… just about bloody anywhere… desperate to make him stop his crushing. He might as well have saved his energy for all the good it did, the blows just bounced off and Hokku carried on grinning and crushing. *The eyes, go for the fucking eyes, Jack,* he thought. But the bigger man, seemingly sensing Gorilla's next play simply burrowed his head in his victim's chest… and still the pressure increased. Gorilla could feel the last of the air escaping his lungs and knew his ribs would start to snap soon. He had to do something if he wanted to survive the next few moments… he had to… think of… something…

Then he knew.

He couldn't reach the guns in the holsters on his hip and underneath his armpit; but if he stretched his body upwards, even just a few inches, he might be able to lean back and reach into his back pocket. The back pocket which held his ever-faithful cut-throat razor. He sucked in the last gasp of air he could manage and stretched backwards, pushing his right hand deep into the rear pocket of his trousers… and relief swept over him when the cold metal connected with his hand and he pulled it free. He swung his body back upwards – Christ, the pain in his ribs was fucking killing him, this bastard was determined to pulverise his internal organs. He heard the crack as one of his ribs gave way and knew it was now or never. He flicked open the razor blade one-handed, grabbed hold of the top of Hokku's head and then very carefully, probably too carefully for a man in his current precarious position, he lay the shiny blade gently along the side of the giant's neck.

The brachial artery runs along the side of the neck and Gorilla knew the cut would need to be deep to be effective. He pressed down and pulled the razor's edge back at the same time, in one smooth and deep motion. The blood instantly began spurting upwards and outwards, like a high pressure fountain and the giant Japanese man roared in shock. At once, he released his grip and Gorilla was left to fall to the ground. He dropped in a heap, right next to the Remington. Looking up, sucking breath in past the agony of the broken rib, he saw Hokku, both hands to the wound, trying to hold the blood back and failing. The giant man was fast going into shock and the colour drained from his face as the blood emptied from his body, but even now he was still trying his best, lurching towards the little *gaijin* who had bested him.

Gorilla was taking no chances, injured himself and exhausted, he knew he couldn't survive another unarmed encounter. He reached over to snatch up the Remington and from a kneeling position, aimed the weapon at Hokku's massive frame. He didn't know what the next load in the chamber was, and he didn't care... he just needed to stop this monster. He pulled the trigger and the solid load split Hokku's head clear in half. The body fell backwards, crashing onto the mat. Gorilla stood and stared, wondering if that was it. Hokku's head looked as if it had been split with a sledgehammer, his face pulverised. There was still a sign of faint breathing coming from the giant, but Gorilla knew it would soon be over for him. He checked the breech of the Remington. Empty. The last round had managed to save his life. He turned to look at Crane. The Special Forces man was dead, with wounds like that, there was no coming back.

Gorilla pressed his fingers against his ribs, wincing at the pain from the one that was fractured, but satisfied to discover it seemed to be the only one. And then he stumbled towards the back of the room, where one final set of stairs awaited him. There was no door in place to stop him this time. It was almost welcoming, in fact. It seemed he was being given free access to the upper level, the most secret inner sanctum and he slowly began to climb up into the Raven's presence. He felt he'd earned it, had paid for it in blood.

Chapter Ten

Yoshida Nakata sat behind his desk and listened to the bloody murder going on below him. He was dressed in the traditional clothes of the *Shinobi*, dark grey trousers, shirt, gloves and the customary *tabi* on his feet. His mask lay before him on the desk. He'd underestimated this *gaijin* and his team. He had hoped to lure them into a trap, isolate them and finish them off in his own way. But he had to admit, these western spies had achieved much and taken down his best assassins.

No firearms were allowed inside the pagoda, it was a fundamental rule, and he'd hoped the use of traditional *Shinobi* weapons would have been enough to cut down this assault team. But Gorilla and his men had been resilient. Even now, he wondered how his clan brother Hokku was faring. Over the past few minutes he'd heard the sound of animals growling, gunshots and the inevitable sounds of hand-to-hand combat. He knew the gunmen were approaching and they would be here in minutes... but so be it... he had gambled and thus far, he'd never lost. Not that the killing was over just yet... he still had options if he was to survive. He'd removed the last remaining sample of the *Kyonshi* virus from the safe built into his desk. The other operational samples were already in use, as part of his plan to destroy his enemies scattered across the world. But this was a concentrated and more powerful version... created for his personal body chemistry. It was his last ditch doomsday weapon, to strike back at those wanting to kill him.

He glanced down at the weapons lying before him on his grand desk. The two razor sharp *Ninjato's* and the syringe which contained the *Kyonshi* virus. They were two very different types of weapons; one from the old world and one from a future world. Yoshida Nakata would never be taken alive. He was committed to taking as many of his enemy down with him as he could. If today was to be his death day, then he would spill the blood of his foes before they killed him.

He heard a guttural shout from the level below him followed by a jarring silence and then, a final boom of a shotgun blast. He gently played his fingers over the cord wrapping on the handles of his swords. He would use them well today. Without hesitation, he lifted up the syringe, studied the vial's orange contents and plunged the needle deep into his arm, just above the bicep. This was the condensed version of the virus. He felt... nothing... but he knew that soon, in fact within minutes, that would all change. He would be gone forever, but his legacy would live on, all over the world. His head snapped back up when he heard footsteps on the stairs. And then at the top of the stairwell he made out the shape of a man. He was diminutive in height, but strong looking, with short blond hair. He was dressed in black, almost like a western version of a Japanese shadow warrior, a *Shinobi*. He looked tired, injured even, but his face was set determinedly... the... he... man... thing... Yoshida Nakata's mind started to falter, flashing backwards and forwards, as the toxins he'd pumped into his system moments before began to take effect. Fury, rage and a detached sense of strength began to filter through his mind. It was almost as if someone had replaced his body... but his mind was in a fugue and he couldn't remember what he had to do... only experienced the insatiable urge to kill.

The last thing he did was pick up his two beloved swords, gripped them in his hands and then the fury engulfed him and the *Karasu-Tengu* was truly born...

* * *

The '39 was dead, empty and obsolete in the holster on his right hip. The only weapon left was his back up gun, the Outdoorsman revolver. It only held six shots, but what it lacked in quantity of ammunition, it more than made up for in stopping power. Killing power, Gorilla hoped. He stood at the top of the staircase and drew the revolver from his shoulder holster. He held it loosely at his side, finger off the trigger, but ready.

The room on the top level of the pagoda was laid out like an office belonging to a high-level business executive; it held a corporate desk, exclusive artwork and paintings, comfortable leather chairs. It was jarring, a stark contrast to the sparse training room below. It took him a moment, through the darkness of the poorly lit office space, to see the thing standing like a living corpse behind the desk. *This* was the man he'd spent six months tracking down, so that he could kill him. The thing, whatever it was now, and which had once been Yoshida Nakata – the Raven – turned and glared at him. It seemed to have grown in size, its bone structure misshapen somehow, and its eyes were blood red. The skin on its body was greying by the minute and its mouth drooled and spat a vicious yellow fluid in alternative moments. It looked rabid. Then it would suddenly twitch, as if it had a tic, causing the black robes it wore to fly out behind it, making the thing appear as if it had wings.

To Gorilla, it looked as if the *Karasu-Tengu*, the Raven Demon of legend, had truly come to life. In its hands were two swords and the monster was slashing them about wildly as it tore up the desk and the chairs and the paintings on the wall with a fearsome ferocity. It took several minutes before the monster sated its initial thirst for violence, then it turned its red eyes one way, then the other, in a quest for a new target.

Gorilla reasoned that if he remained still, the 'thing' wouldn't spot him. Slowly, cautiously, he moved his hand to cock the hammer on the revolver. There was an audible 'click' and instantly, the monster's head snapped around to seek out the source. It glared at Gorilla, twitched in a spasmodic convulsion and let out an ear piercing screech. Everything was rolled into that screech; death, anger, fury – the hiss of an animal from the pits of hell. Then it ran, charging like a rampaging rhino, swords flailing, straight towards him, and all the time, filling the room with that screeching, shrill scream.

The thing had made it less than ten feet when Gorilla lifted the big beast of a revolver with two hands and fired. It was both heavier and more powerful than his '39, and he didn't want to take any chances of missing the target moving at speed towards him. He aimed at the centre of the body mass and fired constantly… once, twice, three times, four times then five. With each round that hit home, and all of them did, the thing seemed to pause in mid-air, before trying to thrust itself forward again, only to be hit by the next heavy bullet and pushed back even further. Its feet seemed to stumble, returning along its original path, past the desk and back towards the large material windows. The sixth shot caused it to fall back through the window, ripping open the thin material that created its covering and then it disappeared into the emptiness of the night. Seconds later, there was a dull thud as the body hit the snowy earth outside.

Gorilla ran to the window and peered down through the gaping slash. The ground, at least sixty feet below, was a mixture of blood and snow smeared together and at its centre was a dark spidery mass, squirming and writhing in agony from the six hard calibre bullets which had blasted it apart. The thing seemed to pause for a moment, as if the messages from its brain weren't connecting to the rest of its body. But the eyes and the scream were still there… the eyes still blazing with fury, the mouth still screeching that whine of hell. Gorilla watched for a minute or two as the body of the deformed and misshapen Japanese assassin struggled and then grew still and all signs of life disappeared.

* * *

Gorilla heard the first 'crump' of an explosion outside and knew he only had moments left to escape. The attack on the pagoda had taken longer than he'd expected. He'd intended to run a nice, quiet and fast attack. Instead, they'd been lured into a trap and fighting a hidden enemy had taken its toll both on his team and the speed of the operation. Now as a result, Hodges whizz-bangs were already starting to do their job.

He was aware of a ball of orange fire as it exploded from somewhere at the base of the pagoda, taking out the supports in one corner. Gorilla dropped the big revolver, pulled out the razor and ran for the stairs, his exhausted legs pumping as hard as he could make them. He wasn't stopping, not for anything, no more fighting – he would just cut and slash and blast past whatever stood in his way. Every level down was like a running through another level of hell as he saw the bodies of the men he'd killed and the men he'd fought beside Another 'crump' shook the building, it rocked from side to side and somewhere behind him he smelled the heavy stench of fire and explosives. On the second floor he came across an assassin, who had miraculously survived and was beginning to climb up the steps. Gorilla wasted no time in kicking the man in the face before slashing at him, slicing open his neck. He sprinted hard for the door leading to the pagoda's exit, lifting up the bolts and running out the main door. He hurtled down the steps, ignoring the bodies lying around, and ran out onto the blood red snow. He slipped and slid his way over the bridge towards the tree line. He heard a voice call his name, and saw Miko standing further along the tree line, waving frantically at him.

"Quickly! Any second now it—" She never finished her sentence because the sound of several larger blasts filled his ears and the shockwave of the explosion flung him into the undergrowth. He landed hard, the wind knocked out of him. Gorilla pulled himself upright and he and Miko stared at the same thing. A blaze of red and yellow flames in the darkness of the night, the fire was a furnace and there was very little of the pagoda which remained recognisable. Hodge's bombs had done their work well and all that remained was a maelstrom of fire and crackling timber and the smell of burning flesh.

"Is it over?" he heard her despite the ringing in his ears.

Gorilla nodded. "I think so, I think we did—"

He stopped mid-sentence, because from out of the inferno, a noise was emitted which sounded half human and half wounded animal. For a few seconds, neither of them could establish what it was. Then from deep within the firestorm, the inhuman cry grew louder. It rose up from the centre of the mass of burning wood, a horror from the pits of hell. Its size and shape were distorted, its body charred and burned, one of its arms severed and it trailed a leg along limply behind it. The remnants of its clothes had been tattered and torn by the explosions it had survived and tendrils of cloth blew behind it like charred wings. But still in its eyes, was the same look of madness and violence Gorilla had seen earlier. It was the *Karasu-Tengu*. It saw them, saw them well, and even in its weakened state the *Karasu* seemed determined to get to its 'feast' and kill them both.

"I've no bullets left," Gorilla muttered out of the corner of his mouth, his eyes never leaving the monster which approached with each passing second.

Miko nodded and brought the rifle up in one smooth motion, steadied herself and fixed the scope on the centre of the *Karasu's* head. "For my father," she whispered and fired. She saw the creature's head explode and watched as it dropped back into the burning pit it had come from. She lowered the rifle and glanced over at Gorilla. They stood together, their hands touching lightly, staring at the flames, watching as the charnel house they'd created burned to the ground. Even at this distance, the intensity of the fire was almost overwhelming.

Gorilla removed the empty '39 from the holster at his hip. He pulled back the slide to make sure it really was empty, an old habit. He traced his fingers once more over the contours of the weapon, remembering its history, what it had helped him do, the number of Redactions it had carried out in his capable hands. Operations gone now, lost forever. The weapon would be a liability, traceable, compromised, and to hang onto it would mean a prison sentence or worse. He knew he could never use it again. He looked at it one last time, then threw it deep into the heart of the blazing inferno. The heat would melt the metal and destroy any evidence... the '39 would be lost forever.

"What was that?" she asked, sounding confused. "Why did you throw it away?"

"It was nothing," he said sadly. "Just a relic from the past..."

Book Four: Retribution

Chapter One

Three days later, Jordie Penn met them both at London Airport. They'd been shepherded into the rear of his Jaguar and whisked through the streets to a safe flat for de-briefing. He'd provided them with a status update, sounding like a newsreader, reading out the information almost in a daze. Initial news reports suggested that the pagoda in Japan had been the subject of an unfortunate fire, there were not thought to be any survivors. The inferno had been so severe, identifying the multiple bodies was proving difficult, if not impossible. There were unsubstantiated rumours that one of the bodies was that of respected businessman Yoshida Nakata, but more would not be known until a post-mortem had been conducted.

On the same day, according to Penn, the Japanese National Police Agency and the Public Security Intelligence Agency received several anonymous tip-off's regarding criminal activities at Nakata Industries of Tokyo. The informant mentioned terrorism-related offences, money laundering and financial links to illegal arms dealing. The officers of the NPA and the PSIA arrived the next morning, with warrants giving them carte blanche to search every room in the multi-storey Nakata Industries office building. Several senior executives at Nakata Industries had already been arrested, and several more had abruptly committed suicide. An in-depth investigation was underway.

Penn handed Grant two final gifts. He'd unfolded the small piece of paper Penn passed to him and raised an eyebrow at the figure in the 'balance' column. It was enough to set him up for the next few years, he would have a chance to start again and provide for the family. Penn had then handed Grant a small automatic pistol. "One's for protection and the other's to keep the bank manager happy," Penn said. "You decide which is which. The Colonel will eventually want to thank you personally, Jack. I'm on my way to meet him later… hopefully… haven't been able to get through to him today. Phone just keeps ringing and ringing."

"He's probably just celebrating, Jordie. The way we used to do it in the old days in Berlin," said Grant, trying to calm his case officer's concerns, but he could see the worry etched on Penn's face. The intervening months of the operation had been hard on him and he'd visibly aged.

The two men shook hands and Grant had kissed Miko briefly on the cheek, the kiss of a friend rather than a lover and wished her well before he left them to catch a train north to Scotland. They'd had their time and now their destinies would send them in different directions.

* * *

Penn and Miko watched Jack Grant through the window as he walked away to catch a taxi. Miko turned to Penn and smiled demurely. "And for me, Mr. Penn? What do you have for me? Money, rewards?"

Penn smiled. "I have an end to this operation, Miss Arato. One final job to do, one final target… if you want it? After that, I have a ticket home, or to wherever in the world you wish to go, compliments of Sentinel."

"And the target?" she asked, intrigued.

Penn gave her all the information he knew about the target. His name, his location, and his dealings with the Raven.

"Weapons?" she asked.

"There is a specialist piece of equipment waiting for you in the boot of my car. A British made Parker Hale rifle."

"Ah, an old friend of mine," Miko said, remembering Lochailort. Now it seemed a lifetime ago.

"An old friend indeed. Are you interested?" asked Penn.

She smiled at him, that sweet smile of hers, both playful and demure. "I think that you and I should go on a little journey, Mr. Penn."

"I think we should, Miss Arato." *She's both beautiful and deadly,* thought Jordie Penn. It was a devastating combination.

Chapter Two

Twelve hours after bidding farewell to Penn and Miko, Jack Grant stepped into the porch of the little cottage, shook the rain from his shoulders and felt the warmth of the hearth from the sitting room filtering through into the hallway. He knew instantly that something was wrong; there was heaviness in the air and the cottage was ominously silent. The cottage didn't work like that; there was always noise, clutter and voices. But silence. Never!

He dropped his bag by the coat stand and listened. He gently shut the front door behind him, and instinctively reached a hand to the pistol in its holster. He would leave it undrawn – for now. As Penn had said, having it was a precaution and he had it ready, near, in case he should need it. He stepped through the connecting door and into the main living room. It was covered in a subdued glow of orange, the light from the fireplace providing both heat and light. In the corner, he took in the sight of May and Hughie, his sister and her husband, sitting on the settee. Their hands were tied, legs bound and each had a gag across their mouths. They looked exhausted, as if they'd been held for quite some time. They both had the desperate eyes of the prisoner who was terrified for their life.

His gaze moved over to the opposite side of the room. He had to squint until his eyes became accustomed to the gloom. He saw the small dining table they normally sat around, the four of them at the end of a working day and talked and chatted and laughed and cried. There was nothing normal about it now; today it looked like a scene from one of Grant's worst nightmares. For sitting in a chair facing the door where he stood, was Frank Trench and on his lap, with a gun pointed at her head, was the girl with the long, black curly hair.

"Take a seat," said Trench, indicating the wooden chair directly opposite his. "You carrying? What am I talking about? Of course you are."

"Don't make me draw my gun, Frank, that would be a death sentence for you," growled Grant, lowering himself into the seat.

"Oh, I'm not stupid Jack. You think I'd let you use your gun? No, put it on the floor and kick it over to me... carefully, fingertips only please. We don't want to have an accident now, do we," said Trench, nodding his head towards the child.

Grant removed the gun from the holster on his right hip and carefully placed it on the floor by his feet, a quick brush with his shoe slid it over towards Trench. Trench expertly back heeled it away, out of reach.

"Who's the girl? She's a pretty little thing," said Trench nodding a head towards the child while he stroked her hair. "Is she your niece?"

Grant narrowed his eyes and fixed Trench firmly in his sights. He shook his head and said simply, "Daughter."

Trench barked out a triumphant laugh. "Well, the ultimate prize, eh! So she's the little secret you've kept hidden all these years? Be a shame if something dreadful was to happen to her, because of her old man."

Grant rested his hands on the edge of the table and glared at the man who had once been his colleague. "What do you want, Trench? The mission is over, the Raven's dead. The best thing you can do is to bugger off and leave us all be. None of this will solve anything."

Trench smiled and smelled the child's hair. "Umm, she smells of strawberries... lovely. I'll tell you what I want, Jack. We're going to play a little game and decide once and for all who's the best stone cold killer in this rotten bloody business. Now, how does that sound?"

* * *

"The rules are simple. If I win, I get to take apart what's left of your family, piece by piece. I'll leave the girl until last… she's a bit young, but I'm sure I could have some fun with her. I'll let the old couple watch, before I finish them off. You'll be dead anyway, so you'll miss it all, unfortunately," sneered Trench.

Trench had made the child sit in the corner by the fireplace, away from the action at the table and Grant's gun laid on the floor beneath his chair. She sat with her knees huddled up by her chin, eyes fixated on the two men squared off at the kitchen table. In the firelight, her black hair had taken on an almost silk-like quality.

"If you win, well obviously, you'll have the pleasure of killing me yourself. One pistol, one full magazine placed directly in front of us both on the table, safety off and ready to fire. On the count of three, first one to grab it and fire… wins." Trench's voice had become more animated now, almost as if he was enjoying himself, ready for the revels that were to come.

Grant considered the proposition. A half chance was better than no chance, at least in his experience. But something didn't smell right…

"Why take the risk, Frank, why take the risk that I could blow your head off? Why not just kill us all now and be bloody done with it?" asked Grant, his fingers gently drumming on the edge of the table, bleeding off the adrenaline which was coursing through his veins.

Trench's mood turned quickly and when he spoke, the hatred in his voice was tangible. "Because, you little shit, I was always in your shadow! All these years; first at Redaction, then working for the Raven! Gorilla, the gunman, Gorilla, the best Redactor in the business… pah… bullshit! You were just an oik from the Army who kissed the right arses, namely that cripple, Masterman – who, by the way, I paid a little visit with last night. He's a cripple no more, if you get my meaning. The old KGB-style bullet to the back of his head; him and his good lady wife. Bastard tried to stab me with a commando knife, he nearly succeeded, so I had to beat him with my gun before he'd settle down. He didn't sing though, still a tough old bugger right until the end." He shook his head violently. "No... I want to settle this once and for all, man against man, speed against speed. No excuses or third parties involved, totally fair. One chance and one winner!"

Grant shrugged. Trench had always been ambitious and egotistical; he just hoped that in the next few minutes it would be one of those things which would give him a tactical advantage over his enemy. Pride and ambition could be terminal for a Redactor.

"I'm going to show you something – don't try anything, or I'll have to hurt the old people," said Trench. Like a magician demonstrating a card trick to a captive audience, Trench moved the gun forward. It was a standard Browning 9mm. He expertly removed the magazine, pulled back the slide lock and ejected the chambered round. Then he placed the vacated round back into the magazine, slammed it back inside the weapon and let the slide run forward, chambering a round. As a last measure, he flicked off the safety making the weapon ready to fire, before gently placing it down onto the centre of the table and spinning it around like a carousel. The gun came to rest with the butt facing Trench and the slide facing Grant.

Both men stared down at it for a moment, pensive, each gauging if the other would make a pre-emptive grab for it. The air was still, the only noise the faint crackle and popping of the fire in the hearth. Then the moment was past and the two gunmen sat back to weigh up their options for this macabre game. It was Grant who broke the silence. "So how does it work then, Frank; you call the numbers, or do we just bluff it out and go for it rough and tumble style?"

Trench shook his head, his eyes hard and cold. Then he lifted an accusing finger and pointed at the little girl sitting in the corner of the room. "She counts to three and on three, we make our play. Fastest to the draw wins."

Grant nodded his understanding of the rules and smiled. He also understood how Trench operated and he doubted if the killer would play by the rules at all, even if he had been the one to initiate them. Trench was a man who wasn't to be trusted... or underestimated.

Grant glanced over at his daughter. "Close your eyes and don't look up, no matter what happens. Understand?"

The girl nodded and dropped her head forward so that it rested on her knees, then as an extra protection against the violence to come, she covered her head with her arms, fingers interlinked, locking them in place.

"Katie, in exactly one minute I'll tell you to start counting. I want you to count to three, one, two, three – exactly like you would in Mrs. Morrison's class. Can you do that," said Grant. He heard a whimper in reply.

Grant turned his gaze towards Trench. Both men locked eyes and studied each other. The seconds dragged by, what seemed like endless hours was in fact, mere seconds. The rain outside, the howling wind, the crackling fire and the grandfather clock's ticking filled the void of silence. For Grant, everything was shut out. Only he and the Browning pistol resting on the table mattered. He flicked a final glance at Trench, dismissed him and then spoke to his daughter. "Start counting, slowly."

The child took a breath and then with a wavering voice she began "One."

The pistol... my hands... the target... the pistol... my hands... the target, that's all, thought Grant. He ignored Trench's stare, noticing instead that the other man's hand was edging slowly downwards, until only his fingertips were resting on the table top. But why?

It hit Grant in a stunning moment of realisation. The main weapon was a ruse, a distraction, because Trench planned to do his killing with a secondary weapon... a back-up gun. Trench's fingers were moving further along the edge of the table, placing his hand to grab the concealed weapon.

"Two," whispered the little girl, her voice catching in her throat.

She'd barely finished saying 'two' when Jack Grant lifted his leg sharply, kicking upwards with full force, his shoe connecting with the rickety table and sending its opposite end, Trench's end, heading towards the ceiling. It looked like a seesaw trying to ascend upwards. Grant heard a sharp gasp from Trench as the gun, through sheer force of gravity, slipped out of his reach and headed towards Grant's stomach, where his hands were waiting to receive it. Grant felt the gun slip smoothly into his grasp and then instantly had it up and out above the table, mere inches from Trench's forehead. Grant pulled the trigger, just once. Trench tried to draw his back-up weapon, but he never made it.

The explosion of noise lasted only a moment. One shot, one kill.

The smoke cleared and Grant was aware of his nemesis, still sitting bolt upright in the chair, surprise etched upon his face and his newly acquired third eye, just above his left eye, had started to weep blood. Trench had managed to access his back-up weapon, a small .25 Colt, which hung limply in his fingers. He heard Trench give out a last exhalation of breath before his chest stilled.

Grant sat in the darkness, staring at Trench for a few moments more until he was satisfied the man was truly dead. He lifted the pistol, removed the magazine and racked the slide back until it spat out the bullet. With the gun safe he slammed it down onto the table, glad to be rid of it from his hands. His mind was already clicking back into professional mode. Dispose of the body; Trench inside a sack weighted with chains, a trip out to the centre of the Loch in Hughie's rowing boat at dead of night... he glanced over at May and Hughie, their eyes agog at what had just happened. "Are you alright?" he said. His sister nodded, and her body crumpled with a mixture of stress and exhaustion.

Grant stood and walked over to where his daughter was still hidden in her own private cave, her arms wrapped over her head. He stood over her, aware of her violent trembling, and gently laid one hand on her black hair and stroked it. "Katie, come here. Come here my sweet, sweet girl. I'm sorry love, so, so sorry," he said.

She looked up, recognised the man standing above her and held her arms out to him. They embraced, holding each other tightly and she whispered into her father's ear. "Daddy, daddy, its fine, don't you worry yourself... you're home now. I read your letter; I read it every day..."

Chapter Three

Sir Marcus Thorne, AKA the Salamander, and now, the newly appointed Chief of the British Secret Intelligence Service, dug his hiking stick deep into the earth of the Welsh mountain Moel Famu, and pushed himself ever onwards up the side of the hill. He loved walking in this region of Wales. The mountains, the wide open spaces, the quiet, the freedom; all gave him the opportunity to think and escape. It was his release. He needed these small moments, perhaps once a month, to let him bleed out the tension of his double life and the nefarious workings of the British Secret Service. This was his luxury.

His hopes of manipulating the *Kyonshi* Crisis had all come to nought. His accomplice – the Raven and his organisation – were defeated… destroyed… at least, if the police reports coming in from Japan were to be believed. He'd grieved for his long-time friend and co-conspirator, had lit an incense candle out of respect. Thorne had spent a decade or more moving the pieces on the chess board that was the Great Game. The inside knowledge on how to extort money from the British government; moving Trench into position; manipulating SIS and MI5 into looking one way, while the Raven moved in another; the 'hit' on Masterman; negotiating as part of the extortion process and promoting that buffoon, Hart, into the role of being the new C …
it had all ended in disaster.

The Salamander and the Raven's original plan had been to both extort money from the British and also to move Thorne into a more powerful position within the government, hopefully a Cabinet position, something which brought him ever nearer to his ultimate goal: becoming Prime Minister. Thorne was to step in once the *Kyonshi* Crisis was in full swing, take the reins as the Deputy Chairman of the Joint Intelligence Committee, and oust the reigning, and failing, Home Secretary. The man was an old fool, who would be out of his depth with this type of attack. That had been the plan… and the world would have been their oyster. Unfortunately, Masterman's private enterprise had put paid to that. Years of planning and strategically moving assets into place had been blown by a few gunmen taking down the Raven and destroying the stockpiles of the *Kyonshi* virus.

Not that it had been a complete waste. There had been a few positives. Trench had left a message in their emergency dead letter box, saying he'd taken care of Masterman at his home and that his next stop was Scotland, to finish off Grant and his relatives. Good man, that Trench. Perhaps he could be used at some point in the future, for quiet, unofficial wet work.

The other achievement was when that buffoon, Hart; the previous incumbent in the role of C had been sacked. Of course, he'd been helped on his way with a little judicious back door pushing by Thorne and his collegiate at the Joint Intelligence Committee. Really, it was inevitable; Hart wasn't up to the job and he had to go… he'd been a good 'straw man'. But who could take on the position at such short notice? Step forward Sir Marcus Thorne, respected Intelligence bureaucrat, former SIS officer and Deputy Chairman of the JIC. His position had been confirmed in an emergency session several days earlier. So not the top spot just yet, but a step or two nearer. One day, he'd be in Downing Street.

Thorne moved further up the incline, stopped and turned to admire the view. God, it was fantastic. The breadth and depth of the mountain range took his breath away. He waved to his police bodyguards and beckoned them to move across to meet him on the far side of the hill.

It was one of the perks of his new position as Chief of SIS – twenty-four hour police protection. Sir Marcus Thorne, the new C, turned one final time to study the magnificent vista of rolling hills and mountains that lay before him. He smiled to himself, feeling safe and secure.

And then he fell…

* * *

Carter, the older of the Special Branch bodyguards was the first to see Sir Marcus fall. He turned and called to his younger colleague, Sergeant Martins. "Tony! Bloody hell, the Chief has slipped and fallen! Come on!" Both bodyguards made their way up the slope of the hill at speed, to the crest of the Tor where the body of their principal lay, not moving. It was only when they reached the prone body that they saw the extent of their VIP's injuries. He'd been shot in the head. The wound had been caused by a large calibre bullet, judging by the damage to Sir Marcus's temple. His head resembled a pumpkin which had been pulped with a hammer.

"Where did the shot come from!" Martins asked, fumbling for his revolver.

"Keep down! It must have been a sniper. Must have had a silencer on it. They could be anywhere!" Carter shouted.

"But there's nothing here! Not even a tree line for over five hundred yards!"

"Well then, they must be a bloody good sniper, mustn't they? For fuck's sake, call it in Tony, call it in right *now*!"

Martins fumbled with the radio that connected them to the Jaguar parked down on the main road. "Ghost man is down. Repeat, Ghost man is down! For God's sake… someone has assassinated the Chief of the Secret Intelligence Service!"

Epilogue

The elderly grandfather shuffled his way across the concourse of the airport terminal, his black lacquered walking stick tap-tap-tapping on the tiled floor as he made his way. The freshly laundered black suit and blue shirt he wore had been delivered to his door that very morning by an anonymous courier; the dark reflective sunglasses he'd provided himself.

He was paid a handsome monthly stipend by the men who represented the Raven and his organisation, and the money had helped pay off the debts from his gambling addiction. For this money, all he had to do was... nothing. Just sit and wait until the call came for him to provide a 'service'. Exactly what that service would be, he didn't know and he wasn't foolish enough to ask questions, especially if it threatened his monthly fee. Along with the suit and shirt, a plain white envelope that contained some basic written instructions and a single key had been delivered. His orders had been to travel to the airport and make his way to the lockers which could be hired by the passengers who came and went. His key was numbered seven, a good omen, he thought. Good for luck and success. From there, he needed to retrieve the items in the locker and take a taxi back to his apartment to await further instructions. It was a simple enough job.

The locker key weighed heavily against his trouser leg as he slowly made his way towards the wall of passenger lockers. The concourse was always busy; it was, after all, one of the busiest airports in all of Asia. The grandfather stopped and appraised the row upon row of lockers until he spotted 'his' one. He felt in his pocket for the key and calmly pulled it out into his hand. There was no need to look around for signs of surveillance. He wasn't a young Triad thug, or a drug smuggler, or a criminal. He was an old man who no one paid any attention to. He approached the locker, inserted the key and turned it. He didn't know, of course; could not know, in fact, that there were a dozen others like him; people of no consequence, nobodies – men, women and children who would be the Raven's final revenge in the event of his demise.

They would even now be opening lockers and cases at airports and train stations in London... Rio de Janeiro... Berlin... Saigon... Lisbon... Cairo. They would snap open the lock, hear the faint pop of the atomiser as it emitted its lethal spray and then their bodies and minds would be plunged into a journey of madness and fury. The grandfather pulled open the locker door and peered into its darkness, felt a gust of air and atomised liquid puffed into his face. He caught the full force of it as he inhaled. He wiped his hand across his face to clear the moisture from whatever had sprayed him and coughed, once, then twice, before he finally recovered his composure. Not an unpleasant aroma... it smelled like almonds. Sweet and comforting.

Without warning, his body was abruptly wracked with pain and his walking stick fell to the floor. He heard it clank as it dropped onto the tiles. A fever rapidly rose in his body, heating his skin unbearably, and his eyes started streaming. When he reached up to wipe the liquid from his cheeks, he was shocked to discover it was blood. He turned to face the people around him in the airport... men and women with luggage, children carrying toys, pilots on their way to their next flights.

Then he experienced a rush of strength... anger... hunger!

He fought it for as long as he could, fought the adrenaline firing around his body... his muscles contracting... his breathing increasing... All he wanted to do was to attack, kill... fight... murder. The stick... the stick could be used to smash... break bones... spear people's eyes...

He submitted to the uncontrollable urge and let the rage consume him.

He saw the innocents all around him... the food... so weak, so easy to kill, and then he ran toward them in a bloodlust.

The *Kyonshi* feasted. It was the Raven's final act of revenge.

Dear reader,

We hope you enjoyed reading *Sentinel Five*. Please take a moment to leave a review in Amazon, even if it's a short one. Your opinion is important to us.

The story continues in *Rogue Wolves*.

Discover more books by James Quinn at https://www.nextchapter.pub/authors/james-quinn-british-espionage-thriller-author

Want to know when one of our books is free or discounted for Kindle? Join the newsletter at http://eepurl.com/bqqB3H

Best regards,

James Quinn and the Next Chapter Team

Glossary

C – Chief of the Secret Intelligence Service (SIS)
CIA – Central Intelligence Agency
Dojo – Japanese training hall for the martial arts
Gaijin – Japanese word for foreigner ('Outside Person')
GCHQ – Government Communication Headquarters; British organisation responsible for electronic and communication intercepts
Giri – Japanese word meaning 'Duty' or 'Obligation'
Gwaih-Lo – Cantonese slang word for foreigners
JIC – Joint Intelligence Committee, political overseer of SIS, MI5 and GCHQ
Karasu-Tengu – A mythical half Raven/half goblin from Japanese culture
Kempeitai – Wartime Japanese secret police
Kyonshi – Japanese word meaning 'living dead' or reanimated corpse
MI5 –British Security Service responsible for counter-espionage within the UK
Ninjato – supposedly the sword carried by Shinobi assassins.
Oyabun – Leader of a Japanese clan or Yakuza family
Ronin – Masterless Samurai, freelance mercenaries with no loyalty
Saiko-Komon – Senior Advisor to an Oyabun/clan leader
Shaken – A metal throwing star used by Shinobi assassins
Shinobi – A covert agent or mercenary assassin in feudal Japan. In popular culture often referred to as a 'Ninja'
Shinobi Shozoko – The uniform of a Shinobi assassin

SIS – Secret Intelligence Service; British overseas intelligence agency, often referred to as MI6

Yakuza – Japanese organised crime family

A message from James Quinn

I hope the adventures of Gorilla Grant will continue to enthral and entertain readers both new and old. Gorilla has, over the past year or so, slowly worked his way into the hearts of the book buyers who have come to know him. He has carved his own little niche (probably with his trusty, cut-throat razor) into the psyche of the espionage milieu and for that I am honoured, humbled and very, very happy.

The story of Sentinel Five and their murderous operation is based, if it is based upon anything, on the Japanese tale of the *47 Ronin*, in which a band of masterless Samurai (Ronin) avenged the death of their late master. I have been a student of the tale for many years and always envisioned putting my own modern twist upon the story.

For the final section of the book, the Raven's Pagoda, I chose a fictional location. However, the pagoda is based, loosely, on Matsumoto Castle in Nagano, Japan. The concept of the S5 team fighting their way to the top level is taken, blatantly, from the original idea that the legendary martial artist Bruce Lee had for the story of his unfinished movie, *Game of Death*, in which a group of fighters have to battle their way to the top level of a mysterious pagoda. That self-contained fighting environment from Lee's vision has always stuck with me and I was desperate to have the best assassins of the age compete against each other inside its walls.

So, what next for Gorilla Grant?

Well, he's back in the 'game' certainly, and he's lost none of his skills in the intervening years between AGFA and S5. And while he still has people he cares about to protect, for now at least, they are safe.

So who knows? What would an experienced assassin do next? SIS doesn't know he's back; he's not even on their radar. So maybe he'll go self-employed, maybe even do a bit of freelancing… after all, it's a dangerous world out there and even Gorilla Grant has to earn a living and keep the wolf from the door.

I hope you'll join him when he returns.

James Quinn

London

2016

Acknowledgements

I am lucky in my books, especially during the initial research phase, to have on hand a fantastic network of contacts who can help me out with their technical knowledge, expertise and experience. Any mistakes found within the book are down to me and NOT down to the superb advice of my contributors. They are, in no particular order:

Anette Wachter, who goes by the handle of "**30calgal**" for all her excellent advice and knowledge in the art of the marksman (and woman) and for helping to bring the beautiful, but lethal, Miko to life.

My friend *Steve Williams* of Georgia, USA for all his knowledge in arming Gorilla Grant for this book and for sharing his wisdom about what would be the most lethal options for close quarter shooting work. I look forward to the day that Steve and I can just kick back and pepper a couple of targets together on a sunny afternoon. One day...

To the real *Colonel "Masterman"* for his guidance and help in negotiating the corridors of the secret intelligence world and for always being a supportive hand that pushes me in the right direction.

To *Miika* and the team at *Next Chapter Publishing, especially my editor Debbie Williams,* for all their hard work in bringing the book up to a fantastic level.

To my good friend *Daniel Webster* (my personal "Armourer") who is always there with good advice and comradeship – both inside the pages of these books and in real life also. We will always have The Shard...

To *Lulu,* for once more writing the last line of the book (it's kind of our little ritual now) and I can't wait for the day that I can return the favour and write the last line of *your* book. You have all my love. xxxx

And last, but never least; to little *Jack* for being an inspiration to me in all he does. He is a gunslinger born and he has never forgotten the face of his father. xxxx

"GORILLA" GRANT
WILL RETURN IN
ROGUE WOLVES

.

About the Author

James Quinn spent 15 years in the secret world of covert operations, undercover investigations and international security before turning his hand to writing.

He is trained in hand to hand combat and in the use of a variety of weaponry including small edged weapons. He is also a crack pistol shot for CQB (Close Quarter Battle) and many of his experiences he has incorporated into his works of fiction.

He lives in the United Kingdom.

For more information check out the James Quinn Website: http://jamesquinn.webs.com/

https://www.facebook.com/Gorillagrant/

Printed in Poland
by Amazon Fulfillment
Poland Sp. z o.o., Wrocław